S0-BSD-752

Let's Kill
Uncle Lionel

Novels by John Creasey

Bruce Murdoch, Mary Dell and The Withered Man Saga

Dangerous Journey

I Am the Withered Man

The Withered Man

Where Is the Withered Man?

Unknown Mission

Secret Errand

Superintendent Folly Mysteries

The Gallows Are Waiting

Close the Door on Murder

First a Murder

Mystery Motive

John Creasey
writing as Jeremy York

Let's Kill
Uncle Lionel

David McKay Company, Inc.
Ives Washburn, Inc.
New York

Radford Public Library
Radford, Virginia 24141

LET'S KILL UNCLE LIONEL
4 · 14 · 76
COPYRIGHT © 1948 BY JOHN CREASEY
REVISED EDITION COPYRIGHT © 1973 BY JOHN CREASEY

All rights reserved, including the right to reproduce
this book, or parts thereof, in any form, except for
the inclusion of brief quotations in a review.

First American Edition, 1976

LIBRARY OF CONGRESS CATALOG CARD NUMBER: 75-37168
ISBN 0-679-50589-X

MANUFACTURED IN THE UNITED STATES OF AMERICA

Let's Kill
Uncle Lionel

CHAPTER ONE

EVIDENCE OF DISLIKE

'SHORT of murdering the man, I don't think there's anything we can do,' said Paul.

'Well, then let's kill Uncle Lionel,' suggested Peter mildly.

'We'll take a show of hands on that,' Paul declared. 'Hands up all in favour of murdering the monster.'

'Darling,' murmured Barbara, 'one of these days someone is going to take you seriously.'

'That hasn't happened in thirty years,' observed Roger, drily. 'I don't see why it should start now.'

'Poor Punchinello,' sighed Paul. 'I am the beginning and the end of tragedy, and my public laughs at me.'

'But we,' Peter told him, 'are not your public.'

'A prophet has no honour in his own country.'

'America loves you, isn't that enough?' demanded Peter.

Paul Briscoe looked at his cousin, his lips pursed in a half-smile which did not touch his eyes. Barbara, his wife, eyed him a little anxiously, knowing that the gibe had stung. There was no telling what Paul would do or say when his vanity was piqued.

Roger, Peter's brother, stepped into the breach.

'Aren't we getting away from the subject?' he asked.

'There speaks the man of common sense,' said Paul, to Barbara's relief. 'We are. The subject is murder.'

'It isn't,' said Roger. 'It's Uncle Lionel and the family dislike of him.'

'But it is,' said Paul, firmly. 'You, more than any of us, would like to see the monster dead, wouldn't you?'

Roger's grey eyes, set in a broad, strong face, turned candidly towards Paul.

'I don't know that I hate anyone,' he said, 'but I certainly dislike Uncle Lionel more than most.'

Paul laughed. 'A masterly understatement if ever I heard one!'

Peter said tartly: 'Aren't you taking a flippant overstatement rather too seriously?'

'If you two are going to spit at each other all the evening, I'm going to leave you to it,' said Roger. 'I thought we might all sink our differences in this common cause.'

'A call to unity!' murmured Peter.

'Straight bat and all that,' murmured Paul.

Barbara slapped the arm of her chair in vexation.

'Roger's trying to put some sense into the situation,' she said sharply, 'and you two seem determined not to let him. He's worth the pair of you together.'

Paul patted her hand.

'Sorry, honey. I'll be good. But as we are discussing Uncle Lionel, we may as well be frank about it. Roger hates him. I would cheerfully see him in his coffin. Peter has particularly good reason to – er – dislike him, since Uncle Lionel dislikes everything French and Peter had to go and marry a lady from Lyons. It isn't any use beating about the bush, is it?' There was a harsher note in his voice as he went on: 'We've got to face this thing. Let's go over the facts before we start discussing the situation arising from them. I would cheerfully see Lionel dead, but not for any personal reason. Both of you will concede that I have one redeeming feature. I am very fond of Jennifer. I have no personal antipathy to Uncle Lionel, and unlike you I don't need his money, but he's planning to shut Jennifer away from the world, and for that reason I would gladly see the life choked out of him.'

There was a challenging ring in his voice; and no one spoke immediately afterwards.

Peter Maitland broke the silence.

He was Roger's brother, but no two men could be less alike. The one so square and rugged, the other tall and willowy, with long wavy hair and a skin as smooth as alabaster. The contrast was as that between rough iron ore and finely-tempered steel. Barbara had known them only for a week, but had reached the conclusion that in spite of these differences, there was a common bond between them; perhaps it was their love for their cousin, Jennifer – the sister-in-law she had heard much about but did not know.

If that were the explanation, then there was also a bond between Paul, her husband, and his cousins. They were much of an age, and had been brought up under the same roof. All had been in their early teens when Jennifer had been born to Paul's mother, then recently widowed. When she had died, soon afterwards, all of them had been transferred to the care of Lionel Chard, their uncle.

This evening, they were in Roger's small farmhouse, on the outskirts of Elborne, a country town some seventy miles from London.

'Yes, Paul's right,' said Peter, 'his redeeming feature is concern for Jennifer.' He bent a glance towards Barbara. 'I'm afraid this is harrowing for you, but we haven't much regard for Paul, you know.'

'I know,' said Barbara.

Roger said nothing; but he smiled at her.

'And I for one didn't think he'd come home for Jennifer's sake or anyone else's,' Peter went on.

'Supposing you stick to the point,' suggested Roger.

'I'm coming to it.' Peter stood up and paced the room, one hand in his pocket, the other clutching the lapel of his coat. 'I think I can paint,' he said. 'I was given to understand that the monster would see me through my growing pains. He did – until I got married. Then immediately he barred my wife from his house, which is my home, and now says he will cut off my income if I continue to live with her. There's a touch of the sadist about the devil, isn't there?' Feeling crept into

9

his voice. 'How dare his favourite nephew marry an artist's model? And a French one at that! If I'd omitted to regularize the position, he would probably have given us his blessing.' He flung out his arms dramatically. 'I'd like—'

'Steady, Peter,' said Roger.

Barbara interrupted. 'Surely Roger's position is as bad as yours?'

Peter dropped his arms in a gesture of hopelessness.

'I suppose it is,' he muttered, 'only he isn't married.'

'You've only got to sell a picture or two, and you'll get through,' said Paul, with an edge to his voice. 'If you painted what people could recognize, instead of giving a poor imitation of Picasso, you'd be all right.'

'We won't discuss that,' said Peter, icily.

Roger was refilling his pipe. Now he looked up with a deceptively placid smile.

'You're all getting worked up unnecessarily,' he said. 'We must discuss the position dispassionately, and find some means of approach to make Uncle Lionel change his mind about Jennifer. You've talked a lot about facing the facts, but you haven't faced the most important one yet. Unless we can stop Uncle Lionel, Jennifer will be in a convent at the end of next month. If it were really her wish, we couldn't very well do anything about it – I wouldn't want to. But it isn't her wish, it's Uncle Lionel's.' He paused, then went on: 'The chief fact we've got to face is that partly due to our neglect, he's gained absolute ascendancy over her. She's hardly got a mind of her own, and willingly submits to any suggestion of his, however outrageous. She simply cannot see him as he really is. Very few people can. Barbara' – Roger looked at her gravely – 'be honest with us – what do you think of Uncle Lionel?'

Barbara returned his gaze evenly, but did not immediately answer. A car passed outside; from further away came the tinkle of a cycle bell.

'Be honest,' Peter urged.

Barbara glanced at Paul.

'It isn't easy for me to give an unbiased view,' she said. 'I've heard so much about him from Paul. When your cable came, telling us what he planned to do, Paul really let loose.' She smiled slightly.

The sun caught her fair hair, lighting it up.

'Go on,' said Roger.

'Since we've been in England, Peter has dotted the i's and crossed the t's of all that Paul's said,' Barbara went on, slowly, 'and you've made it clear, Roger, that you agree with them both. Yet in spite of all that, I—'

'You can't say you *like* the man!' exclaimed Peter.

'I can't honestly say that I dislike what I've seen of him,' said Barbara. She threw her head back, as if she knew how unpopular that statement was bound to make her. 'He was friendly enough; unlike you, Peter, he didn't sneer at Paul at every opportunity, and he certainly gave me the impression that he does everything because he sincerely thinks it's the right thing to do. I haven't talked to him about Jennifer, of course.'

'So he's really taken you in,' Paul marvelled.

'I suppose that's it,' said Barbara. 'You surely can't all be wrong about him, but if you're right, he's—'

'The Devil incarnate,' said Roger, with a dry smile.

'If you'd put some feeling into that, I'd agree with you,' said Peter, abruptly. 'Barbara, there isn't a streak of sincerity, not a drop of the milk of human kindness, not an ounce of charity or a measure of love in Uncle Lionel's make-up. If you knew some of the things we know—'

'That's the trouble, Barbara doesn't,' said Roger. 'Only two or three people, beside ourselves, have any idea of the man's real nature. That's why we're going to find it difficult to take any steps to stop him from sending Jennifer away. Even young Frank Corcoran has a soft spot for the old man, although he's desperately in love with Jenny. I like Frank,' Roger went on, but I'm by no means sure that he's the right man for her.'

'We know he isn't,' Peter said, impatiently, 'but I'd rather see her married to him than shut up in a convent for the rest of her life. You know the truth about him and Jennifer, don't you?' he added, abruptly.

No one spoke.

'If you don't, I do,' he went on, challengingly.

Roger stirred. 'Let's have your view of it, Peter.'

'It's more than a view, it's a fact,' said Peter, hotly. 'He's in love with her—'

'Now, steady!'

'He's in love with all the beastly possessiveness in his nature,' Peter snapped. 'That's the blunt truth. He's always kept her close to him, he's even tried to prevent us from seeing her too often. Now he's afraid that she'll marry Frank – or marry someone. Rather than allow that, he'll bury her alive.'

'Aren't you carrying it a bit far?' asked Paul

Peter looked at Roger. 'Aren't I right?' he demanded.

Perhaps only Barbara saw Roger clearly as he answered.

'I don't altogether agree, Peter, no. In my view, Uncle Lionel has made an idol out of Jennifer. Like all of us, he's seen in her something that's different from most people, that touch of unworldliness which makes her what she is, and I think he believes that he has to safeguard it. I believe he is sincere in thinking that Jennifer is not of this world, and he wants to make sure that she's protected when he's dead. He's considered every aspect of it, and decided that the only way is to send her to a convent. I think Barbara's wrong about Uncle Lionel's general sincerity – well, we know she is,' he added, with a quick smile at Barbara. 'His regard for Jennifer is his one redeeming feature. But he's not in love with her.'

Barbara looked at him. No, she thought, but you are, Roger.

CHAPTER TWO

WILD TALK FROM PETER

THE sun had sunk behind dark clouds, and the room was filled with shadows. As Roger finished speaking, Paul got up and switched on the light.

'I'll draw the curtains,' Roger said.

Barbara rose to help him, glad to get a clearer view of his face and the hurt in his eyes. She was confirmed in her opinion, although when he turned to face the others, he was smiling, and his pipe was back between his strong, white teeth.

'Now that we're pretty well agreed on the facts,' he said, 'we've got to decide on a course of action. Would you rather have dinner first?' He glanced at Barbara.

'It doesn't make any difference,' Peter said.

'Oh, I don't know,' said Paul, jumping up. 'Life always seems gloomier on an empty stomach.'

'You've gluttonized too much on American plenty,' said Peter, waspishly. 'English frugality won't hurt you for a bit.'

'Oh, cut it out, Peter,' said Roger.

'It's true,' snapped Peter.

'It doesn't make any difference what you think about Paul – we're considering Jennifer.'

'We're not,' said Peter, in a high-pitched voice.

Barbara thought: Hallo, here's trouble.

There was a change in Peter's manner. His eyes were suspiciously bright, his lips were drawn back, showing his even teeth. Until then, she had felt angry with him for his constant gibes at Paul; now, suddenly, she understood. He had bottled up his true feelings, but his bitterness could not be wholly repressed, and he had vented it on Paul. Paul, probably, understood that; hence he had taken the insults so calmly.

'We'll have dinner,' Roger decided, and stretched out a hand towards the bell. 'In a quarter of an hour, shall we say?'

He pressed the bell.

'What's the use of postponing things?' demanded Peter, in a thin, vicious voice. 'We say we've been discussing Jennifer's future – we haven't, I tell you. We've come to the conclusion that there's nothing we can do. Uncle Lionel's beaten us. We'll talk to him, plead with him, appeal to a better nature which he hasn't got. And in the end we'll watch Jennifer walk off, and we'll see those damned gates close on her, and know that he's sold her soul in an effort to save his own. What a farce! We're going to stand by and watch a man who's always boasted that he's got no belief in God, a man who tried to destroy *our* beliefs – and probably succeeded where I'm concerned! – a man who's as near anti-Christ as anyone living today, force Jennifer into a convent. That's what we're going to do. That's what we've agreed. That—'

Roger stepped to his side and took his arm.

'Go easy, Peter.'

'Every word is true!'

'I know how you feel, but—'

'You don't know how I feel!' snapped Peter. 'If any one of us really had the guts, we'd say what's in our minds. I tried to and you glossed it over. There's only one way to stop him from doing it, and that's to murder him. And I for one—'

The door opened.

A scared voice sounded into the uneasy silence.

'Did you ring, sir?'

Roger smiled reassuringly at the woman in the doorway.

'Yes, Ellen, we'll be ready for dinner in a quarter of an hour.'

14

Ellen closed the door, leaving an impression of a round, frightened face.

Paul chuckled; an odd, unnatural sound.

'You've frightened Ellen out of her wits,' he said. 'Chuck this wild talk, Peter, it's not going to help.'

'There's only one way of saving Jennifer, and that's by killing Uncle Lionel,' Peter insisted, in an unsteady voice. 'Why don't we face the truth?'

Roger glanced at Barbara. She was quick to see that he was asking her to take Paul out of the room. She rose gracefully.

'I really must tidy up,' she murmured. 'Come on, Paul.'

Paul hesitated, but Barbara took his arm firmly.

At the door, he looked round.

Roger saw the familiar face – familiar not only to him but, in the last year or two, to millions of people. Paul's ugliness had a touch which lent it humour; he was a born actor in his mannerisms, in his appearance, and, by now, in his training. Whatever his shortcomings, Roger believed his devotion to Jennifer to be real.

The door closed.

Roger turned to his brother.

'You've made a pretty fine fool of yourself,' he said.

'I've faced *facts*. I thought that was what we were here to do.'

Roger tapped out his pipe.

'Personally I don't agree that the only way of saving Jenny is to see the old man dead, though talking hot air sometimes does one good. But even if it were, why drag Barbara into it? If you have to shake a tomahawk you might at least keep it to the family proper. We all like Barbara, but she doesn't know Jenny. She can't understand the old man as we do, either.'

'That's quite obvious,' Peter said, heavily.

'And if you must scream blue murder, why scream it in front of Ellen?'

'I didn't know she was coming in.'

'You knew I'd rung for her.'

'If you hadn't wanted to stifle comment—'

'I wanted a word with you,' said Roger, 'to try to stop you from talking that wild nonsense in front of Barbara.'

'If you felt as I do—' began Peter, then stopped abruptly.

Roger said, 'I know how you feel about Lucille, you ass. What I can't understand is how you've come to let that, or anything else, blunt your reason. Supposing it *does* come to a point, and we have to take drastic action to save Jennifer, how are outbursts like yours going to help?'

Peter said: '*What's* that?'

'You heard me,' said Roger, steadily.

Peter looked dazed. 'Are you – serious?'

Roger moved away.

'The old man is Jennifer's guardian in law, although Paul's her next of kin. The formalities for going into the convent demand that he shall give free and full authority for her to take the step. If anything should happen to him, then Paul takes over authority. We have six weeks in which to work. Once she's inside the convent, there won't be anything we can do, and she'll probably want to stay. Whatever it takes, I'm going to prevent her from going in. Do you understand me?'

Peter ran his hands through his hair.

'Good heavens, who's talking! Now *you're* considering murder.'

'I am not,' said Roger, and added calmly: 'But I am prepared to take drastic action if the need arises. A lot might happen in the next few weeks, and there may be ways and means of stopping the old man that we haven't thought of yet. That's what we want to talk about, not nonsense like murder, which Barbara won't forget and Ellen will transmit in due course to all her friends.'

Roger turned towards the door, and then rested a hand on Peter's shoulder. 'Oh, there's one other thing, old chap. I don't want to come the elder brother on you, but you are

16

ribbing Paul a bit too hard, you know. I shouldn't, especially
in front of Barbara. You've always been inclined to judge
Paul too harshly.'

'I like that! You know as well as I do that he funked
fighting and made a nice, soft billet for himself.'

'You've often said so.' Roger smiled. 'It's Paul's business,
anyhow, and you aren't going to help by gibing at him in
front of Barbara. It's unnecessarily hurtful, and – it isn't like
you,' Roger declared. 'Try to guard your tongue a bit.'

Peter shrugged.

'Oh, all right,' he muttered.

Roger went into his room and stood by the open window.
Across the road, the lights of the Round House were on;
someone was talking near the old pump, at which were gath-
ered the usual little party of the girls and young men. From
the other direction he could hear the gruff voice of Simley,
the policeman, much given to pontifical utterances.

Roger heard these ordinary, everyday sounds of the streets
without giving them thought.

He had talked too freely to Peter? True, nothing else
would have calmed him so quickly, but had he been wise to
give tongue to the dark, desperate thoughts which he harboured? Had he ever seriously gone beyond wishing the old
man were dead?

He felt sure that neither Peter nor Paul dreamed of the
depth of his feeling for Jennifer.

The gong rang, summoning them to supper.

Opening his door, Roger saw Barbara coming from her
room. In the dim landing light, she looked quite lovely. She
smiled; and, unexpectedly, held out her hand.

Roger took it.

'Don't let them do anything silly, will you?' she murmured.

'They won't,' Roger said reassuringly. 'Peter's on edge because most of his hopes have been dashed by Uncle Lionel's
latest whim, and Paul—'

'I've never known Paul *feel* anything like this,' said

Barbara. She was still holding his hand tightly. 'Roger, will you be honest with me?'

'Of course.'

'Do you despise Paul?'

Roger said seriously: 'Don't take too much notice of Peter, Bar.' He had never used the diminutive before. 'And don't get it into your head that everyone thinks that Paul failed to pull his weight. Peter was disappointed because he stayed in Hollywood. It wasn't – well, it wasn't what we expected, but Peter's always been inclined to pass quick judgement and then regret it. And he's being hurt badly, so he's hitting out at the weakest victim. Paul's taking it very well.'

'Yes,' said Barbara. 'I didn't realize that—' She broke off.

'Go on,' said Roger.

'We must get downstairs,' said Barbara, taking her hand away. She gave him a quick smile. 'I didn't realize that Paul was so family conscious. I really think that Peter hurt rather than angered him. And – he sets great store by your opinion.'

'And I by his,' Roger assured her.

'Thank you,' said Barbara, in a strained voice. At the foot of the stairs, she went on: 'You don't think Peter was serious?'

'He'll soon have forgotten he made such a fool of himself,' said Roger. 'You haven't seen Peter at his best. If he were to have a stroke of good luck, you'd see a different man.'

'You mean, sell a picture?'

'For a decent price.'

'What would he call a decent price?'

Roger looked at her sharply. 'Now, look here—'

'I've friends in London,' Barbara said.

Roger gave a deep laugh.

'I think they'd have to be colour-blind to buy anything of Peter's! But I'm no judge. Twenty or thirty guineas, I suppose,' he added. 'Now forget it. To buy anything of his except on merit would hurt him terribly if it were ever found out – and those things always are.'

The dark thoughts which had possessed him in the bedroom had gone. It was surprisingly easy to be soothed by
Barbara. She always made him forget the great, over-riding
anxiety which affected nearly everything he did.

During and after dinner, the atmosphere was light and
friendly. Once or twice Peter took pains to defer to Paul,
which was his way of making amends. Roger hoped fer-
vently that this display of good fellowship would last the
week-end.

It was not long before they harked back to the obsessive
question of how to make the old man change his mind.
Roger suggested that if they could only get him to postpone
things, Jennifer could be influenced. In this Barbara might
be able to help.

'If Barbara can make Jennifer envious—' Roger began.

'Jenny envious!' exclaimed Peter. 'She wouldn't envy a
millionaire if she were starving to death!'

'I mean in little things,' said Roger.

'You mean, pretty clothes and frills and coloured ribbons,'
Barbara suggested.

'You've got it.' Roger smiled bitterly. 'It's incredible in
this day and age that she's quite unaware of such things, but
there it is.'

'I think we're going to need something more drastic,' said
Paul, thoughtfully. 'Anyhow, it's worth trying.'

'Of course it's worth trying,' said Peter impatiently. 'I –
hallo, the telephone. That'll probably be Lucille, she promised to ring me this evening.'

He hurried out of the room.

Roger and Paul exchanged glances.

'When are we going to meet Lucille?' Barbara asked.

Roger shrugged.

'It looks as if Uncle Lionel has scared her off relatives.
There doesn't seem much enthusiasm to meet us.'

None of them, not even the old man, had yet met Lucille.

As they heard Peter talking, Roger thought back over the years. All three men had one thing in common – their early upbringing, and victimization at the hands of Uncle Lionel, but Peter's career had been very different from Roger's or Paul's. Probably because of his good looks, Peter had always been the apple of the old man's eye, although no freer than the others from Chard's restrictions and his efforts to subject them to his will.

From his earliest age Peter had always wanted to draw and paint. His masters had encouraged him, though, at first, the old man had not. Peter, like the others, was to enter the jobbing business of Chard & Chard, in the City. 'Jobbing' was a courtesy title. Chard had a finger in many profitable pies, his business interests being varied and wide. His plan had been that the three boys should join him.

Peter had rebelled, taking an ill-paid job in London while attempting to keep up his studies. He had stuck it out for a year, and then had shown signs of giving in. Lionel Chard, seeming to relent, had agreed to him studying at the Slade. Before he had finished there, the war had threatened and he had joined up.

In spite of his delicate good looks and the fact that he was in some ways the weakest of the three, Peter had a remarkable way of getting what he wanted. After the Slade, he had wanted to study in Paris. The first signs of trouble over that issue between him and the old man had been evident before the outbreak of war, but Peter had served on three active fronts and, as soon as the war in Europe was over, had managed to get himself stationed in Paris, where he had studied under modern French masters. The Picasso influence had quickly shown itself in his work, to the regret – almost the despair – of his English tutors. Apparently against his will, Uncle Lionel had undertaken to support him for another three years; after that, if he failed to make a living out of his painting, the axe would fall.

Roger, who had watched the duel between Peter and the old man with growing anxiety, had felt sure of one thing:

Uncle Lionel was still bitter about his defeat. The old man had not given up trying to dominate their lives, as he was in fact dominating Jennifer's. And then Peter, not fully aware that Chard was still nursing a grievance againt him, had gone a step too far. He had met Lucille, an artist's model, married her, and brought her to England in triumph. He planned to use a barn at the back of Chard Lodge as a studio. It had not seriously occurred to him that Uncle Lionel would object to Lucille.

The old man hd not only objected; he had refused her admittance to the house. Next he had delivered one of his ultimatums: Peter was to divorce the baggage, or at least separate from her, or he could go his own way without an allowance and without help.

Not earning enough to keep himself, let alone a wife, Peter needed that help badly. His first reaction had been to get a furnished flat in London, and try to paint there. The effort had failed. He had then gone to Chard Lodge to plead with the old man. He had gained a grudging concession. He, alone, could stay at the house and use the barn. But unless he had parted with his wife permanently within three months, even that concession would be withdrawn. Peter, knowing that conditions in London made it impossible for him to do good work there, had stayed at Chard Lodge, only going back to his wife for week-ends. There he had worked desperately to produce pictures for a ready sale, but again had failed.

Roger, who knew his brother as no one else did, was sure that Peter would refuse to accept the old man's ultimatum, but what kind of life would he, a penniless artist, and Lucille lead? How long would such a marriage last?

Only a few weeks of the three months' grace remained.

This Friday evening, Peter had come to Elborne straight from Hilbury, and he was going to London to see Lucille by the early train next morning; Roger had sugested that Lucille should spend the week-end at Elborne, but the suggestion had been rejected. Roger imagined that Lucille had been frightened to meet any members of the family; and that, surely, was understandable enough.

Peter finished talking on the telephone, and came in, smiling.

'What do you think! Someone called at the flat this afternoon, inquiring about a picture! *One* of these days—' He broke off, with a laugh. 'But I'm always talking of what's going to happen tomorrow! Has anyone else had any bright ideas? What about you, Paul?'

Paul shook his head.

'Barbara?' asked Peter, and then looked at the door. 'What was that?'

'It sounded like the front door,' said Roger. He opened the door, and looked out at the empty porch in some surprise. He went to the gate, and glanced right and left, but the road was clear. He shrugged his shoulders, and returned to the house. Something white lay on the mat.

He picked up a letter.

Peter's voice drifted down the hall.

'Who was it?'

'Someone's left a note,' said Roger. He glanced down at the letter in some surprise. 'It's for you, Paul. I didn't know that anyone knew you were here.'

Paul stared. 'Nor did I.'

'Well, here it is.' Roger handed him the letter, which was addressed in block capitals to *Paul Briscoe, Esq.*

Peter grinned.

'I expect one of your fans recognized you, and wants an autograph,' he said. 'What it is to be a famous actor!'

Roger, watching Paul, noted that he showed little eagerness to open the letter. It had affected Barbara, too; she had lost a little colour.

As he continued to look down on it, Peter said impatiently:

'My dear chap, it won't bite you. Why don't you open it?'

'It—' began Paul.

22

He started to push the letter into his pocket. Peter's eyebrows rose, and he grinned at Barbara.

'A delicate situation!'

Paul flushed.

'Oh, all right!' he snapped. He snatched the letter from his pocket and tore it open. Then he turned it upside down, and Barbara jumped up and seized his arm.

'Don't, Paul!'

He snatched his hand away.

'They'll have to know sooner or later,' he said, roughly.

'Paul, there's no need—'

Paul backed away from her as she tried to take the letter again. He shook the envelope more wildly. Half a dozen white feathers fell out.

As they floated to the floor, Paul glared at Peter.

'Are they a present from you?' he demanded

CHAPTER THREE

WHITE FEATHERS

THE feathers settled on the floor about Paul's feet. Barbara, her face almost white as the feathers, was looking at her husband. Roger uttered a sharp exclamation, while Peter stared with widening eyes at the symbols of cowardice.

'Did you?' Paul rasped.

Peter looked at him. 'Good God, no!'

They stared at each other; and Paul was the first to move his gaze.

'I'm sorry. But it's odd – I didn't know that anyone realized that I was staying here. Who else knows, Roger?'

23

'Only the family,' said Roger. 'Unless you have been recognized in the street. That's just possible. But no one would play a swinish trick like that, surely?'

'They have,' said Paul. 'It isn't my first lot, either.'

'It's going too far,' Peter said, in a strained voice.

'Someone else agrees with you, you see,' said Paul. He got up abruptly. 'I've had half-a-dozen anonymous gifts like that in Hollywood. Bar has, too. If I could find out who sends them, I *would* do murder!'

'I wouldn't mind a few minutes alone with the beggar myself,' Peter said. 'How long has it been going on?'

'Nearly three years.' Paul's voice was without expression. 'There's always a month or so between each delivery. I ought to be hardened by now, but if *you're* prepared to think what you do, Peter, I oughtn't to be surprised at this kind of thing from strangers.'

Peter said: 'But *did* a stranger send them?'

'Oh, let's forget it!' Paul swung round to the piano, and started to play a wild, frenzied piece, his fingers crashing down on the keys.

Barbara watched him for a while, then caught Roger's eye.

He was reviewing Paul's life. He had gone into Uncle Lionel's office, but had never liked it and, after two years, had left England, travelled steerage to America and, as he had often told Roger, thumbed his way across the United States. He had ended up in Hollywood where his ugly, mobile face had attracted attention and earned him two or three small stage parts. A steadier success followed; and then came the war. Roger had expected him to return home, but he had stayed in Hollywood. It was the first real breach between the three men.

Then a cable had arrived announcing Paul's marriage.

Roger had wondered how successful that marriage would be, until he saw Barbara.

Paul crashed the notes in a wild crescendo, and then swung round on the piano stool.

24

Roger thought: I doubt whether he would have returned to England, but for Jennifer.

There had been biting comments in the Press from time to time about English actors who stayed in Hollywood, and, even after America entered the war, found a way of avoiding military service. These had stung Paul, but never to defence. Roger, who was much more tolerant than Peter, had been able to understand a man so genuinely frightened that he had chosen to organize Help for Britain in Hollywood rather than return home to fight. And Paul had done remarkably well in that way.

Paul was now proof against Uncle Lionel, except where Jennifer was concerned, and the only one of the three who was really independent.

Immediately Roger had heard of Uncle Lionel's latest decision, he had cabled Paul, and Paul and Barbara had reached England before the answering cable announcing their visit. Barbara, it proved, was eager to help. She had quickly won the hearts of the family, except that of Uncle Lionel.

Now she quietly collected the feathers, and dropped them into a wastepaper basket. Roger scrutinized the envelope, but there was nothing about it which gave any clue to the sender.

Who else had known that Paul was here?

It was unpleasant to think that one of the family might be responsible. Peter's prompt and emphatic denial had satisfied Paul – and it was absurd to suspect Peter of such a thing as this.

'Let's forget it,' Paul said. 'Throw the damned thing away, Roger.'

'Have you ever tried to trace the sender?'

'No.' Paul looked at Peter. 'In my calmer moments, I've no wish to.'

Peter put a cigarette to his lips, but did not light it.

'Look here, Paul, I know I weighed into you pretty heavily before dinner. I have felt – damn it, I do feel! – sore about you staying in America. But this white feather business is beyond words. If – if I'd known what was happening,' Peter went on, colouring a little, 'I wouldn't have kept ribbing you.'

Roger gave a sigh of relief. There was now a chance that Peter would never again return to the subject; it had cost him a great deal to make that apology.

He smiled to himself. He had been thinking of the two men and judging them. What did they think of him?

He supposed there was not a great deal of doubt; he was undistinguished in every way; a plodder; the only one of the three who had met Uncle Lionel's early domination with outward resignation, never giving way to the fierce longing to revolt. No one but he knew how often he had raged inwardly and, for the sake of the others as well as himself, repressed it. He could have stayed with Chard & Chard during the war; for the first time, he had come into open conflict with his uncle over this issue, and refused deferment. He had been on bombers and had become a Wing Commander, serving without great distinction. At the end of it he had seen, for the first time, a chance of achieving his own ambition, to buy a small farm and work it himself. He had never broached the subject to the old man but, by scraping and saving, he had got together enough money to rent this house and the land beyond it, to buy a small tractor, to repair the byre and put the farm in first-class order. He had finally told Uncle Lionel, when the thing was done, the contract signed; to his surprise, the old man had raised no protest.

Roger remembered being puzzled, and a little worried about that. He had not, of course, told the old man of his longing to bring Jennifer to Home Farm; to set her free from domination and, please God, one day to kindle the spark in her which would lead to marriage. On those long flights over Germany, he had dreamed this dream.

Only a fortnight before, just after the ultimatum to Peter and after Chard had declared his intentions as regards Jennifer, the old man had taken action against Roger, showing that he had not really accepted the decision with resignation, but had been biding his time. He had bought Home Farm over Roger's head, and Roger had received notice to quit.

His two hired men, the house, the farm and all his dreams would have to be forsaken; unless he acquiesced in the plans for Jenny and, afterwards, returned to Chard & Chard.

Could cruelty strike deeper?

Barbara looked up and caught his eye.

'A penny for them,' she said.

Roger smiled. 'Oh, they're worth much more than that! I was thinking of Peter,' he added, untruthfully. 'Are you doing any work now, Peter?'

'How the blazes *can* I work in these circumstances?' growled Peter. 'Oh, I splash about a bit, but it's no good.' He looked at his watch. 'Hallo, it's past ten. I've got to be up at half-past five to catch the early train.' He jumped up. 'Nothing else for the family council to discuss?'

'I don't think so.'

'Then it's bed for me.'

Peter went out, amid a chorus of good nights, and Paul grinned unhappily across at Roger.

'Peter's not having a good time,' he said. 'I fancy his little French piece is badgering him for money.'

'He seems anxious enough to get back to her,' said Barbara.

'Peter would,' said Paul, drily. 'He was always responsive to sex appeal.' He stifled a yawn. 'What were you really thinking about, Roger?'

Roger laughed. 'Nothing in particular.'

'Not me and my sins?'

'Certainly not.'

'Ah well.' Paul turned affectionately to his wife. 'I think we'd better go to bed, and leave Roger to browse among his books. Odd combination, when you come to think of

27

it – books and farming.' He stood up, and pulled Barbara to her feet. 'Pleasant dreams,' he said.

Half-an-hour later, in his room, Roger heard footsteps on the landing. There was a light tap at the door. Paul entered, clad in a colourful silk dressing-gown over which a startling array of dragons and birds of no known species were disporting themselves.

'Can you spare a moment?' he asked.

'Come and sit down. We haven't had a chance for a pow-wow since you arrived.'

'Other things taking precedence,' said Paul. He sat on the end of the bed, and took out cigarettes. 'I come in trepidation, knowing what a mutton-headed gallant you can be at times, but I come all the same.'

Roger grinned.

'What are you getting at?'

Paul moved, a little uncomfortably.

'*I'm* oozing with money,' he said. 'You've got a gun pointing at your head. Let me lend you whatever you think you'll need. A proper business loan, interest at Shylockian rates, secured by mortgage on whatever broad acres you buy – in fact, impose whatever conditions you like. But don't,' added Paul earnestly, 'say "no" and close your mouth like a trap.'

Roger took his pipe from his lips.

Paul's brown eyes showed more than eagerness to help Roger. This was an appeal to him to prove, by accepting the offer, that he held nothing against Paul for his decision to stay in Hollywood throughout the war. Roger understood, then, how much it meant to his cousin. In spite of their new friendliness, the exchanges between him and Peter had gone deep.

'Well?' Paul could not keep silent.

Roger stood up.

'If I'm really in a corner, Paul, I'll accept and be really grateful. On the other hand, this is a scrap between me and Uncle Lionel. He's responsible for the situation, and apart from all claims of blood relationship, family duty and similar blah, which he will ignore, if he takes this place away from me will rob me of some fifteen hundred pounds – the money I put into it. I don't like being robbed. And I don't want to move from here,' he added. 'I've worked hard on this ground, Paul. It's just beginning to show results. I've never had a really head-on fight with the old man, but now I've two scores to settle, my own and Jennifer's. But – I am grateful. And I promise I will come to you if, and when, I am beaten.'

'That's fine,' said Paul, warmly. He held out his hand.

Roger took it. 'Good night, old chap, and—'

There was another tap at the door. Barbara, her hair down and a sober dressing-gown pulled tightly, came in and closed the door quietly. Roger thought that she knew why Paul was there, and was anxious to give him moral support. But did that explain the excitement in her eyes?

'Roger, I think I've solved your problem. I mean Jennifer's problem!'

They stared at her. She went on tensely:

'You *are* sure that if you can get Jennifer away from Uncle Lionel for a few weeks you'll be able to make her change her mind, aren't you?'

'There isn't much doubt,' said Roger, slowly.

'The old man's home is a cage, and Jenny the bird,' Paul said soberly.

'You're absolutely sure it's worth trying?' insisted Barbara, still looking at Roger.

'Yes.'

'Well, why not kidnap her?' asked Barbara.

'Kidnap—' echoed Paul, and then laughed. 'You're getting melodramatic, old girl.'

'You've always said that if you can get her away from Uncle Lionel for a few weeks, she'll see sense,' said Barbara. 'He won't let her go and presumably she won't leave him of her own free will. But if you take her away, sometime when he's not at home, and then make her believe that it's his wish that she's having a change, it might work out.'

29

Paul rubbed his chin.

'There may be something in it. What do you think, Roger?'

Roger said thoughtfully: 'It's an idea, certainly.'

'Is she likely to co-operate at all?' asked Barbara. 'After the first few days I mean?' When Roger did not answer, Barbara stood up impatiently. 'I wish I knew her even a little. I can never get any real sense out of Paul about her. She wasn't always like she is now, was she?'

'No,' said Roger, 'she wasn't always like she is today. When she was quite young there wasn't a merrier, more mischievous little beggar anywhere. If she hadn't fallen ill, I doubt whether this would have happened. Paul's told you about that, hasn't he?'

'He said that she had to go to Switzerland.'

'Yes. She was in an English sanatorium for some months,' Roger said. 'How she first fell ill I don't know. Whatever else, conditions at Chard Lodge were hygienic enough! I would never have thought Jenny would get T.B. But she did. We were all living at the Lodge at the time, and we watched her wasting away – it was pretty grim. Uncle Lionel was as upset as any of us. He moved heaven and earth to try to get her treated in England, but in the end he had to send her abroad. She was away for several years. She came back cured, but with orders to take things carefully. We all coddled her. That's how the present phase began. Then Paul left, Peter and I were caught up in the war, and – well, I knew it wasn't a mentally healthy life for her, at the Lodge alone with the servants and the old man, but she seemed happy enough. It was during the war that the old man really began to subjugate her – I can't think of a better word. I was too busy with my own plans to give it much thought. Even when I was demobbed and went to the Lodge while I was getting this place shipshape, I didn't really notice what had happened to her. Young Corcoran came in and out, he'd met her when she was walking in the village or somewhere. Strangely enough the old man didn't forbid him the house; I suppose he considered him to be beneath suspicion.'

Roger smiled without amusement.

'Well, that's the background, Bar. The damage was done while we were all away. As soon as I saw how the land lay, I had a word with Coppinger, the family doctor.' Roger shrugged. 'He says she's perfectly fit, and as far as he could see, happy enough. And, in a way, she is. I don't think any of us would have tried to upset things, but for this convent idea. It can't be hers!' he exclaimed. 'It must be the old man's!'

After a pause, Barbara said: 'I suppose you thought that once Uncle Lionel was dead, you'd gradually bring Jennifer out?'

Roger closed his eyes.

'It sounds a little crude put like that, but yes, I suppose that was the general idea,' he said.

That was all, but it was enough to confirm Barbara in her first opinion. Paul was now standing with his hands thrust into his dressing-gown pockets, swaying to and fro on his heels.

'Well, really, Barbara!' He laughed. 'Kidnapping one's own sister certainly has the flavour of originality!'

CHAPTER FOUR

PLANS

ROGER could not get to sleep.

At first he had shown no enthusiasm for the scheme. Lionel Chard was not a fool; he knew the antagonism which his decision had roused, and might think a step ahead of them. Even if they did succeed in getting Jennifer away, there would be serious trouble. Whether he thought the family responsible or not, Lionel Chard would go immediately to the police. Getting Jennifer away was one thing, and not impossible. Keeping her away was another.

Roger turned the idea over and over in his mind. The very thought of rescuing Jennifer made his heart beat uncomfortably fast. He found it easy, as he lay looking up at the dark ceiling, to devise ways and means. He even found it easy to imagine that they could keep her away from Uncle Lionel long enough to influence her; that if they gave her a few weeks of really normal, happy life, let her glimpse what life could be like, she would renounce all thought of shutting herself away from it.

Then doubts assailed him.

Was it all Uncle Lionel's fault? Wasn't it possible that, over the years, Jennifer had really become unworldly? Wasn't it even possible that she had thought of the convent herself, and really wanted to take the veil? If that were the case, a few weeks of freedom would not help. He and the others had taken it for granted that the old man was the only one to blame, blindly ignoring the fact that Jennifer *was* unusual. Thoughts like those teased and tormented him, and he began to toss and turn. Always he came back to the original suggestion, to devising ways and means of getting the child away. Where could they take her? For a few wild moments he thought of America, but rejected it.

This house would be no use; nor would the furnished flatlet which Peter and Lucille had in South Kensington. If they took her to a hotel or a small boarding-house, and the disappearance was widely publicized – as it well might be – she would be recognized.

Supposing they did succeed in the first step – wouldn't she become suspicious if she were taken from one place to another? Wouldn't she be aware of curious, watching eyes? Wouldn't whoever was with her be so conscious of the danger of being seen that nervous apprehension would communicate itself to Jennifer? That raised another objection, one he had not seriously thought about; Jennifer could not be left on her own. One of the family would always have to be near her. Yet all members of the family would be suspect, and thus the risk of being recognized would be greater. It was a criminal offence to take anyone from her rightful guardian—

He shut his eyes.

Who could tell what kind of construction would be put on the kidnapping? If it were once suspected that he was in love with Jennifer, if she were suddenly to find herself involved in an affair at once sordid and likely to break her faith in him, would it not harden her decision? Wasn't there a chance of creating more danger, perhaps real disaster, by taking such a step?

He weighed all these possibilities against one another; and, although they were impressive, he always returned to the same question: how to get her away.

At last he went to sleep.

Peter looked into Roger's room, early next morning. His brother was still fast asleep. The bedclothes were dragging on the floor, the pillow had slipped to one side.

' 'Morning, Peter,' came Paul's voice over his shoulder.

'No noise,' warned Peter, hurriedly. 'Roger's all in. He looks as if he's been having a fight with the old man during the night!' He closed the door softly. 'You're up early, aren't you?'

'Habit,' said Paul. 'Had breakfast?'

'No, I'll get it on the train.' Peter looked at his watch. 'I'll have to be off, too, it's ten minutes' walk to the station.'

'Yes,' said Paul, and rubbed his chin. 'Won't change your mind about going?'

Peter shook his head.

'We had some bright notions last night,' Paul went on, lightly. 'Kidnapping. No less!'

'*What*?' cried Peter, standing stockstill.

33

'Hush, man!'

'You seriously mean – why, it's genius! Whose idea was it?'

'Barbara's.'

'Look here, you mustn't talk to Roger about this,' said Peter excitedly. 'The old sobersides won't think of it for a moment – not until we've got it all planned and ready to put into operation.' He fumbled in his pocket for cigarettes. 'You and Barbara must come to town. We can talk about it there, work it out, and—'

'Roger knows, we told him last night.'

'But that was crazy!'

'He saw the objections, but certainly didn't turn it down,' said Paul. 'Supposing you wire Lucille and ask her to come here? Then we can spend the morning making plans. It's got to be talked out,' he added. 'All three of us ought to weigh up the pros and cons, and reach agreement on the way to do it and how to handle the situation after we've got her.'

Peter frowned. 'There's something in that. I suppose I could send Lucille a wire and say I'll be back tomorrow.'

'Look here,' said Paul, abruptly, 'why are you frightened of letting Lucille meet us?'

'Frightened? Don't be a fool.'

'Well, you seem precious nervous about it,' said Paul.

Peter's frown turned into a scowl.

'I'll do it my way,' he said, abruptly.

Paul shrugged. 'Please yourself,' he said. 'Jennifer's our chief problem.'

Peter ran downstairs to the telephone, and Paul went back to his room. Barbara was still asleep. He stood looking at her. She was smiling a little.

Would Roger be agreeable, when he faced the suggestion in the cold light of day?

Roger's first contribution, after a silence which had lasted through most of breakfast, was that he would agree if they could find somewhere fairly quiet for Jennifer to stay, and keep from her the fact that she was there without her uncle's knowledge. He marshalled all the obstacles. The newspapers would carry her photograph – yes, he was *quite* sure that Uncle Lionel would go to extremes to find her – which meant that they would have to keep newspapers away from her. That was only one thing: people would see her photograph, and might recognize her.

'Nonsense,' said Barbara, roundly.

Roger looked at her in surprise.

'Surely not.'

'Aren't we going to try to bring her out?' asked Barbara. 'Pretty clothes and a different way of doing her hair can make a lot of difference.'

Roger looked at Barbara with lively interest.

'You're right, I hadn't thought of that. But she'll still be able to recognize her own photograph.'

Paul raised his hands, palms upwards.

'Come, my friends, a little common sense, if you please! We are going to kidnap Jennifer, are we not? That will mean getting from the house and spiriting away one human being. How much easier, little one, *to steal all the photographs there are of her!*'

Into a stunned silence, Roger said: 'There aren't many.'

'The old man's never encouraged snaps and never had her professionally photographed,' said Peter.

'Her name will be in the papers,' Barbara reminded them.

'A photograph would catch her eye, a name in small print isn't likely to,' said Paul.

Roger leaned back, his eyes narrowed.

'There's bound to be a few days notoriety, but it won't last. We oughtn't to find it too difficult to keep the newspapers away from her for a few days. You know, Barbara, I really think this brainwave of yours gives us a chance. Let's see how far we've got. We'll get Jennifer away. That won't be too difficult, as the old man goes to London once a week. Good! Barbara and Paul will take charge of her for the time

35

being, because they'll be the last of the family to be suspected. They'll have booked rooms at a hotel beforehand.
Barbara – a lot's going to depend on you,' he added.

'I think I can cope,' said Barbara, 'provided she likes me.
After all, success or failure depends primarily on her.'

Roger said slowly: 'It wants working out to the last detail,
and Bar's right, Jenny's going to be the main problem. But I
think we can do it, although—' He paused.

'Go on,' said Paul.

'It's going to cost—'

'My dear chap, why do you think I flew over from the
States?' demanded Paul. 'You can forget that part of the
business. I think we'll have to take charge of certain things
separately. I'll find the place where we're to stay. You'll
handle Jenny, Roger – she's more amenable to you than
anyone else. Some sales talk about the joys of a holiday, for a
start! Then you'll have to pretend that you've got the old
man's permission, and introduce Barbara. She'll take to Bar
like a shot.'

'Do you know,' said Peter, 'I can't believe we're sitting
round this table and talking like this! We've actually found a
way—' He gave an excited little laugh. 'If we save Jenny, I'll
cheerfully live in a garret!'

After breakfast Roger went into the grounds, while Peter
took Paul and Barbara off to the town, as if there had never
been any trouble between them. Alone, Roger felt a little
light-headed; there were moments when the plan seemed
foredoomed to failure, others when it seemed bound to succeed. There was another reason for his brighter spirits, too:
Paul's offer had been meant seriously, the possibility of complete ruin had gone. Was that blinding him to some of the
difficulties that would be created over Jenny?

He smiled as he walked back to the house. He could see
the road easily, and nodded to P.C. Simley who was making
his way ponderously along the street. Then, to his surprise, a
car pulled up outside the front door.

A man and a woman were sitting in it. The car was a big,

36

modern American model, with a silent engine. He thought that they had stopped to ask the way, but the woman jumped out and stood looking at the house. Then she turned to the driver, and spoke in a pleasing voice with a noticeable accent.

'Yes, we are right, it is ze 'ouse.'

She was small, well-dressed and, when Roger caught a glimpse of her profile, proved to have an attractive nose, slightly tip-tilted.

The man, a portly, over-dressed fellow, climbed out of the car heavily. Roger heard him say: 'I haven't any time to waste – I ought never to have come. Crazy idea! Why he can't let you decide—'

'Peter paints ze picture, and he *sells* ze picture,' declared the woman. Roger's eyebrows shot up; for this, it was apparent, was Lucille. 'You yourself tell me you are coming near here, it is no trouble for you. Bring it, please.'

She waited until the man had taken a large picture from the back of the car, then turned and opened the iron gate. Roger walked round to the back of the house.

'No, Miss,' Ellen was saying, 'he's not in, he went out half-an-hour ago and I don't know when he'll be back.'

'That's finished me,' said the man, in his harsh voice. 'I ought to have known better than to come. Next time I want a picture—'

'But, please, we must find M. Maitland quickly,' Lucille said, urgently. 'It is a matter of great importance. Oh!' she exclaimed, for Roger stepped into the hall.

'All right, Ellen,' he said.

Lucille regarded Roger with rounded eyes as the man put the picture down in the doorway.

'Who are you?' demanded Lucille.

'Your brother-in-law,' said Roger.

'Roger!'

Roger smiled. 'Yes, I—'

'Roger, tell me quickly, please. Where is Peter? Zis gentleman wishes to buy a picture, he had ze kindness to come to

37

see Peter, an' now Peter is not here. Always it is the same wit' Peter, he is never where one wishes him.'

'I don't know where he is,' said Roger. He glanced at Kennard, who was fidgeting on the porch. 'But come in, and—'

'I've got no more time to waste,' said Kennard. 'These crazy artists, they think—'

Lucille turned sharply.

'He is not a crazy artist. He is a damn' good artist!'

'I don't care if he's another van Gogh,' declared Mr. Kennard. 'I've come twenty miles out of my way to please you, and he's not here.'

Roger smiled; and when he was smiling, he was at his most attractive.

'Won't you come in and have a drink?'

'And I will fetch Peter!' cried Lucille.

'After all, as you've come so far,' said Roger. 'it would be a pity to miss seeing my brother by a few minutes.'

If this man really wanted to buy a picture, it would be tragic if he were to go off in a fit of pique. 'I think—' He paused, for Kennard shook his head, and turned away.

'*M'sieu!*' Lucille cried. 'It—'

Roger thought: It's no use. It was possible that Kennard had been discouraged by the house, which gave an impression of prosperity; here, perhaps, he thought that price of the picture would go up and, judging from his appearance, he would not be happy unless he were getting a bargain. Roger picked up the picture. Kennard turned and glanced at it.

To Roger, it was just a patch of colour; brilliant colour, without design, but in that first quick glimpse, arresting.

'Oh, it's *that* one,' said Roger, who had not seen it before. 'I'm afraid there wouldn't be any point in waiting for Peter.' He smiled again. 'I'm sorry you've had a wasted journey,' he added. 'Good day, Mr. Kennard.'

Lucille drew in her breath, but did not speak.

Kennard stared at him, breathing heavily.

38

'Do you mean to say that picture isn't for sale?'

'Oh, it's for sale,' said Roger.

'Then what the heck are you talking about?'

'It's a question of price,' said Roger.

'You know ze price?' demanded Lucille, eagerly.

'I know Peter turned down an offer,' said Roger. He studied it at arm's length, with his head on one side.

'What was the offer?' demanded Kennard.

'Fifty-five guineas,' said Roger.

Lucille started. 'But Roger—'

'Maitland's stuff isn't worth fifty,' said Kennard, looking hard at Roger. 'Twenty-five's more like it.'

Roger laughed. 'Well, you probably know what you're prepared to pay,' he said. 'I don't know what experience you have of pictures, Mr. Kennard—'

'Listen,' said Kennard, stepping forward. 'I know a good picture and I know a bad one—'

'You wouldn't have come twenty miles out of your way to buy a bad one, I'm sure,' said Roger. 'Anyhow, Peter's going to keep that one for his exhibition.'

'Eh?'

'We're planning it for November,' said Roger, glibly. 'Are you sure you won't come in and have a drink, Mr. Kennard?'

'I didn't come here for a drink,' said Kennard, sourly. 'I came in to buy that picture. I'll give you thirty guineas for it.'

'Sorry,' said Roger.

Lucille rolled her eyes.

'Paul Briscoe will give sixty guineas the moment he sets eyes on it,' added Roger. 'Did you know Paul was here, Lucille?'

'No, I did not,' said Lucille, in a small voice.

Kennard said: 'Did you say Paul *Briscoe*?'

'The film star,' said Roger. 'Yes.'

'And he comes to buy Peter's pictures?' exclaimed Lucille.

39

'And he's in Elborne?' asked Kennard, slowly. 'I saw he was in England, flew over, didn't he? I wouldn't have expected to find him here.'

'He's out with Peter at the moment,' said Roger. 'If you'd care to meet him – but I'd forgotten, you're in a hurry, aren't you?'

A quarter of an hour later Kennard was starting his third whisky-and-soda. The picture was propped on the top of the piano, and Kennard was looking at it from all angles, nodding his head and saying odd things about colour and distance and feeling.

'Lucille, supposing we let Mr. Kennard look at the picture on his own. Then he won't feel that we're influencing him.'

Kennard nodded in absent agreement, as Lucille jumped up.

Roger led the way to the dining-room. He was mildly amused by her, and at the same time attracted.

Inside the dining-room, he closed the door.

'Well!' exclaimed Lucille.

'How much do you think he'll go to?'

She did not answer, but slowly shook her head, staring at him with eyes rounded in astonishment. Then she began to smile.

'The trouble it gave me to bring zat man here,' she declared, 'and zen you – do you know how much it is worth?'

'I haven't a notion,' admitted Roger.

'None?'

'None. How much *is* it worth?'

'That I do not know. Once I sold a picture. For five hundred francs. Peter said it was worth five t'ousand, never again was I to sell ze picture. But Peter makes ze appointment with M. Kennard for zis morning, he comes, Peter is not there. Roger, how much do we ask?'

Roger shook his head.

'I think we'll play for safety,' he said, 'you go out – and wait, at the corner of the road for Peter. He isn't likely to be

long. Tell him what has happened, and ask Paul to play
up.'

'Paul to play up?'

'He'll know what you mean.'

Undoubtedly Kennard liked the picture. He agreed that it
was the best thing Maitland had done. On the other hand,
Maitland hadn't 'arrived'. It was right and proper that such
patrons of the art as he, Kennard, should be given the opportunity to buy the early pictures of promising painters advan-
tageously. Wouldn't Mr. Briscoe be a sport and allow him to
buy this one? After all, it was an English picture painted by
an English artist, its rightful home was England, rather than
America.

Peter looked at Roger in desperation; he had started this,
it was up to him to get them out of it.

'So I appeal to you as a sportsman, Mr. Briscoe,' boomed
Kennard, 'not to take that picture out of the country. I came
prepared to pay twenty guineas. I'll tell you what I'll do –
I'll double it. There!' He swung round on Peter, and there
was a cunning glint in his eyes.

'What about agreeing on sixty guineas, Peter?' suggested
Roger, thoughtfully. 'It's a low figure, but there's something
in Mr. Kennard's reasoning. It would have to be conditional,
though.'

'What's that?' demanded Kennard. 'Conditions?'

'You would have to release it for the period of the exhibition,' Roger said, swaying to and fro on his heels. 'I told
you about that, didn't I? In November.'

'Oh, that's okay by me,' said Kennard. 'But sixty
guineas—' He shook his head. 'I dunno. I might spring
fifty.'

'Oh, all right,' said Peter, wiping his forehead. 'I—'

'It isn't all right,' said Roger, sharply. 'Sixty is—'

'Now look here, Mr. Maitland, it's *his* picture,' Kennard
protested.

'And I'm selling it for him, said Roger, serenely. 'If you

41

really want to save a pound or two and have the picture, I'll settle at sixty pounds.'

'Okay, okay,' said Kennard heavily, 'but it's a fantastic price. I wouldn't like to do business with you every day of the week, and that's a fact!' He took out a bulging wallet and began to count pound notes.

CHAPTER FIVE

UNEXPECTED VISITOR

'I WONDER why Peter kept Lucille away,' said Paul.

Lunch was over, Peter and Lucille were upstairs, Barbara was sitting in the window seat and Paul and Roger were still at the table. 'I got the impression,' he continued, 'that she was eager enough to meet us.'

Roger smiled.

'Peter's oddly sensitive to criticism. He probably thought we would disapprove as much as Uncle Lionel.'

Barbara looked across at Paul.

'Does it matter?'

'It puzzles me,' said Paul. 'She's an attractive little thing.'

'She's certainly got the French eye for business,' mused Roger. 'Who else would have prevailed upon Kennard to come down here?' He looked levelly at his cousin. 'We're apt to overlook the significance of it, aren't we?' he added.

'What do you mean?'

'If I judge Kennard aright, he's a talker,' said Roger, 'and he doesn't throw money about. Peter says he's a dealer and knows the picture trade inside out. He wouldn't pay sixty pounds for a daub. He must think the picture is worth every penny of it. I haven't pointed that out to Peter yet, but I think it's important. Peter never had a head for business. We'd better get expert opinion on these things of his.'

'A brilliant suggestion,' said Barbara.

'But my dear, you will live to learn that under that solid tweed coat hides a man of unacknowledged brilliance. Believe me, if this business of Jennifer comes to anything, it will be Roger's doing, but no one will give him credit for it.'

Roger laughed. 'It wasn't my idea at all! And we've Bar to thank for the more cheerful atmosphere, remember.' He paused. 'I doubt whether we'll get much sense out of Peter,' he added. 'Shall we start work on our plans again? First of all, when are we going to put them into operation?'

'Fairly soon,' said Paul.

'Yes. I think I'll go and see the old man on Monday,' said Roger. 'And I'll be able to have a word with Jenny. The old man should be going to London on Wednesday. You and Bar had better come on Tuesday,' he added, 'you haven't paid your repects at Chard yet, have you?'

'I have, Barbara hasn't,' said Paul. 'Uncle Lionel saw her in town.'

'Then a visit is called for. Now . . .'

Roger talked at some length. Barbara and Paul made occasional suggestions. The plans became so involved that Roger began to make notes.

He was in the middle of them when a car pulled up outside the house.

'Hallo, more visitors,' he said. 'I wonder who this is.' Roger looked with a certain curiosity at the man who was coming through the gateway. 'It's a stranger. Ellen's out shopping. I'll see who it is.'

When the door of the room had closed, Barbara slipped off the window seat, her face troubled.

'Paul, do you know what I think?'

'No one could!'

'I'm serious. About Roger, and this house. He—'

43

Paul took her hand.

'He's in love with the place,' he said, 'and it's just right for him. Though his chief concern is Jennifer, he hates the very thought of leaving here.'

'Can't we do anything?'

'Only the old man can do that,' Paul assured her gloomily. 'And if he thinks it will really hurt Roger to leave, he'll have the more pleasure in kicking him out. You and I had better be careful.'

'What do you mean?' Barbara looked at the door hearing voices just outside.

Paul lowered his voice.

'I mean that having found a way of revenging himself on Peter and Roger, Uncle Lionel will now find a way of getting at me. When we walked out on him, we made an enemy, my sweet.' He looked round as Roger came in with a worried expression which held a hint of alarm.

Paul jumped up, and Barbara's heart missed a beat.

Roger opened the front door as the stranger raised a hand to ring the bell. The stranger, a tall, big-boned man of middle age, drew back and smiled formally.

'Good afternoon. Is Mr. Maitland here?'

'I'm Roger Maitland,' said Roger.

'I'm glad I've found you in,' said the stranger, and took a card from his pocket. 'Can you spare me half-an-hour?'

'Come in,' said Roger.

He stood to one side, and the stranger passed him. Not until then did Roger look at the card. He read it swiftly, and then looked up in surprise, for the card read:

Superintendent I. G. Marlin
Elshire Constabulary

'How can I help you?' asked Roger, frowning.

'I hope, quite considerably,' said Superintendent Marlin. 'I've come from Hilbury, Mr. Maitland.'

'Oh?' said Roger.

'You know Hilbury, I believe.'

'Fairly well,' said Roger. 'I spent my childhood there – and most of my life, for that matter, and my uncle still lives there.' He forced himself to show no particular emotion, but inwardly he was puzzled and, for some reason, a little agitated.

'So I understand,' said Marlin suavely. 'When did you last see Mr. Chard?'

'About a fortnight ago,' said Roger. He wished the man would look away from him; there seemed to be a challenge in his eyes, and a hint of scepticism.

'As long ago as that,' murmured Marlin. 'Mr. Maitland – I'm sorry. I'm afraid I have a rather curious inquiry to make, and it may startle you. It's about your uncle – have you any reason to believe that anyone has a grudge against him?'

Roger reared back in thought. It was not an easy question to answer, and he sought swiftly for a way out.

'A grudge?' echoed Roger at last. 'That rather depends on what you mean by a grudge, doesn't it? What makes you ask?'

'I'm looking for someone who bears a particularly nasty grudge against your uncle,' said Marlin, 'and I thought you could probably help me. Mr. Chard was the victim of a brutal attack early this morning.' He paused, and Roger took a step backwards, alarmed less by the news than by its possible effect on their plans. 'He isn't badly hurt, but that isn't his assailant's fault,' Marlin went on. 'We don't yet know who the assailant was, but your uncle—' He paused again.

'Yes?' asked Roger.

'Your uncle seems to think that it was one of the family,' said Marlin.

Roger gave a dry smile.

'That is very characteristic of him. But perhaps you'd better come in.' He turned to the dining-room door, and as he opened it Paul's words carried clearly: '... *and he'll try and find a way of getting at me. When we walked out on him*

45

we made an enemy, my sweet.' Roger, being a little in front of Marlin, hoped that the Superintendent had not heard them. He forced himself not to look at Marlin's face, and opened the door wide. Paul jumped up, and Barbara looked at Marlin in some surprise.

'Another unexpected visitor,' Roger said lightly, 'but not one who wants to buy pictures!' He motioned to Barbara. 'Mrs. Paul Briscoe,' he said, 'and Paul Briscoe, my cousin – Superintendent Marlin, of the County Constabulary – or is it C.I.D., Superintendent?'

'The two overlap in the county force,' said Marlin. He smiled and inclined his head.

Roger's answering smile appeared natural enough, but the hint of alarm remained in his eyes, clear for Paul to see.

'The Superintendent brings rather a nasty story. I haven't heard all about it yet.' He moved a chair forward, and offered cigarettes. Marlin took one, and accepted a light. Barbara and Paul watched him closely, while in Roger's mind rang the words: 'A brutal attack' and 'your uncle seems to think that it was one of the family.'

'Now what's all this?' asked Paul.

Marlin smiled frostily. 'It won't take long to explain. Are there any other members of your family here, Mr. Maitland?'

'My brother and his wife are upstairs,' said Roger.

'I wonder if you could ask your brother to come down?' asked Marlin.

'I'll fetch them.'

Roger went upstairs slowly, trying to grasp the full implications of the situation. Someone had attacked the old man; well, there was reason to believe that he had plenty of enemies outside the family. Casual acquaintances might regard him as a genial, even benevolent old gentleman, but his business methods had a mercilessness about them which might have ruined many. It was a relief to know that none of the family could have made the attack.

He thought of Peter's crazy talk of murder; that seemed a

46

long time ago now. His more cheerful spirits that morning had undoubtedly been partly due to the fact that the shadow of violence had, for the time being at least, been lifted from him.

It was a bad thing that the police had been called to Chard Lodge, all the same; it would make it more difficult to get Jennifer away.

As he reached Peter's door, he realized that not once had he felt a tremor of pity for Lionel Chard.

He tapped, opening the door wide enough to mutter through.

'Someone's taken a whack at the old boy, and there's a johnny downstairs, making inquiries. Come down as soon as you can, will you?'

'*What's* that?'

'The old man's been hurt – but not badly.'

'Do you want me, too?' called Lucille. She was staring at the door, her lovely eyes filled with concern.

'No, only Peter,' said Roger.

'I'll be down in two shakes,' promised Peter.

There was a smile on Roger's lips as he went into the dining-room, but it faded when he met Marlin's curiously intent gaze.

'Are they coming?' Marlin asked, sharply.

'My brother will be here in a moment. His wife is resting. I don't think we need her, do we?'

A fleeting look of annoyance crossed Marlin's face. It occurred to Roger that he might be thinking that he had had a hurried consultation with Peter and Lucille, and that the delay in Peter's arrival was due to that. Nothing was said, yet he felt himself under suspicion.

At Peter's arrival Marlin stood up, with his back to the fireplace.

'Now that you're all together, I can tell you exactly what happened,' he said. 'Mr. Chard was attacked outside his bedroom door about half-past six this morning. He was up early, as is, I believe, his custom. He did not see his attacker who

47

struck him heavily across the head, the blow fortunately being broken by the weapon hitting the wall behind him. Your uncle was thrown forward.' Marlin's abrupt words seemed to bring the picture of the scene into the room: they could see Uncle Lionel falling, and the assailant smashing at him.

'He called out for help,' Marlin went on, 'and his niece, Miss Briscoe, and a servant heard him. The assailant took fright and ran off. He appeared to know the house well, for he went by a side door and was immediately lost in the shrubbery – all of you know that shrubbery, of course.'

That was a challenge.

Barbara said sweetly: 'I don't, Superintendent.'

'My wife has never been to the Lodge,' said Paul.

'I see. Will you be good enough, please, to tell me where you were early this morning?' asked Marlin.

Oh, you ass! thought Roger.

No one could have chosen a worse way of approaching Peter, who was already bristling at the policeman's manner.

'What the devil are you getting at?' he demanded furiously.

'Now, old chap—' began Paul.

'I want to know what he's driving at,' snapped Peter. 'I don't like the tone of that question at all. Does he think one of us did it?'

Roger said soothingly: 'Uncle Lionel seems to think it was one of the family.'

'He would,' sneered Peter. 'It's just the venomous thing he would suggest. Well, I've got a great disappointment for him We were all *here*.'

'I'm very glad to hear it,' Martin said stiffly. 'I take it that this can be proved. My question was a formality you understand, it being my duty to find out where the members of the family who bear a grudge against Mr. Chard—'

'What's that?' asked Paul.

'Who said anything about bearing a grudge?' demanded Peter.

'Mr. Chard gave me to understand that all three of you were hostile towards him,' Marlin said. He eased his collar 'Of course, if none of you was near the house at the time of the attacks, there is no need for me to press my inquiries. Can you corroborate the statement?' He looked round.

Roger said: 'What time was the attack?'

'A little after six-thirty.'

'I didn't wake up until after eight o'clock,' Roger said.

'I was about soon after half-past five,' said Peter, slowly. Something had sobered him; possibly he too had seen how this development might affect their plans. 'I was going to London on the six forty-five, but Paul persuaded me to stay for the rest of the day.'

'Indeed?' asked Marlin. 'May I ask—'

'It's the first time we've been together for some time,' said Paul, in a quiet voice, 'and I prevailed, upon him to stay.' He smiled. 'I think it was a little after six o'clock when I spoke to him.'

Peter said: 'And I'd just come from Roger's room. He was fast asleep. None of us could possibly have got to Chard Lodge by half-past six.' He looked triumphant. 'You might break that news to Uncle Lionel carefully, Superintendent, it might cause a relapse.'

Marlin said: 'You don't like your uncle, do you?'

'No.'

Roger shot Peter a frowning glance, and then said rather heavily: 'There are some family differences, Superintendent, but none of us are homicidally inclined, I assure you.'

'You understand that these inquiries are necessary,' said Marlin. He smiled suddenly. 'I wonder if you can suggest anything to help me? Is there anyone, so far as you know, who might have reason to want your uncle dead?'

Roger said sharply: 'No.'

'I see. Do you know a Mr. Frank Corcoran?' asked Marlin.

'Frank!' exclaimed Peter.

Roger said quickly: 'Yes, he's a friend of my cousin Jenni-fer – who is Mr. Briscoe's sister. A nice lad.' He smiled, as if to dismiss the thought that young Corcoran could possibly be involved. 'And he's certainly not the homicidal type, Superintendent! I don't know a quieter youngster.'

Marlin said: 'I don't think there is such a thing as a homi-cidal type, Mr. Maitland. I'm told that Mr. Corcoran is bit-terly hostile to Mr. Chard – there is some matter concerning Miss Briscoe.' He waited, inviting comment.

Roger smiled. 'Frank wants to marry her, Uncle Lionel won't hear of it. But I think you're barking up the wrong tree there, Superintendent. And I'm quite sure that none of us can help you any further.'

Marlin said: 'Mrs. Briscoe and Mrs. Peter Maitland were here during the night, I assume?'

Roger began: 'Mrs. Briscoe—' and then Peter snapped: 'Yes, of course.'

The answer so startled Roger that he looked at Peter in astonishment. Barbara stood up abruptly. Peter eyed Marlin, pale and defiant. The statement had been made so em-phatically that to correct it would stress the fact that Peter had lied deliberately. Roger was wondering unhappily what was the best course to take when the door opened without warning, and Lucille came in.

'Hallo, everybody!' She looked swiftly from Peter to Marlin. 'I come as soon as I can, you understand.'

'There wasn't any need for that,' Peter growled. 'I've just told the Superintendent that you stayed here last night.'

Marlin looked annoyed, as if he realized that Peter was conveying a warning. He looked at Lucille, with evident dis-taste; he was not the type of man to be favourably impressed by her. For the occasion Lucille had dressed in a wine red suit with a low-cut blouse; it had a touch of daring and was just right for Lucille, although it would offend anyone with a Puritan turn of mind. Her amazingly bright eyes were turned towards the Superintendent.

'But of course,' she said. 'Please, what has happened? I do not understand.'

'How badly is Uncle Lionel hurt?' Roger demanded.

'Not seriously,' Marlin said, retreating with dignity. 'He spent the morning in bed, but I understand that he will be up this afternoon. Are you *quite* sure, gentlemen, that you know of no one who bears him a serious grudge?'

'Quite sure,' Roger said.

'In that case,' said Marlin, 'I needn't worry you any further.' He moved towards the door, Roger preceding him. Clearly he was not satisfied with his interview.

Roger saw him off, then hurried back to the dining-room.

'My God, Pete, what a fool you are!' he cried. 'What on earth made you lie like that?'

CHAPTER SIX

SET BACK

'IF you think I'm going to let that old buzzard set the police on Lucille, pestering the life out of her, you're mistaken,' snapped Peter, hotly. 'She's had quite enough trouble with police and officials as it is. She couldn't possibly have whacked the old boy, so what's the fuss about?'

Roger said: 'You must be blind.'

'Now, look here—'

'And a bigger fool than I thought you were,' added Roger, with mounting anger. 'If you wanted to save Lucille from police questioning you ought to have told the truth. One interview, and it would have been over. Now you've compelled the police to investigate further. The man sensed that you were lying, and investigation may go on for weeks. They'll only have to prove you lied, and incidentally made her lie to support you, for the police to assume that the rest of us did, too. We can't produce any evidence showing that we were all here.'

Paul tried to pour oil on troubled waters.

'It was a bit indiscreet, certainly, but—'

'A bit!' exclaimed Barbara. 'It was sheer folly!'

'Listen to me, *please*,' said Lucille. 'I do not understand. Peter said I was here, zen I was here. It does not make any difference. Zere is no need, I hope, to quarrel about it. What a family it is, always quarrelling! It is true, I do not like ze police.' She shivered. 'But zat man, was he really a policeman? He looked not so to me.'

'He was a policeman,' said Roger, heavily.

'Perhaps one of you will tell me what difference it does make,' demanded Peter.

'If you can't see it, I give up,' said Roger. He shrugged. 'I think you did a silly thing, but I can see that you thought it was best. Why is Lucille so worried about meeting policemen?'

Peter said in a savage voice: 'She was in Paris during the occupation, and had her fill of the beggars. She was in the Underground. I—' He strode forward, and, while Lucille stood as if transfixed, he pushed aside the frill of her blouse, exposing an ugly scar at the top of her breast. 'That's just one reason why she hates the thought of the police.'

Lucille shrugged the frill back into position.

'I'h sorry to cause so much trouble,' she murmured.

'It wasn't *you*,' Paul said quickly. 'You had to back Peter up.'

Barbara went across to Lucille.

'Let's not start blaming anyone,' she remarked, cheerfully. 'Lucille, come and help me to get the tea, will you?'

Lucille sniffed, and allowed herself to be led out of the room: while Peter ran his hand through his untidy hair, and

52

gave a high-pitched laugh. Roger, thinking it best to get Peter to unburden himself, spoke mildly:

'Lucille had a rough time, did she?'

'Three times imprisoned by the swine,' Peter said, in a taut voice. 'And they knocked her about pretty badly. The marvel is she came through in one piece. The French *gendarmerie* she struck were collaborators, and a sight worse than the Boche themselves. There was a spot of bother one evening when we were at a club in Montmartre, and the Military Police came in – she fainted right off. Even in London, we've already had one visit from them.'

'Oh?' said Roger.

'There was an error on her passport,' Peter went on, in a milder voice. 'Just a formality, but after they'd gone, she shook and shivered for half-an-hour. It'll pass sooner or later, but the thought of the police questioning her just made me lose my head.' He hesitated, then stretched out his hand to Paul. 'Give me a cigarette, will you?' When it was alight, he added: 'Roger, you weren't serious when you said I would probably make them more curious, were you?'

'I'm afraid I was,' said Roger.

'But why should it?'

Roger said slowly: 'It's fairly obvious that the old man had a nasty shock, and his thoughts flew to us. He'd enjoy making unpleasantness. He knows what we think about him, and he probably wouldn't put it past one of us to have a crack at him. He did the obvious thing, and made the police come down here and question us. We know that we had nothing to do with it, but the police don't. Marlin wasn't too pleased by his reception, and he'll check on us all, as far as he can. If anyone living near you knows that Lucille was at your flat last night, they'll know you lied, and will assume that the rest of us did, too. Don't forget Kennard knows the truth.'

'What a fool I am,' muttered Peter.

Paul said thoughtfully: 'Once they're satisfied that Lucille was at her flat it'll be all right, surely.' He looked at Roger, as

53

if urging him to let the matter drop. 'I'm not very worried about our position, except where it affects Jennifer. We've had a sharp setback there. Presumably the police will be in and out of Chard Lodge for a few days, and we shan't be able to start as soon as we'd hoped.'

'It might be a good thing in the long run,' suggested Roger. 'We were all rather too eager about starting. The thing that most worries me is the fact that someone attacked the old man. We didn't bargain for that.'

'There must be dozens of people who'd do it,' said Peter. Roger shrugged.

'Dozens with reasons for hating him, perhaps, but I doubt if many women go to the length of having a smack at him. I've a nasty feeling that young Frank may be involved.'

Paul looked up with a puckish smile.

'He might have thought that by killing the old man, Jennifer would be saved. It takes us back to yesterday evening, doesn't it?'

Roger said lightly: 'We must have been off our heads. I think I'd better go to see Frank and the old man. One of the family ought to go and commiserate.' He frowned, thoughtfully. 'But wait a minute. Supposing you go, Paul? You've less personal grounds for disliking him, and if you stay there for a few days, Barbara will have a chance of getting to know Jenny. Do you think Barbara will agree?'

Barbara raised no objections, but suggested that it would be wise to telephone before they started out. Paul rang up. Uncle Lionel was affable enough, and said that he would be glad to see them. Paul and Barbara went upstairs to pack their things.

They left just before six o'clock, telephoning soon after their arrival to report that all was well.

On Sunday afternoon, Peter and Lucille went for a walk, leaving Roger to battle with his accounts.

He sat at the writing-table, with the account books in front of him and the bill-headings under his hand, thinking about the detective's visit and its possible repercussions. Although, for Peter's sake, he had treated the matter lightly, Roger was gravely troubled by it. The words had not been used, but there had been an attempt to murder Uncle Lionel. If Peter had behaved less foolishly, Marlin might have been satisfied; he would not be, now. There was little doubt that he would try to discover all the reasons for their hostility to their uncle.

Roger pushed the account book aside.

His thoughts roamed. If the old man had his way, and there was little to stop him, he, Roger, would have only one more set of accounts to get out. With his heightened sensitiveness, the realization of personal disaster swept over him. Paul's offer had been generous, but it would not give him back this farm. He had assumed that, sooner or later, he would have the opportunity of buying it. He was particularly fond of the house itself; it was not large, and the furniture was not particularly good or valuable, but in a comparatively short time he had come to love almost every stick – even the old coloured prints and the etchings on the walls.

He looked round at the panelled dining-room and hatred for the old man welled up in him. He was startled by the depth of his own feeling.

He must get a hold on himself!

He stood up abruptly, and the telephone bell rang.

The ringing was insistent, and he snatched off the receiver.

'Hold on, please, I have a call for you.'

Roger waited impatiently, then a deep, familiar voice spoke.

'I would like to speak to Mr Maitland, please.'

'Oh, hallo!' said Roger, surprised.

'This is Father Hennessy,' the speaker went on. 'I felt I *must* have a word with you.' There was only the faintest trace of Irish brogue in his rich voice, and Roger saw a mind picture of a large, good-natured face and a pair of shrewd,

55

Radford Public Library
Radford, Virginia 24141

understanding eyes. 'Have you heard of the trouble at Chard?'

'A little,' said Roger.

'It was a bad business, indeed,' said Hennessy. 'Yes, a bad business. How did you come to hear of it?'

'The police told me.' There was a laughing note in Roger's voice. 'Cross my heart, I didn't do it!'

'Och, be sensible, man! Are you busy tomorrow?'

'Not particularly. Why?'

'I would like you to have a word with young Frank Corcoran,' said Hennessy. 'I cannot believe he would have done this thing, but the police suspect him, or I'm gravely mistaken. He's at the police station now, but he'll be back before the day's out, I've no doubt. His parents are worried, as you will understand.'

'Yes, of course.'

'I have the police assurance that they're only questioning him, so if you'll come tomorrow—'

'Yes, of course,' said Roger, again. 'Are you sure you wouldn't like me to come tonight?'

'I think tomorrow will be better, Mr Maitland.'

'Right. Then I'll be along sometime. How is Jennifer?'

'She's very well.'

'Is she – of the same mind?'

'Nothing will shift her,' Hennessy said. 'Now don't be worrying, Mr. Maitland. Most things turn out all right.' He gave a jovial laugh and rang off.

Roger turned back to the dining-room, and took out his wallet. He had one, rather faded snapshot of Jennifer. He took it out and looked at it. She looked lovely. Her hair fell about her shoulders, catching the light – but no photograph could do justice to her eyes.

He put it away.

The evening was uneventful; or as uneventful as any evening could be when Lucille was one of the party. She had certainly recovered from the afternoon's encounter, and her gaiety was unaffected. Peter, too, seemed to have thrown off the effects of his gloomy forebodings, and his high spirits matched hers.

Later, Barbara telephoned again. Uncle Lionel had just gone to bed; he had received them amiably and, judging from the tone of her voice, Roger thought that she still found it difficult to believe ill of the old man. He hoped she would never have cause to feel towards him as the rest of them did.

Barbara had spent half-an-hour alone with Jennifer.

'Incredibly charming,' Barbara said, 'but so—' she paused, choosing her words – 'so, unworldly.'

'Haven't we told you that?' Roger asked.

'Of course, but I hadn't realized what you meant until now,' Barbara answered. 'I think we're going to get on, that's half the battle. You haven't heard anything more from the police, have you?'

'No. Has the old man talked about it?'

'Not a word. He says it's a matter for the police, and he's washed his hands of it.'

Goodnights exchanged, Roger put down the receiver and dropped onto his bed. He was tired, but less worried than he considered he had any right to be. It was a warm night, and the window was wide open; he could hear the curtains when the wind blew them gently to and fro. Warm, comfortable and weary, he drifted into sleep.

He awoke, for no apparent reason, while it was still dark. The soft rustle of the curtains was in his ears, but he could hear no other sound. Then, suddenly, something fell downstairs.

He stiffened.

Someone was moving about the house. As he threw back the bedclothes, the door slowly opened.

Peter stood there, a hand on his lips.

'So you heard it,' he whispered. 'Who can it be?

'We'll find out,' said Roger grimly. He switched off the bedside lamp.

57

Together, they moved stealthily to the head of the stairs. As they reached it, there was another noise, as of a chair falling. It was followed by a mutter of words.

'They're clumsy beggars,' said Peter, with a note of repressed excitement in his voice.

'Quiet!' Roger gripped the banister, and began to go downstairs. He was getting used to the darkness, when suddenly the hall light went on.

'What—' began Peter.

Someone gasped.

Roger narrowed his eyes against the light, and hurried down. A man was standing helplessly against the wall.

'Frank!' Peter exclaimed.

Frank Corcoran stood staring at them, his good-looking face pale, his lips unsteady. He stretched out a hand; it was trembling.

Roger hurried towards him.

'My dear chap, what's the trouble? He took Frank's arm, guiding him to a chair. 'Whisky, Peter, quickly.'

Frank Corcoran sank down nervously.

'There's nothing to be afraid of here,' Roger assured him.

Corcoran drew in a sharp breath.

'But – there is! You must hide me. They're looking for me everywhere.'

Roger thought he knew whom he meant, but asked lightly:

'Who?

'The police.'

'What's this about the police?' asked Peter, coming in with a glass in his hand. 'Drink this, you'll feel a different man,' he added, and stood over the youngster while he drank.

Corcoran put the glass on the edge of the chair, and it fell to the floor before Roger could save it.

'They're – after me,' said Corcoran. He leaned back, with his eyes closed. 'I – I ran away.'

His clothes were muddy and untidy, there were dry leaves in his hair, his collar and tie were unfastened. His breathing was steadier now, but he was still trembling. Suddenly he gripped Roger's hand.

'They think I attacked your uncle!' He drew in a sharp breath. 'I didn't attack him, but I wish I had. I wish I'd killed him!' He sprang to his feet, trembling violently. 'You've got to do something, Roger! You mustn't let him do this to Jennifer. I had to see you before they send me to prison – you must stop him, Roger!'

CHAPTER SEVEN

POLICE TRIUMPH

'IF there's anything we can do, we'll do it,' Roger assured the youngster, quietly. 'We're trying to work something out now.'

'You – are?'

'Yes.'

'Then why haven't you told me? Why have you stayed away from Hilbury?' Corcoran took his hand away, and added miserably: 'I think you're only trying to calm me down, and make me forget that you've deserted Jennifer.'

'Don't be an ass,' said Roger. 'If I'd come to Hilbury I'd have told the old man what I thought about him, and that wouldn't have helped.'

Peter stepped forward.

'Has anything happened to make the situation worse? With Jenny, I mean?'

'Could it be worse?' Corcoran brushed his hair back impatiently. 'She's entered the Catholic Church.'

'That was an inevitable first step,' Roger said. 'We can't hope to get quick results, you know.'

'What are you going to do?'

'We—' began Peter.

Roger shot him a quick, warning glance.

'We haven't quite decided,' he said. 'Have you met Jenny's brother?'

'You mean, Paul Briscoe?'

'Yes, he—'

'You don't expect a man like *that* to help, do you?' cried Corcoran. 'Why, he's nothing but a clown and a coward!'

'Who told you that?' demanded Peter.

'Your uncle.'

'Well I'm darned!' exclaimed Peter. 'He – Roger, I wonder if *he* sent those feathers!'

'We needn't worry about that now,' Roger said, impatiently. 'Frank, you ought to know Mr. Chard well enough to realize that you can't believe all he says. Paul's flown over from America to try to help, and he'll do everything he can. When we've heard from him – he's at Chard Lodge now – we'll have another council of war. Whatever happens, don't run away with the idea that we're sitting back and doing nothing. But you're the immediate problem. Tell me exactly what happened.'

Corcoran said wearily: 'I was in the grounds at the time of the attack.'

'What on earth were you doing there at half-past six in the morning?' demanded Roger.

'You don't understand,' muttered Corcoran. 'I saw Mr. Chard the day before yesterday, he wouldn't listen to me and – and he won't let me see Jenny! I – I know Jenny gets up early, I thought if I hung about I might be able to have a word with her.' He broke off.

'And did you see her?' asked Roger.

'Yes – but it was no good. She didn't seem to care.' Corcoran dashed his hand across his eyes.

'Let's get to the bottom of this police business, Frank,'

Roger said, his voice kind and comforting. 'When you were found to have been in the grounds, the police questioned you, did they?'

'They didn't know about that until – until after they'd let me go,' said Corcoran. 'I told them I hadn't been near the place.'

'You ass!' exclaimed Peter.

'You're a fine one to talk,' said Roger. 'Frank, be honest with us. If the police didn't know you'd been near the place, why did they question you?'

'Someone had seen me in the village,' Corcoran muttered, 'and – well, after I'd seen Mr. Chard, I suppose I said some pretty crazy things. I had a drink or two at the Plough, and I talked too much.' He gave a sickly smile. 'I think that's how they got on to me. I thought they were satisfied, and then someone turned up who'd seen me in the grounds. He went into Hilbury to tell the police, and a friend of mine let me know, and so I ran away.'

'Surely you couldn't get far.'

'I didn't expect to keep away from the police indefinitely,' Corcoran agreed. He looked better; there was some colour in his cheeks, and his voice was steadier. 'But I had to have a word with you, because goodness knows what is going to happen to me now. If I'm sent to prison, I can't do anything to help Jenny—'

He broke off.

There was silence in the room, but from some way off there came the sound of a car. Roger thought little of it as he waited for the youngster to go on.

'I just had to see you,' Corcoran finished.

'I could have come to see you, whenever the police lodged you for the night,' said Roger. 'And you, of all people, ought to now that the police won't take any action until they're quite sure of themselves.'

'They'll feel sure, now,' said Corcoran.

'If you hadn't run away—' began Peter.

'It wouldn't have made any difference. As soon as they

knew I'd lied to them about being in the grounds, they'd have come for me,' said Corcoran. 'Well, I've seen you, that's the main thing. You – you do *mean* it when you say you'll do everything you can for her?

He heard the car again; it was coming nearer. There seemed to be something significant in it now. He waited, on edge. Peter looked at the window, and Corcoran stiffened.

Brakes squealed outside.

Corcoran said quietly: 'The police, I expect.'

'It might be,' agreed Roger, unflurried. 'Frank, don't do anything else to make the situation worse, will you?'

As he spoke, there was a heavy knocking on the front door. Peter said: 'I'll go,' and opened the door into the hall. Almost immediately, Lucille cried out:

'Peter! What is zat?'

'It's all right, *chérie*,' called Peter. 'You go back to bed and don't worry!'

Peter opened the door. As they expected, Marlin and several of his men stood there. Peter stepped aside and they tramped into the hall.

Roger took Cocoran's arm.

'Come on, let's face it,' he said.

Corcoran pulled himself free, and ran to the window. He was halfway through as Marlin and two of his men rushed across the room.

'Handcuff him!' The order came sharply.

'The silly young ass,' said Peter, gloomily.

'I will know what is happening here!' exclaimed Lucille. She ran into the room, turned, and recognized Marlin. She stood quite still, her great eyes fixed in terror.

'*Chérie*,' said Peter, desperately.

'Why – why is *zat* man here?'

'On business,' said Marlin sharply.

Peter gripped Lucille's arm.

'For the love of Mike, have some sense!' snapped Roger.

What could Marlin think of this scene? They had harboured Corcoran, or so it must seem, Lucille had lost her head when she had realized that the police were here, and to worsen the situation Peter, by every sign, was about to lose his. Marlin would have every reason to think that they had something to hide.

The tone of Roger's voice had startled Peter. He turned, still keeping his arms about Lucille, and led her to a chair.

Marlin looked first at Roger, then at Lucille. Then he turned deliberately, stretched out a hand and dropped it heavily on Corcoran's shoulder. The words of arrest came clearly, charging the boy with committing an unlawful assault upon the person of Mr. Lionel Chard. Corcoran stood quite still, his eyes feverishly bright; he was not trembling now.

Then Marlin turned to Roger.

'And what justification have you, Mr. Maitland, for assisting the prisoner in his attempt to avoid arrest?'

Steadily, Roger returned the detective's gaze.

'Well, Mr. Maitland?

Roger, fighting back a surge of annoyance, forced a smile.

'You've got the wrong end of the stick,' he said. 'I was trying to prevent him from leaving. I had just advised him not to do anything foolish. But—'

'Well?' snapped Marlin.

'I can easily understand him not wanting to discuss the matter with you,' said Roger, his voice icy.

'Mr. Maitland—'

'Listen to me!' snapped Roger, authoritatively. 'Corcoran came to tell me that he was accused of the attack on my uncle, that he was innocent of it – and I believe him – and that he was anxious to see me before he was arrested. I did not help him to escape and I did not know that he was coming here. Is that categorical enough?

Marlin pursed his lips.

'I *see*. And *why* was Corcoran so anxious to—'

'*Mr.* Corcoran, please.' Roger's voice was sharp, and Marlin flushed.

It was a trivial point, and Roger regretted the outburst almost as soon as he had made it: it weakened his position. Not that his position had ever been strong; had Marlin acted with a little more discretion, it would have been a very awkward situation indeed. The possibility of being accused of helping Corcoran to get away was of comparatively little importance, but the police would obviously demand to know why Corcoran had thought it worthwhile coming here, and what message he had been so desperately anxious to pass on. That would mean telling them something of the story of Jennifer. He could not imagine Marlin having much sympathy.

'Well, why did he come here?' asked Marlin, acidly.

Corcoran spoke in a stronger voice.

'Mr. Maitland is a friend of mine,' he said. 'I knew I should be charged and arrested, and I wanted someone disinterested to take up my case. I also wanted to assure him that I did not attack Mr. Chard.'

Well done, thought Roger. Would it be enough?

Unexpectedly Marlin swung round on Corcoran.

'Have you any reason to believe that either of these men attacked Mr. Chard?'

Corcoran gasped. 'Good heavens, no!'

'Aren't you being rather tedious?' Peter said loftily. 'That was all settled on Saturday.'

'Was it?' Marlin smiled nastily. He turned to Roger. 'Mr. Maitland, I now understand that something was stolen from Chard Lodge – something in which you are intensely interested.'

Roger said, 'Oh? And what was that?'

'The deeds of this house and land,' Marlin said.

It came out of the blue, startling Roger enough to make him back against a chair. It was impossible to assess the full significance of the statement, but it did not take him long to realize what it might mean. If the deeds were lost, it would delay the taking over of the farm; no one but he was interested in that. He could understand now, the accusing look in Marlin's eyes; why the man felt so sure of himself.

'Who told you that they were missing?'

'Mr. Chard, naturally.'

'I see,' said Roger. 'Well, I didn't take them.'

'I would like your permission to search the house,' said Marlin.

'Search—' began Roger.

'You've no right to do that!' snapped Peter.

'I have every right,' Marlin said, and took from his pocket a slip of paper which he handed to Roger. There was a touch of absurdity about the whole proceeding, but one thing was obvious; if he tried to obstruct the police, he would do more harm than good.

He handed the warrant back.

'Quite unnecessary,' he said. 'If you must search, get on with it – Mrs. Maitland wants to get back to bed.'

He smiled reassuringly at Lucille. Marlin turned to one of his men.

'You take charge down here, Abbott. Harrison, take the prisoner to the car.'

Nothing was found in the dining-room

Abbott looked at Roger. 'I'm sorry about this,' he said. 'Come with me, if you like.'

'I will, thanks,' said Roger, warming to the man.

He felt less easy in his mind when Abbott lifted the waste-paper basket in the drawing-room and, with obvious interest, picked out the broken feathers. He glanced up, smiling.

'Have you been plucking chickens?'

Roger forced a laugh.

Abbott hesitated, and then put the feathers and the envelope on the arm of a chair. He finished his search methodically, leaving nothing out of place. Roger had expected him to make only a cursory inspection of the kitchen quarters, but he was as thorough about that as about the living-room.

'Well, that's that,' said Abbott. 'Ours is sometimes an unpleasant job, Mr. Maitland.'

'If everyone made it as pleasant as you do, it wouldn't be so bad,' said Roger.

He led the way back to the dining-room. Marlin had just gone inside. Roger heard him ask:

'Can you give me any information about this, Mr. Maitland?'

Peter said: 'About what? Here, give those to me.'

Roger thought: *More* trouble, and pushed the door wide open. Marlin was standing with a bundle of pound notes in his hand. They were the one pound notes with which Kennard had paid for the picture.

'You've no right—' began Peter, and then laughed abruptly. 'They're the notes with which I was paid for a picture on Saturday. I suppose it surprises you?'

Marlin said abruptly: 'Who bought the picture?'

'A Mr. Kennard.'

'Do you know him well?'

'Not particularly. He does a bit of buying and selling. I don't know where you'll find him, if that's what you mean.'

'I see,' said Marlin, evasively: he could hardly have made it clearer that he was extremely interested. 'Abbott,' he added, 'get your notebook ready. Mr. Maitland, perhaps you will be good enough to read out the numbers of those notes.'

CHAPTER EIGHT

CHARD LODGE

ABBOTT sat at Roger's desk and duly entered the numbers of the notes in his book. Apparently nothing else in the house had attracted Marlin's attention. He was coldly polite when he said that that was all he needed, but that he might find it necessary to ask both brothers for statements, next day.

As the police car drove away, a heavy depression settled on the house.

'Well, that was quite a show,' said Peter, with an attempt to speak lightly.

'Pretty grim,' said Roger. 'Frank's not going to have an easy time.' His eyes swept over Lucille, wan and unhappy. 'We'd better get some sleep,' he said gently. 'We can hold a *post mortem* in the morning.'

Peter looked down at the notes wonderingly.

'I wonder why he was so interested in these,' he said, holding up the money. 'Surely Kennard isn't a crook?'

'Stop worrying about it,' said Roger, tersely.

He wished them goodnight again, and turned into his room. He was glad to get into bed. Tired though he was, however, his thoughts kept him awake. Why *was* Marlin so interested in the notes? Why had anyone stolen the deeds of Home Farm? Why had Frank made that silly effort to escape? Had Marlin seriously thought that he had been helping the youngster? Was Marlin satisfied with Frank's explanation of his visit? And, if Frank had not assaulted the old man, who had?

Of all the questions, that seemed the most important.

Then he remembered the problem which had been raised earlier: the sender of the white feathers. It had been easy to forget that, because it seemed to have no immediate bearing on the main problem; but it might be of some significance. The feathers—

Abbott *had* seemed interested in the feathers.

Roger pushed back the bedclothes and got up, frowning as he hurried downstairs.

He looked into the drawing-room; the feathers and the torn envelope had been on the arm of a chair. They were not there now. He picked up the wastepaper basket, but it only held a crumpled cigarette carton.

Then he remembered, with a sudden spasm of alarm, his notes regarding Jennifer's abduction. The fair copy was in his pocket. The rough draft he had screwed up and left on his desk. He hurried into the dining-room, but they were gone. Perhaps, after all, he had thrown them away? He couldn't remember, and he felt a sudden surge of anger and dismay. Anyone studying those notes closely would surely guess what they were about.

He went upstairs again and read through the fair copy.

The headings were all rather vague; they might not be associated with the plan in mind, but would it be possible to go ahead when such evidence was in the hands of the police?

Had Abbott taken them?

And what significance could he have read into the feathers?

Roger moved uneasily.

If he had gone to see Frank the previous night, as he had suggested, he would have been able to stop at least one ill-considered and dangerous move. For by coming here the youngster had not only greatly strengthened the police suspicions against him; he had implicated them all.

Detective Sergeant Abbott stifled a yawn as he drove from the Hilbury Police Station to the lodgings which he shared with Detective Sergeant Bennison. Bennison, the lucky beggar, had been sleeping the sleep of the just whereas dawn was breaking and Abbott had not had a wink of sleep since the previous night.

He put the car away, let himself in, and went quietly up to his room.

'*Must* you make noise enough to wake the dead?' demanded Bennison, from the snug warmth of his bed. 'Did you find Corcoran?'

'We did indeed,' said Abbott chattily. 'Also some pound notes which Marlin was curious about. His Worship hasn't confided in me, but I think he made a fuss about the notes just to get the Maitland men on edge.'

'So there are two Maitlands now,' said Bennison, wearily.

Abbott grimaced at him, but, now that he had started talking, he found his tiredness receding.

'Oh, I picked up something off Maitland's desk that I didn't tell Marlin about,' he said airily, 'and I took some oddments out of a wastepaper basket.'

'Dear me. Quite the little Sherlock.'

Abbott grinned. 'It was all accidental like! I must have slipped them into my pocket without thinking!' He leaned forward and took the feathers, the torn envelope and a screwed up ball of paper from the table by his bed. 'I don't know why these struck me as odd, except that the envelope's addressed to Paul Briscoe, and there was once some odd talk about Briscoe. You remember the time when some English actors in Hollywood received billets-doux in the shape of white feathers?'

'I don't,' said Bennison.

'Well, they did – and these feathers were with the envelope. Block lettering, as if to disguise the handwriting, too.'

'You're letting your imagination run away with you,' said Bennison, but he stretched out a hand and took the feathers.

'Who knows?' asked Abbott, lightly. He was unscrewing the ball of paper. 'There is something odd, you know, in Corcoran being at Home Farm. Marlin as good as suggested that Corcoran, who dislikes old Chard because he isn't now allowed to see the fair Jennifer, might have attacked Chard under the influence of the Maitlands and, when he was caught, flew to the Maitlands for help.'

'Humph.'

'And there were one or two other odd things,' went on Abbott, smoothing out the paper. 'Peter Maitland was there with a nifty little French piece – his wife.'

Bennison sniffed. 'Pretty women will be the ruin of you.'

'Could be,' grinned Abbott. 'The curious thing tonight was that she got into a panic because we were there. She doesn't like the police.'

'It's an acquired taste,' murmured Bennison.

'Ass! Peter Maitland wasn't too happy about his wife, either. He gave me the impression that he was nervous in case she said too much. Look how eager the old man was to suggest that one of his nephews was responsible for the attack!'

'Chard's no fool,' Bennison said, 'and I've been doing a bit of snooping myself.'

'About what?'

'The family. There's a housekeeper who isn't proof against my blandishments and a whisky or two,' Bennison went on. 'To be strictly honest,' he added, 'the whisky or two comes first.'

He proceeded to outline the story of Roger and the Home Farm, going on to the plan to send Jennifer into a convent.

'And the nephews don't like it?'

'They're up in arms.'

'I don't see what it's got to do with the present situation,' said Abbott, 'but you'd better make a report.'

He had succeeded in smoothing out the crumpled paper, and now he read with kindling interest.

70

'*Paper? ... Make-up ... Barbara to excite envy ... Place ... She can't be alone ... Clothes ... Photographs ... Newspapers ... Quiet spot* ... Hmm,' he said, excitedly. 'I think Marlin might be interested in this.'

At Chard Lodge, that night, Barbara and Paul slept soundly. As Barbara had told Roger on the telephone, Uncle Lionel had received them affably enough and, Barbara had decided, it was that unexpected affability which had first made her see why Paul and the others disliked him. It had lacked sincerity. It was difficult to put a finger on the actual indication of falseness, but it had been there.

She woke up before Paul.

By the clock on the bedside table, it was half-past seven. They were to be called at eight. Probably Jennifer was already up and about; the housekeeper certainly would be, and Uncle Lionel also, unless he was still feeling the effects of the attack.

He was not a man to give way, however.

At seventy-one, he had a surprising physique, and must in his youth have been extremely powerful.

Barbara got out of bed.

The sun was beginning to shine over the pleasant lawns at the front of the Lodge. There was a slight mist in a hollow just beyond the garden. It was fascinating to watch the vague, squat shapes of shrubs and trees gradually getting clearer.

Someone moved in the garden.

Barbara stiffened.

The 'someone' was walking slowly from the far side of the house. She could hear the muffled footsteps, lightly, almost inaudibly, placed.

Jennifer came into sight.

Barbara caught her breath.

There was still enough mist for it to surround the girl; it was as if she carried with her an aura of mystery. The fleeting gleams of sun touched the gold in her hair, emphasizing the untouched youthfulness and purity of her face.

She drew nearer Barbara's window, and stood, dreamily looking over the town.

Barbara followed the direction of her gaze, seeing the austere but lovely lines of the convent.

Barbara instinctively drew back. Perhaps the movement caught Jennifer's eye, for she looked up.

'Good morning, Barbara.' She smiled.

'Hallo,' said Barbara. 'You're out early.'

'I always like to walk alone at this hour,' said Jennifer. 'I hope that I did not disturb you.'

In Barbara's ears her voice seemed to linger, quiet, gentle, not in itself beautiful, but hushed. She gave a slight wave of her hand, walking on, graceful and erect, disappearing into the mist. Barbara thought with fast beating heart: She isn't normal.

Paul stirred.

No, Jennifer wasn't normal. In spite of her smile and the serenity of her expression, Barbara sensed a disquiet deep within her. It was almost as if she carried some burden which she could neither share nor lose.

Jennifer's footsteps were still audible when another sound broke the quiet. Barbara looked towards the gate. A uniformed policeman was walking up the drive. He did not come far, but cut across the lawn. It was obvious that he was looking for someone. As his eyes alighted on Jennifer, he withdrew, satisfied.

'Paul,' called Barbara sharply. 'Do you know that the police are watching Jennifer?'

CHAPTER NINE

UNCLE LIONEL

PAUL leapt out of bed and hurried to the window.

'It's too late to see anything now,' Barbara told him. 'I wonder if Uncle Lionel suspects that we might try to get Jennifer away?'

'He's pretty deep,' said Paul, stifling a yawn. 'So are the police. What's the time?'

'It's getting on for eight,' said Barbara.

She went along to the bathroom, troubled by what she had seen and thinking much about Jennifer. The sight of the girl emerging from the mist had greatly impressed her. Nor could she easily forget the sight of the convent; large, dark, almost sinister.

Dressed, still troubled, she went downstairs and out into the garden. Half-an-hour had made a great difference to the scene. Only a few faint wisps of mist now hung about the distant hollows.

The policeman who had shown such an interest in Jennifer was leaning against the gate. Barbara turned to the left, in the direction Jennifer had taken. When she reached the side of the house, she saw another policeman, just beyond the hedge which separated the garden from a meadow. She could not rid herself of the feeling that the policemen were watching Jennifer, although their ostensible purpose, no doubt, was to make sure that there was no further attack on Uncle Lionel.

'Good morning, Barbara.'

She jumped when Lionel Chard's deep voice came from

73

some bushes near her. There was a smile on his face, as if he had deliberately meant to startle her.

He said perfunctorily: 'You slept well, I hope?'

'Very well, thank you.'

'Tell me, what do you think of my home?'

'I like it very much,' Barbara told him.

'Don't you find it surprising that Paul preferred to live somewhere else?' he asked.

It was the first time he had broached that subject, and it took her by surprise. He laughed when he saw her expression; it was a deep laugh, but it rang hollow.

'I see you don't,' he said.

'Men like to live their own lives,' she said crisply.

'Ah, I see that I must not expect you to side with me. Forget it, my dear.' He rested a hand on her shoulder. The pressure was heavy, almost as if he were warning her. 'Paul has made some success out of life, but success can often be snatched away at the last moment, or spoiled by something long forgotten. Is he happy, Barbara?'

She did not hesitate. 'Yes.'

'I hope he remains so,' said Uncle Lionel. He kept his hand on her shoulder as they walked slowly towards the porch. 'Tell me, what do you think of my other nephews?'

'I know so little of them.'

'They are both self-willed young men, but I think they might live to learn better. Have you met the woman with whom Peter is living?'

'I've met his *wife*.'

Uncle Lionel looked down at her.

'I see. And what opinion did you form?'

'That she is very charming.'

'Charming! The French slut, she—' The old man broke off, as if he realized that he had gone too far. 'You must forgive me, Barbara. I have no love for the French. You must be hungry,' he added, abruptly. 'Come into breakfast.'

Paul and Jennifer were already in the breakfast room.

That something was wrong was immediately evident. Jennifer was standing by her chair, staring at her brother. Paul held an open letter in his hand. Two white feathers were on the table. Uncle Lionel made a curious little noise. Barbara looked at him sharply. He was smiling; *he was amused.*

From that moment, she hated Uncle Lionel.

'Post for you already, Paul?' observed the old man. 'Fan mail, I presume.'

Paul looked up. 'Yes,' he said, abruptly. He thrust the feathers into his pocket, and crumpled the envelope; Barbara had just time to see that it bore a typewritten address.

Uncle Lionel went to his place at the head of the table; a dozen letters were by his side.

Jennifer poured coffee for Paul and and the old man, Tea for herself and Barbara. They helped themselves to bacon and eggs from a hot-plate on a waggon which was pushed from person to person. Uncle Lionel seemed to immerse himself in his letters. Jennifer had little to say, and was obviously deep in thought. Paul's attempt to draw her into light conversation came to nothing.

As soon as she had finished, the old man spoke.

'You have to go to your studies, Jennifer.'

'I am going now, uncle.'

'Don't forget their importance,' said Lionel Chard. He pushed his chair back as she rose. Barbara, looking at the old man, saw that he was watching her with narrowed eyes, and in them was an expression which she did not understand.

He stared at Paul when the door had closed, and said abruptly:

'Paul, please understand that I do not encourage Jennifer in light conversation.'

Paul finished his coffee in silence.

'And I must ask you not to.'

'Jennifer,' pronounced Paul at last, 'is my sister.'

'And my ward. She—'

'And I will talk to my sister in whatever way I think fit, whether you like it or not,' declared Paul, in a quiet voice.

75

He had grown pale, and his eyes were hard. 'You may want to bury her alive. I don't. You may want to keep everything fresh, real, natural and healthy from her, but I don't. She wants the company of younger people, which you have deliberately kept away from her, and—'

'She would have had it if you and your cousins had shown the slightest loyalty,' said Chard, in a taut voice.

'None of us was prepared to risk sharing her fate,' Paul said, abruptly.

Chard said: 'You are forgetting yourself, Paul.'

'No,' said Paul, 'I am just remembering myself.' He got up, and went quickly to the door.

Chard sat back in his chair. His face was white: obviously he was at great pains to repress an angry outburst. He looked at Barbara with bright, hostile eyes.

She wished that Paul had not burst out like that; it might upset all the good they had hoped to do. She was a little afraid of earning a rebuff if she spoke, but she took the chance.

'I'm afraid Paul had a shock this morning,' she said.

'A – shock?'

'Yes. Those feathers—'

'He's a weak-minded fool if he lets a thing of that kind upset him,' snapped the old man. 'Barbara, listen to me. I won't have Paul, you or anyone else coming here and upsetting Jennifer. Do you hear me? I won't have it. If you want to stay here, make that clear to him. If he talks to me like that again, I'll show him the door. And he'd better be careful. So had you.' His eyes were still bright and angry. 'He is doing pretty well for himself, but that might not last. Neither he nor any of the others can afford to do without my money when I'm dead, even if they've managed without it while I've been alive. Tell them so.'

Barbara did not speak.

'And if you and Paul have come here with some silly notion of trying to change Jennifer's mind, you'll have me to deal with,' said the old man. 'Remember that, too.'

Barbara stood up.

'I'm beginning to see why your nephews love you so dearly,' she said.

The remark stung; she saw him wince; and, because of Jennifer, she wished she had not spoken. But it was done, and she went out, feeling hot and angry both with herself and with Chard. She heard a car coming up the drive, but did not look to see who it was.

Paul was not in their room. She thought she saw him in the garden, and hurried downstairs again as Superintendent Marlin entered the breakfast room. She heard Uncle Lionel greet him in a friendly voice. Standing in the hall and looking at her with evident admiration, was a younger man in plain clothes.

'Good morning,' said Detective Sergeant Bennison.

'Good morning.' Barbara hurried into the garden, anxious to see Paul. As she passed the breakfast room window, she heard Marlin say:

'Yes, sir, he is under arrest.'

'I congratulate you, Superintendent. I am not surprised that it was the young fool.'

'We can't be quite sure of that yet, sir,' said Marlin, 'although certainly it looks as if—'

Torn between curiosity and anxiety to see Paul, Barbara hurried on, assuming that the 'young fool' was Frank Corcoran. She looked for Paul in the shrubbery, but could not see him. She knew just how desperately unhappy the feathers made him.

She called out: 'Paul!' but there was no answer.

Moving further through the trees, she caught sight of a summerhouse and a glimpse of her husband standing in the doorway.

His voice came clearly to her.

'You needn't worry about me, Jenny.'

'But I do,' said Jennifer, quietly. 'You looked so unhappy, Paul. When you opened that letter this morning, it was as if you'd received terrible news.'

He laughed. 'It was hardly news. Don't worry about it. Jenny—'

'Yes?'

'Do you really—' began Paul, and Barbara thought: Oh, you ass! But Paul must have realized what he was saying, and added rather lamely: 'Do you really like Barbara?'

'I think I shall like her very much,' said Jennifer, gravely.

'That's fine,' said Paul. 'Why don't you go for a drive with her this morning?'

Barbara, standing in the cover of some trees, saw the girl glance up at the sky and smile wistfully.

'You mustn't tempt me! I have promised Uncle Lionel that I will work this morning. I do not think he would agree to me going out with Barbara.'

'Must you worry about that?' asked Paul.

'Of course,' said Jennifer.

Paul threw up his hands. 'Jenny, he—'

Barbara stepped forward. 'Paul!'

He broke off, startled.

'I've been looking for you everywhere,' Barbara went on. 'Hallo, Jenny, what a lovely spot to work in. If you get finished early, I'd love you to show me round the garden. Paul, we shouldn't waste Jenny's time.'

With forced jocularity Paul took Barbara's arm, and they walked away. He did not speak again until Jennifer was out of earshot. Then: 'Thanks, darling. I was well on the way to making a fool of myself again. How I'd like to take a smack at Uncle Lionel.'

Barbara did not speak immediately.

'Go on, tell me that I'm acting like a child.'

'I was thinking that Uncle Lionel would probably like to do the same to you,' said Barbara. 'Paul . . .'

She told him what had passed between her and the old man.

Paul listened without comment, and was silent for a long time when she had finished. Then suddenly he laughed.

'Come on, let's walk this out of our system! I'm not going to suffer if he cuts me out of his will, but the others won't find it so easy.' He quickened his pace, and they went towards the meadow, climbed a stile and then walked swiftly in the direction of Hilbury. Not once did they look back at the house. Had they done so, they might have seen Uncle Lionel spying on them from a first floor window, and the detective whom Barbara had passed in the hall watching them from the hedge near which they had been talking.

There was no great pressure of work at Hilbury Police Station, and Bennison went off duty before one o'clock. He entered his room, where Abbott was brushing his hair and preening himself in front of the mirror.

'What a pretty boy he is,' scoffed Bennison. 'How did you manage to wake up so early?'

'I didn't. Mrs. Harris wanted to have me up for lunch. What's doing?'

'Nothing fit for your young ears,' said Bennison.

'Come on,' pleaded Abbott.

'Gentlemen!' came a booming voice from downstairs, *'gentlemen, it's on the table!'*

'Coming!' called Bennison, hastily.

He washed his hands quickly and hurried downstairs soon after Abbott, to the small pleasantly furnished dining-room.

Mrs. Harris, both cook and waitress, came bustling in with a tray. Abbott sniffed.

'It smells good.'

'It *is* good,' said Mrs. Harris. 'Would you mind helping yourselves, I'm off to the pictures.'

Bennison wagged a reproving finger.

'Mrs. H., I'm not at all sure that you ought to go to the pictures so often. They might have a harmful effect on you!'

'It's my own business, and I'll thank you not to teach me how to behave,' said Mrs. Harris reprovingly. She wagged a

79

finger at each in turn. 'And don't you forget it, Mr. Bennison. I – oh, there's the greengrocer,' she added. 'Get on with your dinner and don't be worrying me. Coming, Sam!'

Abbott grinned.

'Bless her heart. Don't take the rise out of her too often.'

'It would break her heart if we left,' said Bennison.

'It would break mine if she threw us out!' said Abbott. 'Well, tell us what you've been up to.'

'Plenty of trouble at Chard Lodge, and that's for sure. Threat of murder and all that kind of thing,' Bennison assured him, not without relish.

'You're exaggerating, as usual.'

'I am not! I heard Paul say with real viciousness that he'd like to murder his uncle. Not in so many words, but that is what he meant, and if you ask me, the old devil deserves it,' he added righteously.

'Why's that?'

'For one thing, Briscoe doesn't take kindly to the idea of his sister going into the convent, and Chard won't allow opposition.'

'Hardly a motive for murder,' murmured Abbott.

'There's more to it than that. Chard's made some kind of threat to cut Briscoe and his other nephews out of his will, unless they come to heel.'

Suddenly the door was flung open and into the room stalked Mrs. Harris, dressed for out-of-doors but obviously intent on doing battle.

CHAPTER TEN

MRS. HARRIS OPINES

'ARE you *both* fools?' demanded Mrs. Harris, hotly.

Abbott looked startled.

'What have we been doing now?'

'What haven't you been doing?' demanded Mrs. Harris. 'It's a crying shame, that's what it is, and high time you policemen started to learn your business, instead of persecuting a poor lad like that, and I don't mind who knows it. I've never heard the like, not in all my life, and *you're* to blame.'

'What *is* this?' asked Bennison.

'You know very well what it is. There isn't a nicer lad in all Hilbury.'

'Are you talking about young Corcoran?'

'And who else, I should like to know? Arrested, indeed! Charged with attempted murder, that's what I'm told. Is it true?'

Abbott stood up. 'I'm afraid it is.'

'You're afraid! Then why did you do it?'

'The evidence—' began Abbott.

'A fig for your evidence!' cried Mrs. Harris. 'You've only got to look at the lad to see that he couldn't kill a fly, a quieter, nicer, kindlier, more Christian young man you couldn't find anywhere.' Mrs. Harris drew in her breath and suddenly seemed to wilt. She touched Abbott's shoulder. 'You don't really think he did it, do you?'

'It rather looks like it,' said Abbott, awkwardly.

'Then if he did, he had a good reason,' Mrs. Harris

81

declared, and drew herself up again. 'Not that I think he did, for a moment. It's a terrible mistake, and if you two are worth your salt you'll find out the truth of it.'

'We will,' Abbott assured her.

'You must,' said Mrs. Harris. 'Why on earth *should* he attack the old man? Tell me that!'

Neither of the policemen spoke.

Mrs. Harris sniffed.

'Some people can't see any farther than their nose!'

Abbott smiled faintly.

'It isn't yet proved that Corcoran did attack him, you know.'

'Poor lad.' Mrs. Harris's fingers tightened on Bennison's arm. 'Is there any way I can help him?'

Abbott said: 'I don't know.'

'There might be,' said Bennison, thoughtfully.

'Just say what it is.'

'Someone attacked Mr. Chard early on Saturday morning, and as far as we know yet, only Frank Corcoran was in the grounds. I—'

'You shouldn't really say this,' protested Abbott. 'You'll keep it to yourself, Mrs. Harris, won't you?'

'*I* can keep a still tongue in my head.' Mrs. Harris's eyes gleamed. 'If I told my neighbours what I hear you two talking about sometimes, *you* wouldn't remain in the Police Force for long, and don't you forget it.'

'We'll have to be careful!' said Bennison. 'I know you'll say nothing about this, Mrs. Harris, but if you've any friends at or near Chard Lodge, and can find out if anyone else was near the house, about six o'clock on Saturday morning, it might help young Corcoran.'

'Ben Tippett's the gardener, and his cottage is just along the road from the Lodge. I'll talk to him.'

'You will be careful what you say, won't you?' insisted Abbott.

'You needn't worry.' Mrs. Harris collected the coffee cups

82

absently. 'I'll learn something, never fear,' she said, and hurried out of the room.

'She might, at that,' remarked Bennison a trifle uneasily.

Just before lunch at Chard Lodge, Paul and Barbara were sitting in the drawing-room when they heard Chard's voice raised in an angry shout. A woman answered back, as angrily. There was the sound of a scuffle, and Paul hurried to the door. As he reached it, the housekeeper, wearing her outdoor clothes, and carrying a suitcase, just saved herself from hurtling down the stairs.

'What—' began Paul.

'It's a pity he didn't kill you while he was about it!' cried the housekeeper, her voice thin and high with passion. 'Push me down the stairs, would you? You touch me again and I'll have the police on you!'

Chard's answer, as much in fury, came thickly:

'Get out of my house, or I'll throw you out!'

'I want my money. I've got a right to ask you for my money. I—'

'Get out!' shouted Chard.

Barbara, standing in the doorway, saw his face white with passion and his clenched fists raised. He had scared Mrs. Rampling, a woman whom Barbara had seen only once or twice. There was a moment's pause, and then Paul said quietly:

'Your money will be sent on, you'd better go.'

He picked up her case, and she followed him to the front door. A taxi turned into the drive and, without saying another word, the housekeeper climbed, trembling, into it.

As the sound of the engine receded, Chard clumped down stairs.

'What was all that about?' asked Paul.

Barbara frowned a warning, but Chard answered readily enough.

'I could murder that woman,' he growled. 'I caught her at

83

my whisky – for the third time. When I told her to go, she—'
He paused, drawing a deep breath. 'She said that she had
told the police all that she knows about my happy relationship with my family.'

'How much does she know?' demanded Paul.

The old man looked at him with narrowed eyes.

'A woman in her position can hear a lot and see a lot, if
she's out to pry.'

'Probably. But I'd rather the family's dirty linen was
washed in private,' Paul said coldly. 'By going on at her like
that, you've made sure she'll tell all Hilbury.'

Chard left them, with an angry snort, and went into the
morning-room.

Luncheon was an uneasy meal. The old man referred only
obliquely to the scene on the stairs; he had arranged for
daily help, and Jennifer and the maid could manage well
enough. The scene was etched so clearly on Barbara's mind
that she found herself unable to forget it; the atmosphere at
the Lodge had become unbearably tense. Only Jennifer
seemed unaffected. Paul and Chard hardly exchanged a
word. When the old man spoke at all, it was gruffly, and
usually by way of a question to Jennifer, to which he received a quiet, friendly answer.

As they were finishing, the telephone rang.

Ben Tippett's daughter, small, timid and untrained, came
in to say there was a telephone call for Mr. Chard. Chard
grunted: 'All right,' and went out.

Whoever the caller, he did not appear to have pleased
Lionel Chard. He banged down the receiver, and a moment
later looked into the dining-room.

'I'm going to London,' he announced. 'Tell Tippett that I
want the car at two-twenty, and to meet me off the seven-
fifteen from Waterloo.' He went off without another word.

Jennifer hurried into the hall to telephone Tippett; Barbara leaned forward.

'Paul, we'll get her out for an hour or two.'

'Happy thought,' said Paul. 'As soon as he's gone I'll have

a word with Roger on the telephone.' He laughed. 'A few hours freedom from the old devil won't do any of us any harm! Have you changed your opinion of him?'

Barbara nodded.

'Well, that's a point gained,' said Paul. 'I wish—'

He broke off.

Coming along the drive, walking easily and gracefully, were two nuns. The sun shone on their starched white hoods and their pale faces. Paul went to the window, and Barbara joined him. Paul's hands were working, and his face was set. The nuns drew nearer. Their expressions were peaceful, touched by the unworldliness which so characterized Jennifer.

They disappeared.

Paul muttered: 'If they stop her from coming out, I'll – oh, what's the use!'

Jennifer's voice, quiet and calm, could be heard in greeting.

Paul moved away, distressed at the sight of the nuns, refusing to believe in Jennifer's pleasure at meeting them. He put through a call to Home Farm to hear that Roger had left that morning for Hilbury. He was determined to uncover what evidence he could in Frank Corcoran's favour.

As Paul put the receiver down, Barbara hurried in to say that the nuns had gone, and Jenny had agreed to go out for a spin with them.

Roger saw the car, with Paul driving and Barbara and Jennifer at the back, as it passed through Hilbury. He waved, but they did not notice him. The sight of them cheered him up, for he had not had a particularly encouraging morning.

The police had allowed him to see Frank Corcoran for a few minutes, but the youngster seemed stunned by what had happened and by his own subsequent folly.

The half-hour Roger had spent with Corcoran's parents had also proved a considerable strain. An elderly couple who had made considerable sacrifices for their son, they could not bring themselves to admit that in his love for Jennifer he might have done this crazy thing, while at the same time they were frightened lest he were guilty.

Roger's one cheerful interview had been with Father Hennessy.

He was now on his way to Chard Lodge.

A car pulled up alongside him, and he looked round to see Tippett, in a peaked cap but without his chauffeur's uniform.

'Can I give you a lift, sir? I've just taken Mr. Chard to the station.'

'Oh, he's out, is he?' said Roger. He leapt into the car. 'Well, Tippett, how are you?'

'Right enough in meself,' said Tippett, 'but worried like about Mr. Corcoran.'

'So are we all,' said Roger, sombrely.

'And a nicer lad never breathed,' went on Tippett, who, once launched, rambled on from Frank's innocence to Mrs. Harris and her two policemen lodgers.

'Mrs. Harris wants me to try to find out if there was any stranger near the Lodge on the morning of the attack,' continued Tippett, 'and I must say I didn't notice anyone, although I didn't start work until after seven. There's one man who *might* be able to tell us, sir, but I can't very well approach him myself, and he certainly won't say a word to the police.'

'Who is that?'

'Joe Bryce, poacher.' Tippett smiled sourly. 'I saw him coming away from High Spinney when I was going to work the day before yesterday. If he was working the spinney he'd have to pass pretty close to the Lodge.' Tippett looked at Roger a little oddly. 'I can be frank with you, sir, can't I?'

'Of course.'

'Joe Bryce doesn't exactly *love* Mr. Chard.' Tippett hesitated, and then went on: 'Joe likes his drop to drink, and goes a bit over the line sometimes, sir. He used to work for

Colonel Kingsley, same job as mine, chauffeur-gardener. Driving alone one night he scraped against this car as we passed him, and Mr. Chard made a fuss about it, and persuaded the Colonel to dismiss him. About that time his wife died. Joe's never been himself since then, Mr. Roger.'

'Rough luck,' Roger murmured.

'Well, *I* think so,' said Tippett, 'but don't misunderstand me, sir! He'd do Mr. Chard no harm. What I do think is that he wouldn't lift a finger to *help* him.'

'Or Frank Corcoran?'

Tippett shrugged. 'He was sent to jail last year for a month, after he was caught with a brace of pheasants in his pocket, so it's not likely that he'll open up to the police, Mr. Roger. But he might to you.'

'Where does he live?'

'Up at the far end of Lorne Village,' said Tippett. 'His eldest daughter does for him and looks after the kids. It isn't much of a place, but she does her best.' Tippett slowed down as they approached the Lodge. 'As a matter of fact, sir, Mr. Chard sent in a complaint about the condition of the kids not long ago. I won't say he wasn't justified, they're pretty dirty sometimes. Now there's some talk about the younger children being sent to a home if Bryce doesn't look after them better.'

'I see,' said Roger. 'If you'll drop me at the end of the lane, I'll make my own way.'

As Roger approached the cottage, he saw a man and a woman talking at the gate. The woman, speaking emphatically, was waving her hands in the air. The words drifted easily to Roger.

'If you ask me, Bryce, you're a fool.'

'Ah, but I didn't ask you.'

The man turned obstinately away.

He was a powerfully built countryman, shabby, unshaved, his expression, turned inquiringly towards Roger, cold and hostile. Mrs. Harris, for it was she, turned also, prepared for departure. But one parting shot she allowed herself.

'One of these days, you mark my words, you'll regret it.'

As Roger approached, Bryce spoke frostily:

'You're Roger Maitland, aren't you?'

'You've a good memory.'

'I have that,' the man answered bitterly, 'for all who live at Chard Lodge.'

'Well,' said Roger, amiably, 'if you won't ask me in, you can't stop me from staying this side of the gate.'

'But I needn't talk to you,' Bryce said.

Roger said mildly: 'I came to ask for your help.'

Bryce, in the act of stalking towards his cottage, stopped.

He said harshly: 'And what might that be?'

'Help for young Corcoran,' answered Roger.

'And if I could, I don't know that I want to,' answered Bryce, and there was bitterness in the words. 'Your uncle wouldn't put himself out, I'll warrant.'

'Well, I'm not my uncle,' said Roger, calmly.

'Well if you think I whacked the old sod, you're a fool. But I wish it had come off. I wish he'd died.'

'That's silly talk,' Roger said. 'I don't think you attacked my uncle, but for Corcoran's sake, I'd like to find out who did. Did you see anyone in his garden on Saturday morning?'

Bryce said slowly: 'And supposing I did?'

CHAPTER ELEVEN

TALK OF A STRANGER

'Supposing I did,' repeated Bryce. 'The police won't believe *me*.'

Nonchalantly Roger held his tobacco pouch out.

'I'm not the police,' he said.

Bryce grunted, but he took the pouch and began to fill his pipe.

'Yes, if you want to know, I did see someone. I saw a man come out of the Lodge. He hurried down the drive and cleared off pretty quickly. But no one else saw him, I reckon, and no one will believe me.'

'Did he walk, or was he driven?'

'There was a car,' said Bryce, indifferently, 'but it was a pretty quiet one. Large, too.'

'That might be helpful. There was just one man, you say?'

'I only saw one.'

'You've been in prison, haven't you?' asked Roger, abruptly.

'You know darned well I have!'

'Did you like it?'

Bryce looked at him, suspiciously.

'Now what's your game?'

'Presumably you didn't like it,' said Roger. 'But because you're frightened of questions the police might ask you about your poaching, you'll stand by and let young Corcoran go to prison for years. You can stand by if you like. I'm not going to. I'll try to find someone else who saw this car. If I can't find them, I shall tell the police what you've told me. Unless you're a fool, you'll volunteer the information first. There's been a request in the local paper for information – you've seen that, haven't you?'

'I don't read the newspapers.'

'You hear gossip.'

'I don't take any notice of gossip.'

Roger shrugged. 'It's up to you,' he said. 'If Corcoran were one of your youngsters, you'd feel differently about it.' He nodded, and turned away.

He did not look back, but he was conscious of Bryce standing at the gate watching him.

Back at the Lodge, Roger sat near an open window drinking a cup of tea which Lucy Tippett had brought him.

He saw Tippett drive off to meet Uncle Lionel, and ten minutes afterwards Paul's car turn into the drive. Barbara was driving, and Jennifer was sitting beside her. There was unusual animation on Jennifer's face and, with his heart beating fast, Roger hurried to open the front door.

'Roger!' exclaimed Jennifer. 'Have you been waiting long?'

'Not very long,' Roger assured her.

'I'm so glad to see you,' Jennifer exclaimed, 'I was afraid you were not coming back.'

She gripped his hands, and turned her face towards him. Roger kissed her lightly. No one could doubt the pleasure of her greeting.

'I'm not likely to go away from you forever,' Roger said, laughing. 'Where have you been?'

'As far as the coast,' said Jennifer. 'The sea was so calm, I wanted to bathe!'

'Didn't you have tea?'

'Oh yes, and now I will go and see how Lucy is getting on,' Jennifer said. She turned to the door leading to the kitchen, and then looked back. 'Thank you both very much!' She hurried off, and Roger looked at the others approvingly.

'Success?'

'Roger, it's absurd!' exclaimed Barbara. 'She was a different girl. It was as if she had suddenly seen a world she'd never realized existed. So childlike, yet in other ways she's so mature.'

'There's not much doubt,' said Paul, triumphantly, 'that it's going to be much easier than we'd realized – *much* easier. Why, on the way home, she wanted to know how to drive the car. Roger, we've just one problem – how to get her away. I had half a mind not to bring her back today.'

'We can't do it quite as suddenly as that,' said Roger 'but next time the old man goes to London, we'll have a shot.'

Tippett telephoned to say that Chard was not on the train, but there was another in an hour's time. He would wait. The hour passed quickly, and they were in the hall when the big car turned into the drive.

'There'll be a spot of bother over taking her out this afternoon, I expect,' Paul said. 'I hope it doesn't put him on his guard.'

'Why should it?' asked Roger.

'Bar's got some fool notion that the police are watching her, as well as making sure there isn't another attack on the old man,' said Paul. 'But we needn't worry about that now. You'd better make yourself scarce, Roger. There's bound to be a dust-up over this afternoon's jaunt, and there's no reason why you should be dragged into it.'

'I'll give you moral support,' said Roger.

They stood watching the big, old-fashioned Daimler come up the drive, tense with the expectation of unpleasantness to come.

Tippett jumped down from his seat, shot them a scared glance, and opened the door. The old man was sitting back in a corner, his eyes closed. He looked blue about the lips, and his skin had a yellowish tinge. Roger and Paul joined Tippett as Chard opened his eyes. Refusing help, he clambered out of the car. He was breathing heavily, and although he kept a fairly steady course, it was obvious that he found walking difficult. He reached the hall, then turned slowly.

'I shall not come down to dinner. Send Jennifer up to me in half-an-hour's time.'

Slowly, laboriously, he dragged himself up the stairs. They stood watching until he was out of sight, and then Tippett said in a nervous voice:

'He was all right when I met the train, Mr. Roger. Then he spoke to someone in Hilbury. I've never seen the man before. And he just seemed to fold up. But he snapped my head off when I suggested taking him to Dr. Coppinger.'

'He just spoke to a man and *this* happened?' exclaimed Paul.

'Yes, Mr. Paul – he was quite himself, spoke to me as he

always does, and then we were stepping into the car when this man came up.'

'You had better tell us about it later,' Roger said. 'Paul, telephone for Coppinger. Bar, tell Jenny that he's not well, will you, and that he wants to see her soon. All right, Tippett,' he added, when he saw the anxious expression on the chauffeur's face, 'you did what you were told, you've nothing to worry about. But he's a sick man.' He walked towards the stairs as Paul went to the telephone.

Tippett followed him.

'Have you ever seen him like this before?' Roger asked.

'Not so bad,' said Tippett. 'It's his heart, isn't it?'

'It looks like it.'

Roger did not tap on the old man's door, but went straight in. Uncle Lionel did not see him immediately. He was trying to unfasten his shoes.

It took all his strength. With reluctant admiration for such spirit, Roger went forward. He did not ask whether he could help, and would not have been surprised at a vituperative outburst for his interference.

Uncle Lionel's colour was still bad, and his eyes were bloodshot; he looked as if he were in considerable pain.

Roger went down on one knee, lifted the old man's foot and untied the lace. Soon shoes and socks were off. Gently he began to remove the coat.

It was a slow, laborious business, but at last the old man was in bed, still blue at the lips, his breathing heavy.

When he spoke, his voice was hoarse and low-pitched.

'I suppose – you enjoyed – that.'

Roger did not speak.

'Tell the truth,' sneered Uncle Lionel. 'You're gloating over me. You think I'm helpless. You enjoyed every minute of it.' He gasped for breath, clutching the bedclothes, the veins of his hands standing out like those of a very old man. 'You think I'm finished. *I'll* show you whether I am, you gloating fool.'

'If you go on like that, you'll finish yourself,' Roger said.

'I know my own strength.' Chard gulped for breath. 'In an hour you won't know there – there's been anything the matter with me. Who – who told you to come up?'

'I didn't need telling,' said Roger. 'I've sent for Coppinger, he'll be out soon.'

'You've done what!'

'Coppinger will be here soon.'

'I won't see him! I—' Roger went forward and eased his uncle gently down on to the pillows; meeting unflinching eyes filled with a hostility which was not far removed from hatred.

Then the door opened, and Jennifer came in, carrying two hot water bottles. She gave Roger a fleeting smile, hurried to the bed, and slipped the bottles under the clothes. Chard groped for her hand and held it. She leant over him, smiling into his face; the hostility faded. He smiled, and the pain seemed to ease from his body. Roger was astonished at the transformation, at the effect of her touch and her presence.

'I will look after him, Roger,' Jennifer said.

Roger went out. Tippett, still looking scared, was standing by the head of the stairs. They went down together; Roger wondered whether it were possible that a chance encounter had caused such an attack. Whatever the cause, the most important thing was that, for the first time, he realized that his uncle was gravely ill. An attack such as this might prove fatal; the speed with which Jennifer had acted proved that it was not the first of the kind.

Paul came hurrying out of the drawing-room.

'How is he?'

'I think he's easier,' said Roger. 'Come in, Tippett.' He led the way into the room, where Barbara was standing by the window. It was a dark room, facing north, and it struck cold. The heavy Victorian furniture increased the gloom; it was a room which Roger had always disliked.

'Now, just what happened?' he asked Tippett.

'It was just as I told you, sir.' Tippett had recovered some

93

of his poise, although his square face was still touched with alarm. 'I was waiting at the barrier to take Mr. Chard's case, and we walked towards the car. A man got out of a big Chrysler, and spoke to him. Mr. Chard jumped – I'm not exaggerating, sir, he jumped as if he'd been stung!'

'What did the man say?' asked Roger.

'Only a few words, sir – "How are you, Lionel?"'

'Nothing else?'

'No, sir, *nothing*. Mr. Chard said "What the devil are you doing here?" or something like that, and the other man just grinned at him. He didn't say another word, just snapped his fingers under Mr. Chard's nose. That – that's everything, sir.'

'What was the man like?'

'He was rather big and coarse, Mr. Roger, if you know what I mean. Red-faced. He wasn't the type of man Mr. Chard usually has anything to do with. Not that he didn't *look* all right, he was dressed well enough, a bit flashy, p'raps, that's all.'

'Did you notice the number of his Chrysler?'

'I've been thinking about that,' said Tippett, unhappily. 'I ought to have made a note of it, but everything happened so quickly that I didn't. It was a London registration, I know that, but I can't think of the numbers. I'm sorry, sir.'

Roger smiled. 'My dear chap, you had plenty on your hands. I shouldn't worry – I think he'll be all right. How long ago is it since you last saw him looking anything like this?'

'Quite a while – several months. He wasn't anything like so bad.'

'Do you remember what office he came from?' asked Roger.

'I can't say I do, sir, but I'll try to call it to mind.'

'Do that,' said Roger. 'Now you get off, you must be hungry. And don't worry, Tippett.'

Tippett touched his forehead and went out, and hardly had he driven the car to the garage than Dr. Coppinger arrived.

Coppinger was a tall, youthful-looking man whose appearance belied his sixty-odd years. Roger knew him well, but had never succeeded in getting past the rather acid exterior. He listened, poker-faced, to Roger's explanation; then nodded brifly.

'Don't trouble to come up with me, I know the way.'

'I've never liked that fellow,' Paul said, when he had gone.

'He's a good doctor,' Roger observed.

'I wonder how ill Uncle Lionel really is,' said Barbara.

'I shouldn't base any hopes on a quick way out,' said Paul. 'He'll live forever, if only to spite us.' He laughed mirthlessly. 'I wish I knew that stranger's secret, don't you? I'd give a lot to be able to frighten the old man simply by looking at him.'

Roger said 'The strange thing is that just such a man and car were seen by Bryce on the morning of the attack.'

'By Bryce?' asked Paul, quickly.

Roger told them of his encounter with the poacher, and was not surprised at Paul's comment that it seemed to let Frank Corcoran out.

'It might help him a bit, but I wouldn't go any further than that yet,' Roger said shrewdly. His words were cut short by the ringing of the front door bell. He rose to open the door, but Lucy had reached it before him.

Standing in the porch was Superintendent Marlin.

CHAPTER TWELVE

QUICK RELEASE

It had struck Roger that Marlin and Dr. Coppinger had much in common. Both were tall and thin, Marlin looked sour and Coppinger cynical. Then Roger remembered that Coppinger was the police-surgeon; he did not know why that realization gave him a twinge of alarm.

He went forward.

'Good evening, Superintendent.'

'Good evening,' said Marlin frostily, 'I understand that there has been an accident to Mr. Chard.'

'Then you have been deceived,' said Roger.

Marlin looked taken aback.

'I was informed—' He broke off, then started again. 'One of my men informed me that Mr. Chard arrived not long ago, looking extremely ill. Is that the case?'

Roger wished that he did not dislike the man so intensely. 'My uncle is ill, certainly. I believe it to be a heart attack. Dr. Coppinger is with him now.'

'I see,' said Marlin. 'What brought on the attack?'

'Has this anything to do with you?' Paul asked abruptly.

Marlin turned on him.

'It has, Mr. Briscoe. In view of the recent attempt on his life, anything affecting the well-being of Mr. Chard is of concern to the police. Will you be good enough to tell me what you know about it?'

Paul shut his mouth stubbornly, but Roger saw no point in being obstructive, and repeated briefly what Tippett had told him. Marlin watched him closely as he talked, nodded when he had finished, and had the grace to say:

'Thank you, that is most helpful. Is Tippett here now?'

'He's at his cottage.'

'Corcoran couldn't have had anything to do with *this*,' Paul murmured, provocatively.

'Corcoran is no longer in custody,' Marlin announced.

⚜ ⚜ ⚜

Abbott and Bennison could have told Roger and the others Frank Corcoran had been released, earlier that evening. In his bleak, bitter way, Bryce had told them what he had seen on the morning of the attack.

There was another thing. The stick with which Chard had been attacked had been found. It was a smooth, ebony walking stick, and might easily have cracked the old man's skull. There were no fingerprints on it, so the assailant had worn gloves. From the statements made and the evidence collected, it was known that Corcoran had not been wearing gloves that morning. There were other things; two or three footprints had been found on the porch and on the drive, suggesting that the assailant had run quickly, for the marks of his heels and toes were deep. They were larger than Corcoran could have made.

Somewhat reluctantly – for Marlin liked quick results in his cases – he decided that evidence against Corcoran was insufficient to justify his detention. Nevertheless, he ordered a close watch to be kept on him.

'I want you to be on duty tonight,' he told Abbott, 'and you to take over at six o'clock in the morning, Bennison. Your task will be to keep Corcoran under surveillance, and you will allow nothing to distract your attention.'

Corcoran had been released, Abbott was following him as he went by taxi to his home, and Bennison was thinking that it was time he left the office, when one of the constables on duty at Chard Lodge telephoned to report that it looked as if Lionel Chard had had another 'accident'.

Bennison thought hopefully that he would be summoned to the Lodge with the Superintendent, but Marlin had other ideas. He reminded Bennison of his early morning task, and took another sergeant with him. Feeling angry with Marlin, Bennison went to his lodgings.

At a quarter to ten that night, however, the sergeant who had been with Marlin telephoned Bennison.

'There's nothing in it,' he said. 'Just a heart attack. Coppinger told Marlin that the old man's subject to them. Here's a bit of news though. Who do you think was waiting for Marlin when he got to the office?'

'No time for guessing games,' said Bennison crossly. 'Who was it?'

'None other than Folly of the Yard,' said the other with relish.

Bennison said sharply: 'Are you sure?'

'You could hardly mistake Folly, his chins alone put him in a class to himself. We haven't sent for the Yard, have we?'

'Not to my knowledge. There's no reason why we should.'

'Well, he was there,' said the sergeant. 'Cheerio.'

Bennison walked slowly away from the telephone.

Superintendent Folly, of New Scotland Yard, was a legendary figure. Three years before, the Yard had been called in on a murder case which had puzzled Marlin, but the subsequent behaviour of Superintendent Folly had made the local man wish he had never heard the name. Folly had taken complete control, cutting through the case like a brig in full sail, spreading alarm and confusion among all ranks and giving most of the staff the impression of a man colossal in figure but even vaster in conceit. The only two men who had a good word for him were Bennison and Abbott. At the time, they had been Detective Officers. Folly had specifically asked for them to be assigned to him, and as they had worked fairly closely together, they had been able to see beyond the accepted facade to the workings of a remarkable mind.

Bennison, remembering this, remembered also Marlin's dislike of him. After such an experience it was more than unlikely that Marlin would risk a further encounter by calling in the Yard.

Bennison, bursting with his news, could hardly wait to tell Abbott. He decided to walk towards Corcoran's house, a mile or so from Chard Lodge.

Arriving, he could see no sign of Abbott, but as he stood looking about, Bennison saw a dark shape near a summer house in the garden adjoining the Corcorans'.

'Is that you, Abby?'

'Hallo, what's brought you?' asked Abbott.

'News, old boy. News.'

'Don't say old Chard's dead.'

'Unfortunately, no. Folly's around.'

At first, Abbot refused to believe him. Then they discussed their memory of Folly and agreed that if he were going to stay in the district, they were in for a good time.

The shrill ringing of a telephone bell disturbed their whispered conversation.

Next moment, the light in the front room of the Corcorans' house went on, and Frank Corcoran appeared in the room. Of one accord the two men drew nearer, taking care that Frank could not see them.

They saw him lift the telephone, and heard his: 'Hallo.'

There was a pause, then: 'Yes, yes, I'll come at once!' He rushed out of the room, and they could hear him talking in a high-pitched, excited voice, although it was now impossible for them to hear what he said.

The front door opened, and Frank appeared, his mother, elderly and grey, standing just behind him.

'Don't be long, dear,' she said.

'They wouldn't have sent for me if it weren't about Jenny,' said Frank. 'If I'm going to be long, I'll give you a ring.'

He struggled into a raincoat, said 'good-bye' and hurried down the short drive.

99

Bennison waited in the shadows.

As the front door closed, Abbott drew up in the car.

'We won't need this,' he said.

'You'd better have it,' Bennison told him, 'he's going to the Lodge, and someone might drive him back. I'll walk after him, you go ahead.'

By now, Frank had reached the main road. He was walking at a furious pace, and Bennison had to exert himself to keep pace with him. About a quarter of a mile from the house there was a short cut, across the meadow. Frank turned into the field.

The going was more difficult here, and the pace slower.

Young Corcoran seemed to have no idea that he was being followed. It was a bright, starlit night, and Bennison could see him clearly.

They neared the hedge and the stile.

Corcoran climbed over.

Bennison saw another shape, beyond the hedge, one that appeared so quickly that he had no time to cry out, no time to wonder who, or what, it was.

The next moment, he saw an arm raised and heard a cry.

Bennison rushed foward, shouting. He saw Corcoran pitch forward, saw the other man beating at him savagely. He reached the stile and leapt over it. At the same moment something hit him in the stomach. Pain shot through his body, and he fell heavily, hearing nothing, unaware of what was happening.

At the drive gates, talking to the policeman on duty there, Abbott's first intimation of trouble was a cry which seemed to come from a long way off. The two men stared towards the sound. There was another cry, more urgent. Abbott snapped: 'Come on, it's near the house!' and broke into a run, but the steep drive made it impossible to make much speed. The constable laboured after him, and when they were halfway up the drive, they heard the blast of a police whistle coming from their right.

'Over there!' gasped Abbott.

Someone from the house had heard the cries, for lights went on and there was a shout. Dark figures rushed from the porch towards the stile. Abbott jumped to the steep bank alongside the drive, cursing the darkness. Someone cannoned heavily into him.

For a second, Abbott reeled back, shaken by the collision, then plunged after the unknown man who had leapt down the bank and was making for the drive.

He would have lost him had the other not slipped. Abbott drew level and grabbed his shoulder.

'That's enough,' he said, roughly.

The fugitive tried to free himself, but Abbott held on. The light was bad, but there was something in the appearance of the man, and in his shadowy face, which seemed familiar.

'Damn you, let go!' exclaimed the other.

It was the voice which enabled Abbott to place him: he was struggling with Peter Maitland, the artist.

CHAPTER THIRTEEN

GRIM SIGHT

ROGER, Paul and Barbara were in the small morning room, when the first shout alarmed them. Roger got up at once, and Paul followed him into the hall. Jennifer was coming down the stairs, and called out as they appeared:

'What was that?'

'I don't know,' said Roger.

'There's a whistle!' exclaimed Paul. 'The police.'

'Come on!' called Roger, and pulled the front door open.

Running back for a torch, he called to Barbara and Jennifer to stay indoors, then pounded after Paul. The whistle was still blowing, the trouble centre seeming to be the hedge separating the garden from the meadow. Paul had judged the direction well; Roger could see him as he ran.

Gradually Roger overtook him.

Neither of them spoke.

Shouts and the sound of men running added to the din, but Roger did not stop in his headlong rush. He began to flash the torch over Paul's head. The beam reached the hedge and beyond. It shone on someone who was climbing the stile; the man jumped into the meadow, out of sight.

Someone else appeared suddenly in the beam; a ghostly figure, his face twisted. Roger did not recognize Bennison, but saw that he was clutching his stomach, as if in pain.

Roger shone the torch on the ground. Something lay there. The light showed up a battered head, the blood glistening. Roger drew in a sharp breath, and the torchlight wavered. Bennison gulped, then managed to speak more clearly:

'Direct the torch downward.'

Slowly, Roger did so.

The man's head was so badly battered that there was no hope of him being alive. In spite of that, Bennison went down on one knee, and peered at him more closely. Then he felt his pulse. Only when Bennison moved the victim a little did Roger recognize Frank Corcoran.

'Frank!' he exclaimed.

Bennison straightened up.

'Yes, it's Corcoran.'

The night seemed cold. There was no wind, but he began to shiver. The beam of the torch trembled.

'There's no hope, I suppose?' Roger asked.

'I'm afraid not.'

'If we move him—'

Bennison shook his head. 'Better not.' He was thinking of what Marlin would say about this. He was less affected by fear of reprimand than by the fact that his was the responsibility; had he been five yards nearer, he could have saved the lad's life.

Roger thrust the torch into Bennison's hand, and went down on his knee. As he took Frank's limp wrist in his fingers, he heard a car coming up the drive, its headlights full on. By their light he saw Barbara and Jennifer approaching.

Barbara called: 'Roger, what's happened?'

'Someone's been hurt! *Go back!*'

He felt a sudden, overpowering fear that Jennifer would see Frank as he was now, and the thought made him panic. The tone of his voice was enough to frighten them, but he must stop Jennifer, he must—

The beam of the torch still shone on the bloody head.

Jennifer and Barbara must have seen the thing at the same moment, for Barbara uttered an exclamation.

Abruptly, Bennison switched off the light.

Jennifer's voice came, quiet and controlled.

'Who is it, Roger?'

She was visible, although the figure on the ground was not.

'Who is it?' insisted Jennifer.

Roger said: 'I'm sorry, Jenny. It's Frank.'

She moved forward, and Barbara made no attempt to stop her. She went down on her knees, and Bennison exclaimed:

'Don't touch him!'

She ignored the order, laying her hands on Frank's head. She turned it gently, as if she wanted to make sure that she had been told the truth.

There was utter silence.

A shrill, testy voice broke the spell; it was a voice which Roger had never heard before. Bennison switched on the torch. It shone on the face of a mountain of a man, who closed his eyes and put up his hand as if to keep the light away.

'Put that out, you idiot! What has happened?'

Chard Lodge was in a turmoil.

It seemed full of policemen and detectives; of men with cameras and others with bags of plaster of Paris, another with a small case of grey powder and some feathery brushes; men who asked questions, who went hither and thither at the orders of the newcomer whom, Roger now understood, was Superintendent Folly. Folly had come with Marlin to see Uncle Lionel and it was characteristic of the man that he had chosen that particular moment to arrive. He seemed to be in complete control, dominating everyone; even Roger felt the influence of that domination and, perhaps because of the speed of events and the shock of finding Corcoran dead, did not resent it. Frank's body was now on its way to Hilbury. Photographs had been taken before it had been moved, and the flashlights had lit up the scene in garish fashion. Every member of the household was closely questioned, although none could give any explanation of what had happened. One thing soon transpired; Folly was from Scotland Yard, and had come to see Uncle Lionel. Dr. Coppinger, however, who soon arrived on the scene, forbade an interview at that juncture.

Statements had been made by the two detective-sergeants, Abbott and Bennison.

There was some talk – and only this was treated with any secrecy – of Abbott and one policeman meeting a man on the drive; the man was now a prisoner somewhere in the house. Who he was, Roger did not know; certainly he did not give a thought to the possibility that it was Peter.

As far as anyone could find out, there had been two men as well as this 'stranger' near the hedge. Paul and one policeman had followed the two across the meadow but a car had been waiting, and the men had escaped. They had left behind them the cudgel which had been used to attack Frank; the ugly looking weapon was now on a small table in the morning-room, resting on an old newspaper.

Now Roger, Paul and Barbara were in the drawing-room, where Lucy had arranged coffee and sandwiches. Of the two girls, Barbara seemed the more upset; Jennifer's calm had been uncanny, and she had wanted to go to see Corcoran's parents. Dr. Coppinger had persuaded her against this, and Marlin and one of the sergeants had gone to break the melancholy news.

The door opened gently.

✦ 'May I come in?' The gigantic Folly came into the room on small, almost dancing, feet. It was the first time that Roger had seen him without any distraction, and Folly astonished him. He had the figure, even the expression, of a *bon vivant*. Innocence, and a childlike air of anticipation, exuded from him. His face was round, and deceptively cherubic. In fact everything about him appeared to be round, gently tapering to unusually small, exquisitely shod feet.

'Believe me, I am distressed indeed by what has happened here tonight,' said Folly, his voice was flutelike as a choirboy's 'It must have worried you all, especially after the earlier, happily less disastrous, incident.' He smiled at them in turn. 'I wonder, now, if any of you have any theory to advance?'

'Isn't that your job?' asked Paul.

Folly's eyebrows shot up.

'My dear sir! What a quaint idea. It is easy to tell that you have lived a long time out of this country! In America, perhaps. There, I am told, the police alone have theories. In England I find that everybody indulges in them. Upon my soul, I don't think I have ever worked on a case without everyone connected with it, and a great many not connected with it, submitting a theory. In some cases – I should say, a few cases – tenable theories. Therefore, one hopes.' He paused, as if for breath, and Roger, suddenly warming to him, smiled.

'That ours may be tenable ones?'

Folly smiled upon him.

'Exactly. Can you imagine anyone with a greater claim to

theorizing in this instant than you and your cousins, Mr. Maitland? The crime, when all is said and done, was committed on your land.'

'My uncle's land,' Roger corrected.

'Yes, yes, it is as well to be precise. I wonder if I may sit down?'

'But of course.'

Folly inspected several chairs with care, and chose the most comfortable. He beamed.

'How rare an event to find an armchair large enough for me! Your family must have known big men, Mr. Maitland.'

'My uncle isn't small,' said Roger.

'So I am told. I am looking forward to meeting him, and I am most distressed to hear that he has had a heart attack. A frequent occurrence, perhaps?'

'Not to my knowledge,' said Roger.

'It *is* surprising how little one knows about one's relatives,' remarked Folly. 'Sometimes I feel it is almost better not to have any!' He smiled again, but there was something in his voice which added a barb to the remark; Roger began to respect this man. 'Now, I asked you for a theory, and—'

He stopped abruptly.

He was staring towards the table, and the others looked round, in some alarm, for Folly seemed greatly affected. All they could see was the rest of the room and the coffee cups and tray.

Folly's expression became one of great fatigue, or that of a man in instant need of sustenance.

'I hope you will forgive me, but do I see coffee?'

Barbara said weakly: 'But of course, you must have some.'

'I do apologize, but I would be most grateful for a cup,' declared Folly. 'My vocation is a thirsty one.' He smiled sweetly at Barbara. 'May I?'

Roger leaned forward and rang the bell. No one spoke until Lucy came in. Folly seemed content to sit with the tips of his fingers pressed together, surveying them in the role of a genial host. He was smiling, but became serious when Lucy entered.

'Some more coffee, please, Lucy,' Roger said.

Folly raised a hand.

'Dare I?' he murmured.

'Dare you what?'

'I am ashamed to ask, but if there could be a sandwich – or even a biscuit, I would be grateful. I came from London before dinner, and have managed only to get a snack at Hilbury Police Station. I cast no aspersions on canteen snacks, but still–' Folly shrugged delicately.

Barbara said warmly, 'I'll get you something.' She seemed glad of the excuse to leave the room, of the homely comfort in such a task.

'I am making a nuisance of myself,' said Folly, humbly, 'and yet needs must – we policemen are not arbiters of our own fate. Now, gentlemen, while we are alone I will ask you again – have you any suggestions to make about the attack upon this unfortunate young man?'

Roger said slowly: 'I haven't.'

Paul shook his head.

'Nothing at all?' Folly looked disappointed, but did not wait for another negative. 'One thing does strike me as obvious from the beginning. No doubt you will see it yourselves when you have had time to think, so there is no harm in telling you. The blows over the head were similar to the blows aimed at your uncle's head, and a not dissimilar weapon was used.' He looked at Roger, but darted a quick glance at Paul. 'Don't you agree?'

'Well, yes, that is a point,' admitted Roger.

'Ah! So here we have a crime in which the suspect of one of a lesser degree is the victim of one of a much higher degree. I wonder if the same man could have been responsible?'

'Have you any further reason for thinking so?' asked Paul.

Folly chuckled. 'My dear sir, no! First the theory, then the

search for grounds to support it. And to come to the point –
for there is a point about all this, Mr. Maitland! – can you
give me any idea of any motive for attacking both your uncle
and young Corcoran?'

Roger said slowly: 'I can't imagine why anyone should
want to kill Corcoran.'

'But you can imagine someone wanting to kill your uncle,'
murmured Folly.

Again they had a glimpse of the man for what he was, and
saw the danger which he might bring to the house.

Roger said slowly: 'My uncle isn't the most popular of
men, Superintendent.'

'Ah! You are frank. You will be surprised, Mr. Briscoe,
how true it is that honesty pays with the police. You may
have some private knowledge, something which might be
considered a guilty secret, you do not see how it affects the
case under review, you keep it from the police and they discover it through someone else – it is really astonishing how
things get around – I speak figuratively of course. There is
no greater foolishness in such an investigation than reticence.' He pursed his lips, and then flung his bombshell.
'Have *you* any reason for wishing your uncle dead, gentlemen?'

'Our uncle isn't dead,' Roger said, quickly.

'Let us be frank,' said Folly. 'His murder was attempted
and might yet be carried out. In murder, as in other matters,
prevention is better than cure. Has your brother Peter any
motive for wishing him dead, Mr. Maitland?'

Roger smiled grimly.

'Hadn't you better ask him? He's staying at my house in
Elbourne.'

'I – ah! Coffee and sandwiches. How charming of you,
Mrs. Briscoe!' Folly's eyes lit up. When Barbara put a tray
on a table near him, he quickly lifted the lid of a serving
dish. His eyes shone. 'How really charming! Scrambled egg
on toast! How few, how very few can scramble eggs at the
right consistency! Is Miss Briscoe downstairs yet?'

'I haven't seen her,' said Barbara.

'I must have a word with her soon,' declared Folly. 'Dark horses, you know, and still waters, if I may mix my metaphors.' With pleasurable anticipation he poured himself out some coffee, seemingly unaware of the effect of his words. 'I have heard a great deal about your sister, Mr. Briscoe, a great deal. She is – somewhat estranged from the rest of you, I understand.'

Roger opened his lips, but repressed a comment. Paul, less wary, looked up angrily.

'Your understanding is at fault!'

'Indeed?' said Folly. 'I am sorry. But then, I had my information secondhand, you understand. There is no estrangement? I was given to understand that there was, if I may put it this way, a schism in the family – your sister and your uncle against the rest of you, as it were.'

'You're quite wrong,' Roger said, briskly. 'You can put that idea out of your head.'

Folly, delicately forking his way, looked crestfallen.

'Delicious,' he murmured, and turned to Roger. 'You see how right I was to see you for a few minutes on your own. The wrong impression can have such distressing results. So Miss Jennifer and all the family are on the best of terms – excellent! What about you and your uncle, gentlemen?'

'We have differences,' Roger conceded, 'but it *is* Frank Corcoran who is dead, isn't it?'

'Yes, of course, of course.' Folly's fork hovered, about to pounce. 'But I cannot help but feel there is a connection between the two crimes, Mr. Maitland. And that is why I wanted to see whether you could tell me of any possible motive against both victims. It seems that you cannot – very well, I shall have to find one by other means.' Folly pursed his lips and looked at Barbara. Just as he had dominated the police, so he now dominated the room. Roger felt the spell of his presence, Paul looked uneasy, Barbara frowned. 'Yes, I shall have to find one,' Folly went on, and his voice, high and pure, became oddly impressive. 'I must find a murderer, too.

It is not, perhaps the most attractive of tasks, but it is my duty. I give you my assurance, I shall find the man.'

Roger said hoarsely: 'On your own?'

Folly looked at him reprovingly.

'No, sir. I am but the thin edge of the wedge.' He kept a completely set face, but the allusion was so absurd that Roger grinned, and the tension was broken. 'Lest you are curious, gentlemen, I am happy in the confidence of the county police.'

'They didn't lose any time in consulting you,' Roger said, drily.

'My dear sir! *I* consulted them.' Folly dabbed his lips daintily with his handkerchief, and stood up. He was surprisingly agile. 'I do appreciate this hospitality, Mr. Maitland – in fact, I must thank all of you. And I am sorry that we police are likely to make such nuisances of ourselves, but as the murder was committed in these grounds we shall have to operate part of the time from here. I understand that Mr. Chard is too ill to see me, so I must turn to someone else for permission to use a room, no matter how small, for the time being. It would be most helpful if there were a telephone in it,' he added.

Roger said: 'There is the morning room.'

'Thank you,' said Folly, blandly. 'Thank you again.' He reached the door. 'Oh!' he exclaimed, and turned back. 'There is a matter I had forgotten. I am told that your brother, Mr. Maitland, was at your house on the morning of the attack upon Mr. Chard. Is that the case?'

'Yes.'

'Are you quite sure?' Folly asked, softly.

Paul broke in. 'I saw him myself. I was talking to him at the time of the attack.'

'Oh, I see,' said Folly, nodding and almost closing his eyes. 'Then that puts the matter beyond any doubt. Did he know Frank Corcoran?'

'Slightly,' answered Roger.

'Were they – friends?'

'There's quite a difference in their ages,' Roger said.

'Oh, yes, but age is no bar to friendship, I am happy to say. Be frank, please. Were they *enemies*?'

'What are you driving at?' demanded Paul, angrily.

'I am trying to find out the truth, sir,' said Superintendent Folly, 'and I shall do so, whether it annoys you, or frightens you, or causes you misgiving.' His face was set and his voice had altered again, becoming deep and imposing.

There was a tap at the door.

'Come in!' cried Folly, before any of the others could respond, and immediately the door opened.

Into the room came Abbott, his hair a little dishevelled, and behind, handcuffed to him, came Peter.

CHAPTER FOURTEEN

ARREST

PETER looked much more dishevelled than Abbott. His collar was torn, and his tie was pulled to one side. There were scratches on his hands and face, and his eyes held a wild, angry look.

Folly continued as if nothing had happened.

'I *know* that Mr. Peter Maitland had a motive for attacking his uncle, that goes without saying. I must insist, here and now, on being told why he killed Corcoran.'

Roger stepped to Peter's side, and from there looked at Folly. In spite of the flush of anger and shock, he found time to admire the man's tactics; this was showmanship indeed. He understood that Peter had been brought in at that juncture by arrangement.

111

Folly, pressing his advantage, made his accusation in the form of a question, and glared at Peter.

'Well, sir, why did you do it?'

Peter said: 'How many more times have I got to tell you that I know nothing about it?'

'A fine story,' said Folly softly. 'You came secretly to this house. You telephoned Corcoran, knowing he had been released. You and your accomplices lay in wait for him, and struck him down. There is the truth.'

Peter threw up his hands.

'I didn't telephone him and I didn't know that he was coming.'

'Perhaps you will now deny that you were in the grounds, behaving most furtively, that you assaulted first a police constable and then a sergeant and were persuaded to stay here only by superior force. Had you had your own way, you would have left the grounds and failed to disclose the fact that you were present. Isn't *that* true?'

Peter did not answer.

'There is guilt writ large upon your face,' said Folly grandiloquently.

Roger said drily: 'Have you charged my brother?'

'He has been charged.'

'With what offence?'

As he spoke, Folly looked at Roger as if he could not quite assess him at his true value. Paul and Barbara were hanging on his words, and Peter was staring at him, his lips parted.

'Assault upon the police and complicity in the murder of Frank Corcoran,' answered Folly at last. 'Is that sufficient for you, Mr. Maitland?'

'Quite,' said Roger. 'Peter, you'll want legal aid. Until you've seen a solicitor, and I'll send one along later, don't say a word.' He smiled at Folly with self-assurance. 'You see, Superintendent, how much I admire your methods.'

Folly rasped: 'A short while ago I congratulated you on adhering to the truth. Now you are advising your brother to be evasive. It will do him harm; it may do you harm.'

'Oh, no,' said Roger. 'Tempers are frayed, none of us is being reasonable – not even you. We all want to cool down a bit.' He rested a hand on Peter's shoulder. 'Don't worry, old chap. It will work out, even Superintendent Folly will become convinced that you didn't kill Frank. Where's Lucille?'

'She—' began Peter, and then added quickly: 'She's gone to London. I expect she'll stay with friends.'

'Oh.' Roger did not believe him, nor did he think that Folly was convinced, but he made no further comment. 'I'll get in touch with her as soon as I can. Again – don't worry. We'll have you free in no time.'

'One would think,' said Folly, silkily, 'that you know who killed Corcoran, Mr. Maitland.'

'Yes, wouldn't they?' asked Roger. 'But I shouldn't theorize too much if I were you.'

He had brought about an impasse; but he was in no mood to take pleasure in Folly's discomfiture.

'Roger's right, Peter,' Paul said.

Peter brushed his hair back from his forehead.

'Yes, of course. Thanks, Roger. I'm afraid I lost my temper when these oafs sprang at me. Sorry.' He turned to Folly. 'I'll go quietly,' he said, with a faint grin.

'And about time, too.' The Superintendent nodded to Abbott, who took Peter out. There was silence in the room for some minutes, and then they heard the front door close; soon the engine of a car started up. Folly, who appeared to have been listening for just that, relaxed, and thrust one hand into his pocket. He surveyed Roger moodily.

'You think yourself very clever, I have no doubt.'

'Well, you ought to be a good judge of vanity,' Roger retorted.

There was a quick, amused gleam in Folly's eyes; Roger was surprised. It passed in a flash, and again Folly looked moody and dissatisfied.

'I have no desire to make it appear that any innocent man is guilty,' he said, 'but I must remind you that the evidence

113

against your brother is strong. And undoubtedly he assaulted the police.'

'Under provocation,' murmured Roger. 'That isn't going to worry us very much. You don't object to me getting legal advice, do you?'

Folly rose, and walked the length of the room.

'Mr. Maitland, I am going to be frank with you. Grave crimes have been committed, and they centre on this house. They are, perhaps, graver than you realize. I shall not rest, the whole police force in this country will not rest, until this matter is resolved and the guilty brought to justice. Do not trifle with the police; do not trifle with the law. Good night to you.'

He went out, closing the door gently.

The others stayed where they were, doing nothing.

At last Roger ventured: 'I wonder what Peter was doing here.'

'And I wonder where Lucille is,' said Barbara. 'He shouldn't have lied about her.'

'The police must know how scared she is of them by now,' Paul said.

'I think we'll find that Folly knows pretty well everything we do,' Roger said gloomily. 'Well, the first job is to get a lawyer.'

Paul raised an eyebrow.

'Right. Well let me say – money no object.'

'Thanks,' said Roger.

'Shall we get someone from London?' asked Barbara.

'I don't think we need do that yet,' said Roger. 'I know Tubby Edwards, of Edwards & Edwards, fairly well. I'll give him a ring.' He smiled grimly. 'I suppose we can use our own telephone!'

A policeman was on duty in the hall, and the morning room had already been taken over. Roger caught a glimpse of Marlin's face. It surprised him, because he got the impression that he was angry and that Folly was trying to smooth him down. Abbott was standing by the door, and gave Roger a friendly grin. The police were a puzzle in themselves, thought Roger, as he telephoned Tubby Edwards, who promised to come to the Lodge immediately.

Abbott and Bennison expected that one of them would be assigned to Chard Lodge that evening, and were startled and disappointed when they were told to return to Hilbury. They went ahead of Folly and Marlin, who were in Folly's big car.

Outside the main entrance of the police station stood a Rolls-Royce.

Abbott whistled. 'Hallo, the Chief Constable's here. They're not losing any time, are they?'

They waited in their office, not sure what to expect. When a policeman came and said that Marlin wanted to see them, they exchanged glances, prepared to hear the worst. Marlin was alone, but in the office next to him they could hear Folly as he talked to the Chief Constable.

'You sent for us, sir,' murmured Abbott.

'Certainly I sent for you, to tell you that I'm profoundly disappointed in you, Abbott, and in you, Bennison. You had clear instructions. Abbott should have followed Corcoran, and his dereliction of duty has had the most serious consequences. You, Bennison, were not on duty, but your failure to prevent the murder when you were so close at hand is a grave matter.'

Neither of them spoke.

'I have reported the situation to the Chief Constable,' Marlin went on with a certain grim enjoyment. 'He wishes to see you both in the morning. You will report here at nine-thirty. Until then you are relieved of duty. That is all.'

Silently, the two sergeants walked to the front door, and down the steps. Silently they got into the small car and drove to Mrs. Harris's, still without saying a word. They parked the car, and went into the hall, where the hands of a wall-clock stood at half-past twelve.

In silence Abbott shook his head at Bennison's brief suggestion of a snack. In silence they went to bed.

In spite of their troubled thoughts, however, they soon went to sleep; and they were both asleep when Mrs. Harris tapped on the door at half-past seven next morning. Abbott was first to wake at the rattle of tea cups.

' 'Morning,' he grunted.

'Half-past seven, Mr. Abbott,' said Mrs. Harris severely, 'and you must wake up *properly*. There's a gentleman waiting downstairs to see you.'

Abbott dropped a teaspoon.

'A gentleman, for *me* – for *us*?'

'*As* I said,' Mrs. Harris bridled. 'At *once*. He's not a gentleman as'll stand *waiting*.'

'For the love of Mike tell us, who *is* it?' pleaded Bennison.

'A Mr. *Folly*,' Mrs. Harris hissed cryptically from the door.

They looked at each other in sudden alarm, and then Bennison flung back the bedclothes. He stopped abruptly, for the door began to open. There on the threshold stood Folly. Shaved, bathed, brushed he stood looking at them, a rosebud in his buttonhole. At the clink of a dislodged tea cup his gaze lowered.

'Dear me, morning tea, how very refreshing.'

'There's a cup poured out,' said Abbott eagerly, handing a cup of tea to Folly. 'Have this one, sir.'

Folly took it, beaming.

'Your landlady appears to look after you very well,' he remarked, a speculative gleam in his eye.

Both men murmured an enthusiastic assent.

'I am told that The Crown is the best hotel in the town,' Folly went on, 'but the food!' He threw up his hands. 'But I digress.' He sipped his tea. 'Put those shaving things down, Bennison, and drink your tea like a Christian! Ah, that's better. I didn't come here to put you on the parade ground, I came to exchange notes. I thought it better to come, let us

116

say, surreptitiously – I suspect that Marlin has not forgiven you for finding favour with me when I was last here. Is that so?'

'It's not far out,' mumbled Abbott.

'Have you two men ever thought of applying for a transfer to Scotland Yard?'

Bennison gaped.

'Don't look like a startled goat,' said Folly, crossly. 'Have you?'

'No,' muttered Abbott.

'Then you should. We are still short of good men at the Yard, and I think a transfer could be effected. You might not find such pleasant lodgings, but that should not be an insuperable obstacle. When this affair is finished, I recommend you to make formal application. May I have another cup of tea, Abbott?'

'Yes, *sir!*' exclaimed Abbott, his eyes glistening.

'Thank you. Now, I am not here as Superintendent Folly, I am here as a private individual, and you are private individuals, so nothing any of us says is to be taken officially. Is that clear?'

'Quite clear,' they choroused.

'Good! You know more of the local situation than I do. You need not worry about Marlin trying to keep you off the case, I have sufficient influence with your Chief Constable. You will receive a severe reprimand I've no doubt, but the policeman who's never been reprimanded has never risen above a sergeant's rank. Forget your personal anxieties. Concentrate on this particular case. Tell me everything that you know about it, especially about Lionel Chard and his relatives. Marlin has told me a little, and I have discovered some things for myself, but I want to know more. Do you fully understand?'

'Yes, sir,' said Abbott.

'You start,' suggested Folly, 'and when Bennison thinks that you have forgotten anything about any particular subject, he can interrupt.' He paused, and as Abbott was marshalling his thoughts, added abruptly: 'Perhaps I had better tell you this: at Scotland Yard, some of the activities of Lionel Chard have been watched with much interest. That is why I am here.'

CHAPTER FIFTEEN

FOLLY LEARNS ALL

Thus encouraged, Abbott talked at great length.

Now and again Bennison made some point, but there was little that Abbott neglected. He mentioned the white feathers, the letter, the notes scrawled in Roger Maitland's handwriting, the talk he had heard between Barbara and Paul, Lucille's fear of the police, everything he had picked up by astute observation; it made an impressive array of facts and suspicions, and before he was half-way through, Folly was nodding with evident satisfaction. Only twice did he ask for clarification of a point; both concerned the attitude of the nephews to Jennifer Briscoe. When Abbott had finished, Folly regarded him with a smile of congratulation.

'Very satisfying. I doubt whether Marlin is aware of half of that, and I am quite sure that he would not realize its significance if he were. Marlin troubles me. He will discard so many things as irrelevant when in fact they might have an important bearing on the case. The dismissal of the housekeeper, for instance of which I learned from the maid. But never mind – and remember, this is a private chat! I am constrained to ask one thing: all the men concerned are fond of Jennifer Briscoe?'

'Very,' said Bennison.

'Is any one of them *so* fond that, fearing the girl might be put into this convent at her uncle's behest, he would be prepared to kill the uncle? And, at the same time, is that same one so fond of her that, fearing Frank Corcoran would persuade her to marry him, he was moved to kill the youngster?'

Abbott and Bennison gave a murmur of interest.

'Peter and Paul are. both married,' went on Folly thoughtfully, 'and both apparently in love with their wives. So that leaves Roger.'

Bennison said: 'Isn't that a bit far-fetched?'

'Perhaps a trifle,' admitted Folly, surprisingly, 'but such an explanation is feasible. It does seem to me that the murderer and Lionel Chard's assailant are one and the same. I have some information for you,' he added. 'A large and powerful car, a Chrysler, was parked near the meadow next to Chard Lodge last night. You remember the poacher's story that a powerful car was waiting for Lionel Chard's assailant? You remember also the story of the man from a Chrysler who caused such distress to Lionel Chard and brought about another heart attack. Now Chryslers do not grow on trees. The men who murdered Frank Corcoran doubtless escaped in that car.'

'But—' began Bennison.

Folly raised a hand.

'The murderers, I say, doubtless escaped in that car. Earlier, they had telephoned Corcoran, in Peter Maitland's name, and asked him to go to the house. They knew he would cross the meadow, and they waited by the stile. They had, we must assume, an excellent motive for murdering Corcoran.'

'Do you mean you've ruled Peter Maitland out?' demanded Abbott.

'My dear good man, no! He may have been with the murderers. He may have instigated the crime. Until we know why he was in the grounds and are satisfied the reason is a good one, we must continue to suspect him. Remember, too, that the others of the family may be shielding him, and may be prepared to commit perjury to defend him from the charge of the assault on his uncle. I most certainly do not rule out the possibility that Peter Maitland, or any other member of the family, is concerned in this. We must assume that all of them would like to see the uncle dead. I had no choice but to arrest Maitland – and in any case Marlin would have insisted. Not without reason, for he questioned the maid at Home Farm, and discovered that she recently interrupted a family conclave at a point when Peter was talking of murdering Lionel Chard.'

'Did she, by jove!' exclaimed Abbott.

'So the arrest had to be made but I am less hopeful of convicting Peter of the murder than of using him to force the others to be frank with us. For I must admit that I, even I, make mistakes' – he smiled engagingly – 'and all has not yet been told to me.'

Abbott asked thoughtfully: 'How do the nephews come into the other side of the picture – the Yard's interest in their uncle?'

'I don't know, yet,' said Folly. 'I will tell you that we suspect Lionel Chard of sending money and valuables out of the country in direct contravention of the law. Big money – he is a very wealthy man, much wealthier than most people realize, probably much wealthier than his family knows. And he is suspected of contravening the Defence of the Realm Act in a large way. No more than suspected, but we are watching him, and when I heard what had happened I came down almost at once. I don't know that the nephews are concerned in that side of his activities; I can only say that they might be. We will find out.'

'Where has he been sending the money?' asked Bennison.

Folly wagged a finger.

'We only suspect that he has been sending it. The amounts involved would be large, and the issues concerned might be larger than we yet appreciate. Lionel Chard, as you pointed out, is a tyrant in his family; and he has the habit of dictatorship. What we have to learn is whether the differences between him and his family are only domestic or whether this other matter affects them. I understand that all of the nephews rejected his offer to take them into the family business, and that he has exerted some pressure upon them to make them change their minds.' 'That's right,' said Abbott. 'I got that from the housekeeper at the Lodge.'

'Quite so. And Chard has since sent her packing. I must have her questioned. Well! Time is getting on,' said Folly. 'You have to be at the office at nine-thirty, I understand. So I'll wish you good-bye.'

Half-an-hour later, after a strident call from Mrs. Harris, the two friends went downstairs. Abbott, the first to enter the dining-room, stopped short.

'What's worrying you?' asked Bennison. 'I—'

Then he saw Folly, sitting at the table and beaming up at them.

'Mrs. Harris very kindly agreed to provide me with breakfast,' explained Folly in his flutiest voice. 'I told her how much better was the aroma of her food than at the hotel. Sit down, my dear fellows, set to! We have a hard day in front of us.'

Uncle Lionel did not come down to breakfast next morning, although Jennifer reported that he was much better. She had tended the old man with great care, and seemed delighted at his progress.

'We mustn't let this business prevent us from working on Jenny,' said Paul.

'We can't do anything about that yet,' Roger answered, quietly. 'We'll have to get this settled first. Apart from everything else, we've got to get Peter out of trouble.'

After a long pause, Paul nodded agreement.

'Do you know why he was here last night?' he asked.

'Not yet. Tubby Edwards promised to come in this morning.'

It was now ten o'clock. The morning-room was locked.

Roger wondered what Uncle Lionel would have to say when he heard that the police had more or less commandeered it.

Soon afterwards, a post office telephone van arrived, and another line was put into the morning-room. So the police did not mean to allow anyone of the household to overhear what they said!

Roger intended to go into Hilbury after his interview with Tubby Edwards, to see Peter and the Corcorans. In the bright light of morning, it was difficult to realize that Frank had been killed only a few yards away.

Paul said fretfully: 'I wish we knew where Lucille was. Suppose I go up to town and see if she's at the flat?'

'Not a bad idea,' said Roger. 'It would certainly give Bar a rest from the house.'

At half-past ten, the telephone bell rang. Edwards was sorry, but he would not be able to come out until after lunch; they were 'not to worry'. Paul was irritated, but refused to give up his visit to Lucille's flat. He and Barbara would be back soon after lunch, and Roger could tell them what the solicitor had said.

'You'll have to tell the police what you intend to do,' counselled Roger.

'I'll go without asking anyone's permission,' Paul said, angrily.

He went upstairs, and Roger reflected moodily that perhaps he had taken too strict a view, but it seemed important not to antagonize the police.

As he followed Paul, anxious to heal the breach, he heard his cousin's voice raised in angry exasperation.

'That's right, agree with anybody except me! It's always the same, I'm wrong before I open my mouth.'

'But surely—' Barbara began.

'And there's another thing, while we're at it. It's Roger this and Roger that and you follow him about like a little dog. He—'

'Paul!'

'Well?' sneered Paul.

Barbara's voice, clear and cold: 'It is certainly true that I like Roger and admire him. And it's just as certainly true that I *don't* like you in these moods.'

There was a pause, and then Paul spoke in a different voice.

'I'm sorry, Bar. It's those damned feathers, and everything happening at once. My nerves are shot to pieces. I try to keep steady and then some little thing happens, and—'

'I know,' said Barbara, quickly.

'I'll have a word with the police,' said Paul.

He ran down to the telephone, while Roger went on to his room.

The door of Paul's room was open, and Barbara was sitting at the dressing-table. Roger was shocked at her expression. She caught sight of him in the mirror, and turned to face him, forcing a smile.

'Did you hear?' she asked.

'Yes,' said Roger.

'I – I'm so sorry,' Barbara said.

'My dear Bar!'

She sat watching him; and he stood undecided in the doorway. He remembered their meeting on the landing at Home Farm, and as if his vision had suddenly cleared, he realized that he had come to hold her in very high regard.

Downstairs, Paul said jubilantly: 'Okay, Folly! Thanks.'

He came bounding up the stairs and, in his mercurial way, beamed at Roger.

'You were right again, Folly's granted us a licence!'

'That's fine,' said Roger. He moved away. It was strange how the image of Barbara stayed with him, almost ousting that of his cousin Jennifer.

But there were more urgent problems to face. Edwards had advised him to keep away from Peter that morning.

He went to Hilbury, and saw the Corcorans. The uselessness of such a visit hurt him. In the face of grief there is nothing to be done. He had come by bus from the Lodge, and decided to walk back. He was approaching the house when he recognized Joe Bryce walking across the meadow.

Roger waited.

"Morning,' greeted Bryce, gruffly. 'I hope you're satisfied.'

'About what?' asked Roger.

'If you hadn't talked at me I wouldn't have talked to the police,' Byrce said, 'and the boy wouldn't be dead. Even I'd rather be in prison than dead.'

'It seems that way,' agreed Roger, 'although you're not necessarily right. He might have been killed later.'

'And your brother?'

Roger smiled faintly. 'He'll soon be released.'

'That's what you think,' said Bryce. He fell into step. 'I'll know better another time when to keep my mouth shut.'

Roger looked at him curiously. The man was speaking with the sullenness which was to be expected, and yet there was something puzzling in his tone and in his expression. They walked on in silence. Twice Bryce started to speak, but broke off. They passed the gate.

Then he said abruptly: 'That boy's death's on my mind, Maitland.'

'It's on mine, too.'

'If I hadn't talked—'

'You're tormenting yourself unnecessarily,' Roger assured him. 'There's only one thing for us to do now, that is find out who killed him.' There was a pause. 'It wasn't my brother, you know.'

Bryce made no comment.

'But the attack was very like the one on Lionel Chard,' Roger went on. 'It might have been by the same man. If so, your information about the car will be important. Have the police come back on you at all?'

'No.'

'I didn't think they would,' Roger said. 'They're fair, you know.'

'Fair! They—'

Roger smiled. 'Now look here, you've done all you could to antagonize them in the past. You're sore because you were jailed for breaking the law, but the wise thing would be to forget that and make sure you don't run foul of them again.'

'That's easy to say. How am I going to live?'

'Get a regular job.'

Byrce spat into the dust.

'Who's going to employ me?'

'Your reputation isn't as bad as you think it is,' said Roger. 'When this business is over—' It was on the tip of his tongue to suggest that Bryce should come to Home Farm, but he stopped himself in time; momentarily, he had forgotten that. Home Farm might not be his for long. 'We'll see about it', he added, weakly.

They reached the end of the lane leading to Lome. With a casual nod of his head Bryce walked off, a solitary, lonely figure.

Roger had luncheon alone with Jennifer. There was a difference in her. She had become, he decided, less child-like, more mature.

Over their coffee she looked at him seriously.

'Is it true that Uncle Lionel is trying to force you to leave Home Farm?'

'How did you learn that?'

'I overheard Barbara and Paul talking. And is it true that he has forbidden Peter's wife to come here?'

Roger said slowly: 'Yes, both things are true.'

'Why has he acted like that?'

'He thinks it's for the best, I suppose,' said Roger. He was surprised how embarrassed he felt. He had never discussed such subjects – or, indeed, any subjects – with Jennifer. Were he and Peter responsible for her childishness? Could they have affected a change by treating her more normally?

'He has always been angry with you all for refusing to enter his business,' mused Jennifer. 'And now – he feels it much more.'

Roger looked up sharply.

'He is in some trouble connected with the business,' Jennifer went on. 'I don't know what it is, Roger, but I know that when he returns from London he is often worried and ill. More than once he has said that if he only had someone at the office whom he could trust, he would not have to worry.' She smiled gravely. 'Why have none of you done what he wanted?'

'We've our own lives to live, Jenny.'

'Is that the only reason?'

'Yes, of course.'

'You don't – *disapprove* of his business?'

Roger looked at her perplexedly.

'No. We just haven't any interest in it. Financial gain is its only object, and that hasn't seemed the only thing worthwhile to the rest of us. Peter and Paul are too clever in their way to spend their lives grubbing for money, and I–' He smiled. 'I'm fond of the land. I'm never really happy away from it, Jenny.'

'I know,' said Jennifer. 'Sometimes, Roger, I think you are most unhappy, I wish you were not, and – I hate to think that it is because of Uncle Lionel. You don't like him, do you?'

Roger hesitated.

'Be honest with me,' pleaded Jennifer.

'No,' said Roger. 'I don't like him. Chiefly because he always wants his own way, and gets vindictive, even vengeful, when he can't have it. He's got into the habit of telling us what to do, ordering our lives, being the only one to make decisions. We've all rebelled against it.'

Jennifer's cool grey eyes were very close to his.

'I haven't rebelled,' she said, 'and he has always been so kind to me – in every way, Roger. I don't dislike him. I admire and respect him. I used to think that I loved him, but – recently he has been different. Last night, he talked wildly about you and Peter. He dislikes you both, but I suppose you know that.'

'It's hardly a state of mind that can be overlooked,' said Roger a little bitterly.

'But Roger, can't you try to reach an understanding with him? Sometimes I think that he regrets much that he has done, but he is stubborn.' She smiled at Roger's expression. 'You're surprised that I have noticed these things and thought about them, but I should be a fool if I hadn't,' said Jennifer. 'And there are some things that you have judged wrongly.'

'Oh,' said Roger. 'What are they?'

She stood up. 'All of you blame him for wanting to send me away, don't you? But I do assure you that it is my own wish. I discussed it with Uncle Lionel and, after a while, he agreed that I should become a novice. He did not suggest it to me.'

Roger said quietly: 'Then if that is so, we've certainly got it wrong, Jenny.' Inwardly, he was in a turmoil. It was impossible to doubt her word; she would not lie. He was hearing her as if she were someone whom he had never met before, seeing a depth, an understanding and a purpose of which he had not thought her capable. The hurt was like a physical pain. He saw their plans falling to pieces in front of him. As he watched the calmness of her eyes, he knew that she was telling the truth. He stretched out a hand, and took hers. 'Jenny—'

She smiled.

'Jenny, are you quite sure you're right about wanting to become a nun?'

'I'm quite sure.'

'Won't you leave it a little while longer?'

'I have thought about it for so long,' Jennifer told him. 'I suppose you are thinking that I enjoyed the outing yesterday. In a way, I did, but—'

He broke in, fiercely: 'Jenny, you haven't lived a normal life, you've been too secluded, you haven't met people, you haven't been about, you've had none of the pleasures, none of the joys of life – and few of the real hurts. You don't know what you're planning to leave. This house has been your world, but it's not *the* world. If you haven't been really happy here, it isn't because there's no happiness to be found. It's there for the asking.' He did not realize how tightly he was gripping her hand, nor how passionately he was pleading. 'Jenny, let me – let us – help you to find what life is really like. Jenny, don't—'

'I saw a little of it yesterday,' Jennifer said, quietly. 'First with Barbara and Paul, then, when Frank was killed. Is *that* your world?'

'Jenny, you mustn't think that, it's an isolated matter, there's much good in the world.'

'Frank was in love with me,' said Jennifer. 'He begged me to marry him. He talked like you do now. He's gone. You might go, Roger, and I should know great sorrow and loneliness. Roger, shall I tell you the truth?'

He did not speak.

'I am frightened of your world,' said Jennifer.

The door opened. Roger swung round, to meet the cold grey eyes of his uncle. He realized that the old man had been listening outside the door, and must have heard most of the conversation. Chard's gaze shifted to Jennifer.

'Hallo, my dear! I'm glad you're trying to put some sense into Roger's head. Roger, I want a word with you, and this is as good a time as any. Come into the business with me. I need the help of someone I can trust. Let bygones be bygones. Put the idea of farming out of your head, come in with me. You won't regret it.'

Roger hesitated.

Jennifer sent him a bright smile, and slipped out of the room.

Chard laughed.

'She's done some good, bless her! You've made the mistake of blaming me for everything, but I'm not behind this idea of hers. I don't like it much more than you do, but if it's for her good and she wants it, I won't interfere. And you've no right to. Well, what about accepting my offer?'

'You know as well as I do that it would never work,' Roger said.

'Don't be a stubborn fool. D'you think I've taken a high hand about Home Farm just to make you squirm? Do you think I've rapped Peter over the knuckles for the sake of it? I've got to bring you two young fools to your senses. You're dabbling in something you know little about, and there's no future in it. Let Peter keep his French cocotte if he wants her, she'll make no difference, but before I'll help him he'll have to come into the business. And so will you. Stop fighting against something you can't beat. Stop dreaming, be practical. I'll give you some time to think it over,' he added, abruptly, and turned and went out of the room.

Roger felt confused and bewildered. Had anyone else heard the old man, he would have been impressed by his apparent sincerity. But what did he really want? What was he feeling? How far was Jennifer right in what she thought about him?

He stayed there for half-an-hour, and then went in search of the old man. He must talk to him; the olive branch mustn't be peremptorily rejected. If Peter were allowed to continue his work happily, even at the cost of Home Farm, something would be achieved. It was no longer any use blaming Uncle Lionel for Jennifer's decision; that she had made the decision herself put the matter in an entirely different light. Uncle Lionel might even be an ally, not an enemy, in an effort to keep Jennifer away from the convent.

Roger was seething with new thoughts.

Jennifer had said that their uncle regretted some of the things he had done. The old man might genuinely have repented, age might have mellowed him. The possibility that he had judged too harshly was clear in Roger's mind as he hurried to Uncle Lionel's room, and knocked lightly on the door. There was no answer. He knocked again, and, after a pause, pushed it open. His uncle was sitting at a writing table near the window.

Roger stared ...

On the floor and on the desk was a layer of white feathers; some were clutched in the old man's hand. A sudden reversion of feeling swept over Roger. Here was the store of white feathers; it was the old man who had sent them to Paul!

But the immobility of the man in the chair was disquieting.

Roger hurried across the room; Uncle Lionel was dead.

CHAPTER SIXTEEN

FOLLY IN A HURRY

SUPERINTENDENT FOLLY had worked miracles. Marlin doubtless called them something else, but Abbott and Bennison preferred to call them miracles. The reprimand from the Chief Constable had been surprisingly mild and they had been assigned to the case, as special assistants to Folly. A pep talk followed. The good name of the County Force was largely in their hands, their responsibility great. They understood, of course ...

And that was that.

It had been a quiet morning, and the afternoon promised to be as quiet.

The telephone-bell rang in their office just after three o'clock. Abbott answered it.

'Superintendent Marlin isn't in his office,' said the operator, 'will you take a call from Chard Lodge?'

'Yes, put it through.' He waited for some seconds, then said: 'Ah, Mr. Maitland. This is Sergeant Abbott ... *What!*' He listened for two minutes, with growing tension, and then snapped: 'Yes, at once.' He jumped up. 'Chard's been murdered – shot. Come on!' He rushed along the passage to the room which had been placed at Folly's disposal, and burst in. Folly, quietly sitting behind the desk and dreaming of who knows what Lucullan feast, opened his eyes suddenly. On the desk in front of him was a block of chocolate, the silver paper wrapping in disarray.

He sat up. 'Now, Abbott, control yourself!'

'*Chard's been shot!*' cried Abbott.

Folly blinked. 'Repeat that.'

'Lionel Chard's been murdered.

Folly stared. 'Good gracious me! Has he, indeed.' He rose, not without difficulty, to his small, exquisitely shod feet, and moved towards the door; and as he walked, he talked. 'Bennison, you will stay here. Send orders for every road to be watched, all cars to be stopped and drivers questioned – how long ago was it?' he asked Abbott.

'No more than half-an-hour, according to Maitland.'

'Within a radius of forty miles,' said Folly. 'Look especially for a Chrysler, the fools might use the same car again, have everyone who has travelled from Hilbury checked closely.' He reached the passage as Abbott opened the door. 'And tell Marlin as soon as he comes in,' he added over his shoulder. 'Telephone me at Chard Lodge about any matter of importance, I am expecting a message from Scotland Yard. Hurry, Abbott!'

He beat Abbott to the head of the stairs, and went down them with remarkable speed. A policeman on duty at the foot of the stairs leapt to one side as Folly passed him like the wind.

A woman was approaching the police station; slim, *chic*, attractive. Abbott just caught sight of her and heard her exclaim, but it was not until he reached Folly's car that he remembered who she was.

'Super—' he began.

Folly, in his haste, had tried to get into the car without taking due care. He was stuck. He held the door with one hand and the roof with the other, the steering wheel wedged against his stomach. His face was screwed up in both agony and temper.

The woman had started to run after them.

Savagely Folly pulled himself free, and, crouching, attempted once again to bypass the wheel.

Successful, he settled down, grunting. The woman was rapidly approaching Abbott who stood by the open door.

'Get in, man!' snarled Folly. 'D'you think we've all day?'

'You!' cried the woman. 'You, ze policeman!' She reached Abbott's side and gripped his arm. 'I must see you, now!'

'Send her away!' snapped Folly.

'I will not—'

'It's Peter Maitland's wife!' cried Abbott, desperately.

'I don't care whose wife it is.' The big car began to move. 'Send her away and get in.'

Suddenly the car stopped.

'*Who* did you say she is?'

'Peter Maitland's wife.'

'God bless my soul! Why didn't you say so in the first place!' exclaimed Folly, his choirboy voice rising to a pure soprano. 'We'll take her with us. In with her!'

'I insist—' began Lucille.

'We're in a hurry, Mrs. Maitland,' Abbott said, 'but we'd like to talk to you.' A look from Folly gave him courage and he seized Lucille by the elbows and moved her towards the car. Lucille, seeing that there was nothing else to do, got in, and Abbott followed. The car started off, a boy on a bicycle only just swerving clear of the swinging door.

'I wish to see my 'usband,' said Lucille, in a small voice. 'I do not want to be here.'

'You can see him later,' said Folly. He turned his head to look at her, and a car in front, pulling into the side, missed them by inches.

'Be careful!' cried Abbott.

'What fools there are on the road,' said Folly, glaring at the unoffending driver.

'I come to see my 'usband,' repeated Lucille.

'Yes, yes, of course,' said Folly, glancing round again. 'We are on urgent business, but you wouldn't want to wait—'

'Where is he?' demanded Lucille.

'At the police station,' said Abbott, 'but—'

'Zen take me back!' cried Lucille. 'You 'ave not ze right—'

'Your husband's solicitor will be at the Lodge,' said Abbott, desperately. 'That's where we're going.'

'Sol-icitor?'

'Lawyer, not Counsel. You will be able to see him and he will arrange for you to see Mr. Maitland,' said Abbott.

'Where will ze solicitor-lawyer-counsel be?'

'At The Lodge, where we're going.'

'Chard Lodge?'

'Yes.'

Lucille waved her arms wildly.

'I will not go zere! Zat man has insulted me, I will not go to see him, take me to Peter.'

'But—' began Abbott.

Folly, now on the open road and driving at furious speed, looked over his shoulder again.

'If you mean Mr. Lionel Chard has insulted you, ma'am, you need not worry, he will not do so again.'

'What is zat you say?'

'He was murdered last night,' Folly said.

'*Murdered!*' gasped Lucille.

Abbott was about to correct Folly and to say: 'This afternoon,' when a glance of indescribable cunning from Folly stopped him.

'Last night, yes,' said Folly, 'he was brutally murdered. Your husband—'

'Not Peter! No, it was not Peter!' She clutched Abbott's arm. 'Tell me, it was not Peter, he was so angry, he was so wild, he—' She stopped abruptly.

To Abbott's surprise, the car was slowing down, although they were still half-a-mile from Chard Lodge. Folly pulled

133

into the side of the road. Lucille was staring at Abbott as if she were frightened out of her life. Folly performed an incredible feat, and turned in his seat.

'Now, Mrs. Maitland,' he said, 'your husband is in great *danger*. You know that.'

'*Peter*,' sighed Lucille, and caught her breath.

'Did you see him last night?'

'I – but yes,' she said, 'yes, I saw him. I did not know why he did not return.'

'To London.'

'To – the hotel,' said Lucille. The vitality seemed to have been drained from her. 'We were in – Hilbury.'

'I see,' said Folly. 'You and your husband came to stay in Hilbury for the night, and your husband went to the Lodge, angry with his uncle. Is that right?'

She hesitated, and then nodded. 'Yes.'

'He was *very* angry?'

'Most angry,' Lucille said. 'He – of course he was angry!' A spark of vitality returned. 'He was right to be angry, it was a wicked zing zat his uncle wrote to him.' She opened her bag – a newspaper cutting fell to her lap. She searched further, and brought out a letter. It was addressed to Peter, at Home Farm. Lucille's fingers were trembling as she handed it to Folly.

As he read, Folly's eyes narrowed; he nodded, as if everything were explained.

'It was unkind to write such a letter,' he said, slowly.

'It is lies!'

Folly looked at her for some time.

'I have no doubt that what he says is untrue,' he assured her. He glanced at Abbott. 'Mr. Chard wrote to Mr. Maitland making unpleasant accusations against Mrs. Maitland.' The formality of the words was lost in their meaning. 'And when he received this letter he hurried to Hilbury and, against your wishes, Mrs. Maitland, he went to see his uncle. Understandable, of course.' He spoke to Abbott in an aside as if he did not mind Lucille hearing. 'That is why he would

134

not tell us why he had gone to the house, and why he kept away from the others. He did not want to see them, he wanted to see the old man, it was a strictly personal matter. Our Peter Maitland is a chivalrous young man.' He looked at Lucille. 'I should like to keep this letter until we reach the house, Mrs. Maitland, but I ask you not to worry too much. Your husband did not kill his uncle. I made a slight mistake, it was this afternoon when your uncle was murdered, not last night. Do you know a Mr. Corcoran?'

'*Zis* man,' said Lucille, and touched the paper cutting.

'What does that say?' Folly asked Abbott.

Abbott looked down. It was a stop press notice in which there was a brief mention of Corcoran's death and the fact that Peter had been detained for questioning. As Abbott read it to a running commentary from Lucille, Folly sat silent. Lucille had seen it in the hotel lounge and asked someone there what it meant. The 'someone', obviously had given her to understand that it meant Peter had murdered Corcoran; and Lucille had immediately rushed to the police station.

'And you did right,' said Folly, unctuously. 'I should not worry, Mrs. Maitland.' He started the car again. 'I think the delay well worthwhile, Abbott. We now know why Maitland was at the house, his business was not with Corcoran but with Chard – it is the unexplained which always causes so much trouble. What is the man Edwards like?'

'Maitland's solicitor? Pretty good.'

'A man of sense?'

'Oh, yes.'

'Then he will have got this story out of Maitland and will persuade Maitland to tell us.' He talked as if oblivious of Lucille. 'Mrs. Maitland's dislike of the police worried her husband, of course, he did not want us to interview her, and he did not think she would so easily triumph over her fears when she knew he was in danger. Madame!'

Lucille started. 'You spoke, *m'sieu*?'

'Why do you fear the police?' asked Folly.

She stared at him. 'You would not understand,' she said quietly.

They reached the drive gates, and Folly swung the car into the drive, scraping one wing on a gate-post. Abbott wished he had read Chard's letter. He was mentally exhausted. Folly swept through arguments to reach his conclusions, which seemed wildly dangerous to one nurtured on the cautiousness of Superintendent Marlin.

Was Folly right in assuming that Peter Maitland was not Corcoran's murderer, nor implicated in the crime?

Folly pulled the car up with a screech of brakes. The three of them approached the house slowly. Roger, waiting at the porch, suddenly moved forward, his face showing unusual animation.

'Lucille!' he exclaimed. 'What are you—'

'Mrs. Maitland was anxious to come here and we gave her a lift,' said Folly. 'I must ask you to—'

Roger ignored him. Lucille ran into his arms, her face puckered with unhappiness.

'I must see Peter,' she exclaimed.

'You will, very soon,' Roger assured her. He looked over her head at Folly, with an unspoken question: did Lucille know about Chard's death? Folly nodded; Roger held Lucille's arm, and led her into the house. 'Paul and Barbara have gone to London to see you,' he said. 'I suppose you missed them.'

'I am sorry to be so insistent,' Folly said, 'but there are urgent matters which must have our attention. I have told Mrs. Maitland that she need not worry unduly about her husband.' He actually patted her shoulder. 'Now, Mr. Maitland, what has happened here?'

'My uncle was shot in the head, apparently through the window and from a distance.'

'And Mr. and Mrs. Briscoe are out?'

'They went to London. Surely you—'

'Yes, I remember. Miss Briscoe?'

'She went for a walk.'

'I see.' With a brief nod, Folly stalked up the stairs. Abbott had unlocked the morning-room door, and was telephoning; Roger heard the name 'Coppinger'.

It was the sight of Lucille which steadied Roger. The discovery of the old man surrounded by feathers, evidence that Uncle Lionel had been responsible for the malicious campaign against Paul, had been enough to upset him. And he had made another discovery: the deeds of Home Farm were on the desk, and in a moment of revelation he realized the truth: they had never been stolen.

He had hurried downstairs to tell the sergeant-in-charge of his uncle's death, but the man had been in the grounds and it had been some time before a constable had found him. Roger had then telephoned the police-station. Once the sergeant had taken formal charge, and a policeman had been set to work searching the nearby grounds, Roger had looked for Jennifer.

She had not returned; and he had seen no sign of her. The policemen remembered that she had gone out of the gate towards the convent. She might be back at any time, but the longer he had to wait to break this news to her, the worse Roger felt. Memory of how she had talked to him was still vivid in his mind. The words which stung him most were: *'Then – Frank was killed. Is that your world?'*

What would she think now?

The two murders seemed, at that juncture, unimportant compared with Jennifer. He had not really accepted the fact that she herself wanted to take the veil, and had not yet adjusted himself to the necessary change in his attitude towards her. In her mind, it was now apparent, there was a sharp contrast between the evil which went on about her, and the sanctuary of the church. Being Jennifer, that sanctuary appealed to her in a way which he could not personally understand. He thought that there was a chance of dissuading her, but after this, she might make up her mind finally.

The old man, in death, might influence her even more than he had in life.

Now he had to deal with Lucille.

He had been astonished to see her, but was glad that she was here. It was an immediate problem, and it cleared away some of the confusion.

'Shall I be able to see Peter soon?' she asked, in a small voice.

'The police wouldn't have told you you'd no need to worry, if it weren't true,' Roger assured her. He could not understand why Folly had said that, yet he accepted the man's word. 'You know what happened, don't you?'

'Only a little.'

'Come and sit down, and I'll tell you,' said Roger. 'And we may as well have some tea.'

Lucille looked at Roger searchingly.

'You do not seem very worried about your uncle,' she said.

The statement shocked Roger. If she had noticed that, Folly and the others would notice it, and they might draw the wrong conclusions.

'It doesn't seem quite real to me yet,' he said, 'and in any case, we weren't close friends.'

'I should zink not!' exclaimed Lucille.

She was filled with emotional excitement, and anger against the dead man, which did not at first seem to have any reasonable explanation but which gradually impressed Roger. He sorted her story out as she went along. The letter which Peter had received, the malicious terms of it – how well that squared with the white feathers and the deeds of Home Farm. Then Peter's decision to visit his uncle, his furtive visit, leaving Lucille at a small hotel in Hilbury, his failure to return, and Lucille's increasing anxiety until she had seen the notice in the newspaper, and had gone rushing to the police.

His reaction was much the same as Folly's had been, and was coupled with profound relief. It seemed to him a fortunate thing that Peter had been in prison when his uncle had been murdered, for his motive for murder was stronger now than ever it had been.

Who *had* killed Uncle Lionel?

He talked to Lucille, over tea, but all her thoughts were centred on Peter, and very soon she fell silent. Now and again Roger looked out of the window, in the hope that Jennifer would appear, but she did not. He thought vaguely that Tubby Edwards was a long time coming, and then saw two cars turn in at the gates.

The first was Dr. Coppinger's Talbot; the second, presumably that of Tubby Edwards.

It was.

At Roger's approach he gave a friendly wave of the hand.

'Sorry for the delay, old chap. Got stuck at the Assizes. Didn't think I'd have to go there this morning, but it couldn't be helped. What's on here?'

'More murder,' said Roger, drily.

Tubby's round, plump face and merry blue eyes became a mask of astonishment.

'Well, well! Someone's making quite a business of it. And *this* wasn't Peter. Who—'

'Do you know Peter?' demanded Lucille, quickly.

'Peter's wife, Lucille,' Roger explained.

Tubby's face lit up.

'I *am* glad to see you! Peter was telling me about you this afternoon. The silly ass didn't want to talk at first, but I got the truth out of him at last.' He glanced at Roger. 'Have you heard about the letter?'

'Yes.'

'Well, well. If the police had known about it last night, I doubt whether they would have been quite so high-handed,' said Tubby. 'But I think they'll see reason and admit they haven't. now, any real grounds for detaining Peter. Just as well the silly fellow was getting free board and lodgings for the night, don't you think?'

Lucille raised a hand. 'What does he say?'

Tubby beamed at her.

'I think we'll have your husband out in no time,' he said, 'you're not to worry.' They went indoors. 'Any idea who's responsible for the new outburst of violence?' he asked lightly.

'No,' said Roger. 'I think – hallo, who's this?'

A man had turned into the gates and they saw him running up the drive. As he neared the house Roger saw that it was Joe Bryce.

Roger went towards him, filled with alarm; it would take a lot to move Bryce like this.

'What is it?' he asked.

Bryce drew a deep breath, and then said: 'Miss Jennifer.'

A cold hand seemed to grip Roger's heart.

'What about her?'

Bryce said slowly and deliberately, pausing between each word:

'She has – been – taken – away.'

CHAPTER SEVENTEEN

TOO MUCH AT ONCE

No one else was within earshot. Roger waited in an agony of impatience until Bryce's breathing eased.

'What happened?'

'I was coming across the fields,' Bryce explained, his voice still harsh and rasping, 'when I saw Miss Jennifer. She had been to the convent, and was – alone. A car pulled up. Two men got out, and they – made her get in.'

'What kind of car?' asked Roger. He must keep calm.

'A small one.'

'Which way did it go?'

'On the Bournemouth Road.'

Roger saw the morning-room door standing open, and hurried towards it, followed by Bryce. Abbott looked up with a glance of bright inquiry which faded at sight of Roger's expression.

'Miss Briscoe has been kidnapped,' Roger said, steadily enough. 'Bryce here saw it happen. A small car, with two men in it, and it took the Bournemouth Road.'

Abbott lifted the telephone. It was then that Roger realized how shaken he was, and how weak he felt at the knees. After their plans to do this very thing, it seemed incredible that someone else should have carried it out. But Bryce would not lie to him. Thank God for Bryce! Had he not seen what had happened, hours might have elapsed before an alarm was raised.

He dropped into a chair, while Abbott rapped out terse instructions. That done, he put the receiver down and turned to Roger.

'Mr. Maitland, there is really no need to worry overmuch. There's a very good chance that we'll pick this car up. We're already watching all the roads out of the town for another car, one used by your uncle's murderers.'

'What are you saying?' demanded Bryce.

Abbott explained briefly, adding: 'It looks as if a rifle were used, range several hundred yards, probably. Did either of you hear a shot?'

Both men shook their heads.

Abbott shrugged his shoulders.

'The trouble with this show is that too much is taking place at once.' He got up. 'I must go and tell Folly what's happened.' As Roger got up he smiled and went on: 'Seriously, I shouldn't worry too much about your cousin. Whoever took her off can't have realized that the roads are being so closely watched. We ought to have news quite soon.'

Roger nodded briefly, hardly hearing what Abbott had said. Jennifer – *missing*. It did not seem real, any more than the conversation with her after luncheon had seemed real. But here was Bryce, still by his side, solid and somehow dependable.

'I'm sorry I had to bring ye bad news,' Bryce muttered.

Roger said: 'You've been very good, Bryce, and I won't forget it.' He saw Tippett hovering about outside, pretending to work, but obviously unable to settle down. 'Oh, Tippett! See that Bryce gets some tea will you,' he said. 'I'll try to see you before you go, Bryce, but if I don't, we'll have a word later. And again – thank you.'

'Glad to help Miss Jennifer,' muttered Bryce.

Tippett said: 'I – I couldn't help overhearing what was said, sir. Is – is – Miss Jenny—' He broke off.

'We'll get her back,' said Roger, roughly.

He did not want to see anyone, but Lucille and Tubby were together in the drawing-room, and he could not leave them alone much longer. They hardly knew Jennifer; the news would startle them, but he could not expect them to feel much concern for her. Paul and Barbara would not be back for an hour or more. Oh, what was the use of letting it get on top of him? Abbott was right; too much had happened at once, it was difficult to take it all in. There was his uncle, lying dead upstairs, and Corcoran, in the mortuary, and Jennifer—

'Roger!' exclaimed Lucille, as he went into the drawing-room. 'Roger, what is ze matter?'

Tubby Edwards stared at him, looking equally startled at his appearance. Roger caught a glimpse of his face in a mirror. It was chalk-white.

'What is it?'

Roger told them; and there was nothing they could say, no comfort they could bring.

Then he heard a voice at the head of the stairs; a voice which grew louder and clearer as Folly descended. Roger did not particularly want to see Folly at this juncture, but of all the policemen, Folly seemed to him most likely to get results. And now it was not a matter only of finding a murderer, of avenging a death; Jennifer must be found.

He jumped up, as Folly paused on the threshold, and then came forward, one hand outstretched.

'My dear fellow,' he said. 'My dear fellow, what a shock this must have been.' He gripped Roger's shoulder. 'I can understand how you feel, and I want to give you this assurance: we shall leave nothing undone to catch a murderer, but now we have to find someone even worse – a kidnapper – and on our shoulders rests the responsibility of finding a most charming girl. That will be our first charge, it will have absolute priority.'

'Thanks,' muttered Roger.

'I am going to make sure that everything is put in hand, and then I shall have to ask you a few questions about the other matter. I'm sure you understand.' He paused, and looked pointedly at Tubby.

'Mr. Edwards, of Edwards and Edwards, Superintendent—'

'Oh, Peter Maitland's solicitor!' beamed Folly. He shook hands. 'I am very glad to meet you. I have just been informed that you were shrewd and able enough to persuade Peter Maitland to tell you – and us – what happened last night, and what he was doing here. I do congratulate you.' He shot a quick look at Lucille. 'I understand that Superintendent Marlin has recommended that your husband should be released, subject, of course, to his assurance that he will not leave the district for the time being.'

Lucille seized upon one word.

'Released!'

Looking at her, Roger thought: Well, someone is happy.

The commotion which had followed Folly's first visit to the house paled into insignificance compared with the turmoil during his second visit. Roger did not know what the police were looking for, but they seemed to be in every room, in all the outhouses and in the garage. Men had come in from Hilbury, and Marlin was among them. Policemen, in uniform, with Abbott at their head, searched the grounds, although it seemed pointless to Roger. He could not get thought of Jennifer out of his mind. He had reached the drive when one of the searchers raised something high above his head, and shouted:

'I've got it!'

Immediately, Abbott hurried towards the man, and Roger joined them. The find was a small bore rifle. It had been discovered near a tree from which there was a clear view of the window, covered with bracken and dead leaves.

Abbott hurried back to the house, with Roger in his wake. He did not utter Folly's name, but obviously he was agog to show Folly this discovery.

They were half-way towards the house, when Abbott spoke.

'By the way, Maitland—'

'Yes?'

'Do you recognize the gun?'

Roger smiled wryly.

'Yes,' he said. 'I've often used it, it's one of several which have been here for years.'

Abbott seemed bereft of words.

But for Jennifer's disappearance, Roger would have found the discovery of the gun worrying: he had no doubt that it was one which he had often used as a boy, and he was able to show Abbott where the others were kept, in a small pantry near the kitchen. All the family knew about them.

He did not know what Folly said; but he did know, a little later, that no prints had been found on the gun, and that there were no footprints near the tree which would help them, although there was evidence that the tree had been recently climbed. Dimly, it dawned upon Roger that the family was now in grave danger, for only someone who knew where to find the gun could have used it. Folly had surprisingly little to say about it; Marlin looked as if he would like to say a lot, but did not dare.

Only Lucille seemed completely unaffected; the promise of Peter's release was all that mattered to her.

When Barbara and Paul arrived home, Roger was alone in the drawing-room. He heard Barbara walk from the car to the front door. She went straight upstairs, and he caught a glimpse of her set face.

More trouble?

Paul came in after he had garaged the car. He was also on edge, and poured himself out a stiff drink.

'Lucille wasn't at home.'

'I know,' said Roger. 'She's here.'

Here?' exclaimed Paul. 'I thought she so hated Uncle Lionel that—' He broke off at sight of Roger's expression.

Roger told him of the two crimes; and Paul seemed hardly affected by Uncle Lionel's death, but desperately anxious about Jennifer.

Whatever bother there had been between Barbara and Paul on their return was forgotten in the new emergency, but once again a sense of helplessness fell upon them. Only Lucille was untroubled, waiting for Peter.

⁓ ✦

'Yes,' said Folly, as he drove towards Hilbury, with Abbott by his side, 'someone at that house of tragedy is happy, and we should be pleased about it, Abbott. Have you ever pondered on the importance of human contentment? Can you imagine a world in which everyone is contented? If that were possible, there would be no need for you and me, there would be nothing for us to do. On the whole, perhaps, I prefer the world as it is!'

'You mean the French girl,' said Abbott.

'I do indeed. A charming creature, and she matches her husband – what a handsome couple! One of the main obstacles to his future happiness has been neatly removed. A removal in which he himself could have played no active part. Reason enough for felicitations. Can he paint, do you know?'

'I haven't seen any of his stuff.'

'I made some inquiries about him before I left London,' Folly said. 'He is, I am told, of the modern school. One can be too modern; perhaps he is. I am also told that he has great promise, and we have to remember that a man in the trade thought it worthwhile visiting him at Home Farm and buying a picture for sixty pounds. Do you consider that a lot of money for a picture?'

'It would be for me,' said Abbott.

'You must try to get away from the personal angle on all these matters,' Folly said, reprovingly. 'The question is whether, on the open market, a picture by that young man is worth sixty pounds. It might have an important bearing on the case.'

'Oh,' said Abbott.

'You don't see it? Then look at it this way,' Folly advised. He was now keeping his eyes steadfastly on the road, and driving with extreme caution. 'Chard has been murdered. I think we must accept the fact that all the nephews have good reasons for wanting him dead. Undoubtedly they did wish it. And in two cases, Roger's and Maitland's, the motive could be gain. But if Peter Maitland can paint a picture and sell it for sixty pounds – well, he is not really so poor as it might appear. If he has arrived as an artist, his motive would be much weaker than it was.'

'I can see that,' Abbott said, 'but Peter Maitland couldn't have killed his uncle.'

Folly shot him a quick glance.

'Indeed, no. But he could have conspired with the others to do so. Roger could not have fired the shot, because one of our men heard it while Roger was indoors. Paul could.' Folly smiled. 'I am very glad I had Paul and his wife followed, the report on what they did should be most interesting! I wonder if he knew that he was followed?'

'I doubt it,' said Abbott.

'We shall find out,' said Folly. 'But they might, all three, have agreed that the old man must die, and if they did, if they played any part in the conspiracy, each is equally guilty. Remember the maid's story at Home Farm. She overheard some pretty wild talk about murder.'

Abbott did not speak.

'Don't you agree?' asked Folly, sharply.

Abbott hesitated and then said: 'I thought you'd ruled Peter out.'

'For Corcoran's murder, yes. For complicity in the murder of his uncle, no. Complicity is the keyword. Or conspiracy. Each of them, I repeat, might be equally guilty as accessories before the fact, and they must therefore all be closely watched. Motive is always of such importance, and we know a lot about motives, now. By the way, Abbott, didn't you tell me something about finding some white feathers at Home Farm?'

'Yes.'

'I thought I remembered something about that. Now white feathers are insignificant things, except in one connection.'

'You mean, as an emblem of cowardice.'

'Exactly! You see, you do realize these things, they're all tucked away in your mind, but you haven't developed the habit of taking them out and inspecting them,' said Folly. 'That's where you and Bennison fail, it is lack of practice or lack of training as much as anything else. Which of the family would be likely to receive white feathers from Uncle Lionel?'

Abbott's eyes gleamed

'Paul, of course! He stayed in America throughout the war. And that torn envelope was addressed to him!'

'Precisely. Uncle Lionel, then, sent white feathers to his nephew. Unkind of him. The sort of thing that would make a spirited man, especially if he felt a little guilty, very angry indeed. So would Roger be angry if he discovered before Chard's death that Chard had never lost those deeds, but reported them missing in order to make difficulties for Roger. Chard was, undoubtedly, a sadist. He enjoyed seeing

147

his nephews suffer. However, have we a motive for murder in the deeds or the feathers? Neither in itself, I think, but each might be a contributory motive. I do not think there is much doubt that all three nephews had various reasons for hating their uncle, and it is the last straw which breaks the camel's back.' Folly beamed. 'We must take that into account, mustn't we?'

'Yes,' agreed Abbott. 'The trouble is—' He broke off.

'Go on,' urged Folly.

'What are we trying to find out? Who murdered Chard? Who murdered Corcoran? Or who has kidnapped Jennifer Briscoe?'

'Now, now, that's not worthy of you,' said Folly. 'It really isn't worthy, my dear fellow. Think about it. Talk it over with Bennison. I am going to see Marlin, I must make my peace with that fellow, every time I go near him he bridles.'

Abbott grinned. 'I'm not sure what bridling means.'

'Nor am I,' said Folly blandly, 'but I like the sound of it. Well, here we are!'

Bennison was in the sergeant's office, with two other sergeants. He had little to report. No news had come in from cars stopped on the road.

After a sketchy tea in the canteen, Abbott and Bennison returned to find a note from Folly on Abbott's desk. He would not require their services until later in the evening, and suggested that they should rest while they could. They went home to find that Mrs. Harris was out, and another note saying she would be back at half-past seven, in time to give them their supper.

Supper was a *rabbit en casserole*; and as Mrs. Harris was serving it, there came a ring at the front door followed by a voice they were beginning to know well.

'My dear fellows, what a fortunate moment I have chosen,' said Folly, coming in brightly. 'Mrs. Harris has kindly suggested that I have a snack with you.' Preening herself, Mrs. Harris stood there, fully aware she was being

148

subjected to wheedling and cajolery, but thoroughly enjoying it. 'If ever you were to marry again, Mrs. Harris,' Folly went on, what a fortunate fellow your husband would be!'

'I wouldn't be such a fool,' declared Mrs. Harris.

She went out, smiling. Folly cocked his head on one side.

'Wouldn't she, I wonder? We'll see. Still, that isn't the point just now.' He sank down with a sigh of contentment. 'Well, have you discussed that little matter with Bennison?'

'Yes, and we haven't got anywhere,' Abbott said.

Folly helped himself to vegetables.

'You ask me which of the three crimes we are investigating. The obvious answer is *all* of them, and you know that. What you really mean is, on which am I concentrating? The answer is again: *all* of them. You may be persuaded that these three crimes are all separate; or that two are connected and the third is separate. I won't allow the possibility for one moment. There may be different motives, perhaps, but there is a single thread, connecting them all. So, we have to concentrate first on finding out why anyone should wish (a) to kill Lionel Chard, and I believe that to be the first intention, (b) to kill Corcoran and (c) to kidnap the girl. If she has been kidnapped,' he added, with a sniff.

They stared at him expectantly.

'She could have gone of her own free will,' Folly said, airily. 'I won't say that I think that is the case, but at least it is possible. We have only the evidence of the poacher, who saw the incident from some way off.'

'That girl wouldn't go of her own accord,' said Abbott positively.

'Perhaps not. But I think we will call the kidnapping her "disappearance" until we have evidence to the contrary,' said Folly. 'Well, that is the point I wanted to make: the crimes, or incidents, are all connected, one would not have happened without the others. The family may be guilty; it is just possible that someone outside the family is responsible, although I am a long way from convinced of that.'

'You mean, it might be concerned with Chard's financial racket,' Abbott said.

'Yes. I will tell you a little more about that. There has been an illegal transfer of assets, but there has also been a transfer of jewels to America. During the occupation of Europe, the Germans looted, as we well know. Not all the French are patriots. The French Government believes that criminals took from the Germans a very large store of jewels, and shipped them to England for transhipment to America – where the money is, my lads, where the money is. In addition to his ordinary business, Lionel Chard has large dealings with the French, as an exporter and importer.' Reluctantly Folly rose from the table. 'I see there is apple pie to follow. Alas, at my time of life discretion, though all too frequently flouted, cannot be entirely ignored. With regret I leave you to it.'

His voice could be heard in praise and valediction receding down the hall.

Abbott and Bennison soon followed him, Bennison deep in thought.

'The French,' he muttered, then suddenly turned to Abbott with shining eyes. 'Lucille was in Hilbury this afternoon, *she* could have fired that shot! She was in the Resistance Movement, wasn't she? Abb, we've got something!'

Abbott looked thoughtful.

Bennison telephoned the police station, gave a description of Lucille, and asked for efforts to trace her movements that afternoon. Then he and Abbott took paper and pencil and worked out a timetable. Chard had been shot between 2.30 and 3.30. Anyone could walk from the centre of Hilbury to the Lodge and back in an hour. Certainly Lucille could have killed Chard and returned to Hilbury in time to see Abbott and Folly about to leave.

'I'm going to follow this up,' Bennison said. 'What hotel was she at?'

'White House,' Abbott said.

Bennison went to White House, and Abbott went to the station. Events moved quickly. Within an hour, they knew that Lucille had been seen walking from the direction of Chard Lodge half-an-hour before she had encountered Abbott and Folly.

Lucille was obviously frightened. Yes, she could use a rifle – certainly! Yes, she had been on the road, had she ever denied it? She had intended to see Roger, but, half-way to Chard, had taken courage and returned to see the police. Folly did not detain her.

'I know, I know,' Folly said to Bennison. 'It's interesting. It might be damning. We will make inquiries as to whether she was really near the Lodge. But remember this: if she *is* concerned, if the motive is the French business, there are bigger fish than Lucille. She will lead us to them. And we must remember that Chard did everything he could to poison her husband's mind against her. She might have hated him for that reason, too. It is up to you to find out if she was near the Lodge at the time of the shooting.'

Bennison said: 'I'll do that all right.'

'First find out if she *could* have fired the shot,' said Folly. 'And we want to know where the Briscoes went while in London, too. They might have returned earlier. The report should be here soon.'

Bennison, however, was not satisfied, and back at his lodgings grumbled to Abbott.

'I'm sure he's wrong about one thing,' he commented.

'What's that?'

'Jennifer Briscoe. She was kidnapped all right, and—' He broke off, seeing a sudden change in Abbott's expression. 'Now what's got into you?'

'Of *course* she was kidnapped! ' exclaimed Abbott, pulling out his wallet. He searched for a slip of paper, and eagerly produced it. 'Ben, we've got something. Come on—'

Folly opened his eyes abruptly when they reached the downstairs room.

Abbott thrust the paper in front of Folly's nose.

'What do you make of this? *"Make-up ... Barbara to excite envy ... Place ... She can't be alone ... Clothes ... Photographs ... Newspapers ... Quiet spot ..."* Well?' he demanded.

Folly took the paper.

'And what am I supposed to make of it?'

'They're the notes which I found screwed up by Roger's desk at Home Farm,' said Abbott, excitedly. 'And now Jennifer Briscoe's been kidnapped!'

Folly read the notes again.

'I see.' He nodded, and then bent an approving glance upon him. 'Do you know, Abbott, I think you've got something here. Just such notes might have been made if they *were* planning to kidnap the child. Remarkable! Now we've got something else with which to confront Roger Maitland.'

'Something else?' asked Abbott, quickly.

'Yes indeed. The will. I have seen a copy.'

'Have you, by George!'

'I do not lose time,' said Folly, 'and a copy was found at the house – that was one of the things on which I was able to congratulate Marlin. Yes. A most interesting will.'

'Who gets what?'

'How crude,' said Folly, wincing, 'but how pertinent! Paul gets nothing at all. Peter gets a fair share only if he gives up his painting. Roger gets twenty thousand pounds, unconditionally. The residue goes to Jennifer, unless she goes into the convent, in which case she gets £300 a year and the rest goes to charity. And the rest is more than seventy thousand pounds, my lads!'

CHAPTER EIGHTEEN

FOLLY VERSUS ROGER

ROGER tried to keep his temper, although for half-an-hour Folly had been doing his best to make him lose it. The subject of the notes had not yet been touched upon. Folly had hinted at a conspiracy among the nephews to murder Lionel Chard, and had dropped further hints about the motive for such an act which each one of them had. Roger was rendered more uneasy by the terms of the will. He had freely admitted that the old man's death would greatly benefit him. There was now no danger of being forced to leave Home Farm and, he had agreed, if Jennifer were back and safe, he would have no complaints.

Folly swayed up and down on his toes.

'Tell me Maitland, why are you so concerned about your cousin? You show a remarkable affection for her, if I may say so.'

'I see nothing remarkable in it,' said Roger.

'Then tell me this: were you and your cousins and your brother prepared to go to extreme lengths to get her away from the atmosphere of this house?' demanded Folly.

'We should have liked to get her away.'

'So you would have liked to get her away.' Folly raised a finger. 'Maitland, earlier in this unhappy business I congratulated you on your frankness. I wish I could do the same now. Unfortunately you are being evasive and I have every reason to believe that you are withholding material facts. That is a serious matter.'

Roger said, 'I know nothing about any of these crimes.'

153

'So you say, so you say, Maitland, but you *do* know something about your cousin Jennifer's disappearance.'

'Indeed I don't.'

'Why lie to me?' thundered Folly. 'Don't you realize that we have been gathering evidence, that we now know your plans, your hopes, your ambitions? Don't treat us as fools. *Tell us where Jennifer is.*'

Roger said slowly: 'I don't know.'

'I tell you—'

Roger snapped: 'For God's sake do your job and find her! This waste of time—'

'Waste of time!' echoed Folly. 'Now listen to me, Mr. Maitland. For a variety of reasons, you hated your uncle; the main reason being his influence over his niece. You decided to get her away from what you considered to be his evil influence, and you plotted to kidnap her.'

Roger drew a sharp breath.

'Deny it if you dare,' said Folly dramatically.

Roger did not speak.

Folly relaxed; at the moment when Abbott and Bennison had expected him to thunder, he dropped his voice and became sweetly reasonable.

'My dear fellow, I know how worried you are, I know how hopelessly involved this situation has become. Don't worsen it. You planned to kidnap your cousin. You would not, of course, have done it yourself, you would have employed other people. This you have done. They have performed their part. You were not to know that the murder of your uncle would make the move unnecessary. Now, please, admit the truth and tell us where she is.'

Roger said wearily: 'We did make tentative plans to get her away, but we didn't carry them out. I've no idea where she is.'

Folly frowned. 'I see. You ask me to believe that you planned this disappearance, and someone else put it into practice. Do I look as gullible as that?'

'I've told you the truth,' said Roger.

'You may have told us part of the truth, very much too late,' said Folly, 'but that is all. Take courage. Tell us the rest. We shall not be vindictive. If you considered it a wise and necessary step to take this child from the care of her lawful guardian, we shall not blame you. But help us now. Unless you do, you may find yourself facing graver issues and graver charges.'

Roger did not speak.

'Come,' whispered Folly.

Roger said: 'There's nothing more I can tell you.'

Folly pursed his lips. Where an outburst might have been expected, none came. He moved towards the door, then turned and spoke again.

'Talk it over with the others, Mr. Maitland. I think you are troubled by a mistaken sense of loyalty to them. Tell them that now the truth must be told and only the truth will serve.'

He went out.

Roger sat alone for what seemed a long time.

Somewhere, perhaps miles away, Jennifer was with those two men, and he was sitting here, helpless.

The door opened.

'Roger,' said Barbara, gently.

He looked up.

She closed the door behind her, and approached him, smiling faintly.

'Does it hurt so much?'

He tightened his lips.

'You're in love with her, aren't you?' she asked quietly.

It did not really surprise him that she knew. He nodded. She put a cool hand on his, and kept it there.

'It's odd, but Folly's guessed,' said Roger. He was surprised that it was so easy to talk about. 'That man is clever, you know, and – but what does he matter?' He laughed, mirthlessly. 'It's been for so long,' he said. 'She's no fonder of me than of the others, no fonder than she was of Frank Corcoran.'

'You sound so sure.'

'If you'd heard her this afternoon, you'd know why,' said Roger. He jumped up. 'Bar, what a fool I am! What a callous fool! I'm talking as if she's upstairs, as if she might open that door and come in at any moment, instead, she's—'

'There's nothing we can do,' Barbara said, in a more practical voice, 'and if that man Folly is clever, he—'

Roger said abruptly: 'He thinks we've taken her away.'

Barbara stared.

'It's true. How he found out, I've no idea, but he knows we were planning to get her away. And he thinks that if we were prepared to do that, we might have been prepared to kill the old man.' He looked at Barbara steadily. 'I was,' he added, abruptly.

'Roger—'

'I was, I tell you! I quietened Peter down because he was talking wildly, but I was always prepared to see the old man dead rather than that Jennifer should go into the convent. So was Peter.'

Barbara said: 'So was Paul.'

Neither of them saw the door, which was slightly open, move a little wider. Outside, Bennison was standing.

'But talk like this won't get us anywhere,' Roger said, after a long pause. 'We didn't have to do it, someone else did it for us.' He laughed, harshly. 'Whether we'll ever be able to convince the police of that, I don't know. I doubt it.'

'None of us could have killed him,' said Barbara, quickly. 'Paul and I were in London, you and Peter—'

Roger said slowly: 'Of course, but – who did you see in London?'

'No one.'

'No one at all?'

Barbara shrugged. 'We went to Peter's and Lucille's flat, but there was no answer, so we came straight back, stopping at a roadhouse for tea. Why do you want to know?

'Folly will ask,' said Roger. 'And we've got to be practical.

Jenny's missing, we're all suspected in a greater or lesser degree of conspiring to kill both Corcoran and Uncle Lionel. Folly made that clear,' he added. 'And he made it equally clear that we all had pretty sound reasons. We mustn't forget that there's an over-riding one, too.'

'And that?'

'Inheritance,' said Roger, drily. 'He threatened to alter his will. That would give point to any motive Peter and I had. What a mess it is!' He touched her arm. 'And what a mess we've brought you into.'

'Don't worry about that,' said Barbara.

'It does worry me,' said Roger. 'You and Lucille oughtn't to be caught up in it, but there it is. I know one thing. Folly's dead right when he says that it's time we made a clean sweep of everything we've done and said and planned. He suspects a lot. If we tell him everything, the story from start to finish, it's going to save us from a lot of shocks when he finds out first one thing and then another. Where's Paul?'

'In the dining-room with Lucille and Peter.'

'I'll go in and see them,' said Roger. 'I hope they'll agree. It's all got to come out,' he added, 'from the white feathers to Uncle Lionel's pretty little way of blackmailing us into doing what he wanted. Don't you agree?'

'If you say so,' said Barbara.

The words were curiously submissive; Roger thought about them a great deal, later in the evening.

A little after eleven o'clock, the family sat together, listening to Folly's car departing. There had been some argument before Peter and Paul had agreed with Roger; and Barbara's pleading of his case had undoubtedly helped them to make up their minds. Roger had sent for Folly; Abbott and Bennison had taken down the statements in shorthand. During the recitals, Folly had sat like the chairman of a board meeting, asking an occasional question, sometimes calling them to order when they had become irrelevant. It was surprising how little fuss the man had made, how naturally he seemed able to accept their statements as normal. Now Folly understood everything of the cross-currents in the family.

When they had finished, he surprised them by asking questions about Uncle Lionel's business. Did they know the other people employed? Did they know the volume of his business? Had he business enemies? Did they know of anyone else who disliked him enough to murder him?

Roger had been able to tell him more than the others.

He had mentioned Uncle Lionel's appeal, just before his death; the talk of needing someone whom he could trust; his assurance that he was doing nothing out of spite, but everything because he needed help from the family. But none of them knew a great deal about the business.

From little asides, Folly had revealed that he knew a great deal more than they did. He had given them to understand that their uncle's financial dealings and influence were considerable. And he had asked, several times, whether any of them knew any business acquaintance of the old man's who owned a Chrysler.

After the last negative answer, Folly had said:

'Well, no doubt I shall learn something from London about that before long.'

Now the sound of the car faded into the distance.

'I wonder what he meant about the business,' Peter said.

'Folly's obviously on to something we don't know about,' answered Roger. He drummed his fingers on the arm of his chair. 'I wouldn't care a hoot about anything, if we could only get word of Jenny.'

'She'll turn up,' Paul said lightly. 'The point is, is Folly as good as he thinks he is? He doesn't seem to be doing anything about the actual murder of the old man.'

'What *can* he do?' asked Roger, reasonably. 'Someone could see him sitting near the window, took a shot, and that was that. It was someone who knew he often sat there.'

'What's the good of mulling over it? Why not try to get a good night's rest?' suggested Barbara practically.

Roger remembered her expression when he reached his

room. It reminded him of their encounter on the landing at Home Farm. His thoughts drifted from Barbara to Jennifer. Sleep seemed a long way off. He remembered there was Lucille to consider. It was true that she had plenty of reasons for hating Chard, and was a self-confessed marksman with a rifle.

Who did the police suspect?

Who, among the family, could have fired that shot?

He could; but he thought the police knew he had been in the house from before luncheon until the discovery of the body.

Lucille could, of course. Paul and Barbara had been out and, on their return, had shown signs of one of their differences; and Paul *was* keyed-up.

He flinched; he had forgotten something: Jennifer had been out and could—

Oh, nonsense!

He was dozing when he heard a rustle at the window. He heard it again, and decided that it was the wind blowing the curtains. Then it came for a third time. Now wide awake he stared at the patch of sky, bright with stars; and he saw something move.

He sat up abruptly, flung back the bedclothes and got out of bed. He saw the stars gradually blotted out, as a man climbed in. He put out his hand to touch the bedside lamp, and the man spoke.

'No light.'

The voice was hoarse, yet somehow familiar.

'Who—' he began, and then he realized that it was Joe Bryce.

'I'll tell you why I'm here in a minute,' whispered Bryce.

'I'm going to put the light on,' said Roger. 'Stand away from the window.'

Bryce obeyed, as Roger fumbled for the switch.

'Now what's this about?' he asked authoritatively.

'It's Miss Jennifer,' Bryce muttered.

Roger stiffened. 'What about her?'

159

'I've had a message from her,' said Bryce. He put his hand to his pocket. Roger watched him, feeling almost suffocated by the quick beating of his heart. Bryce seemed so slow. He brought out a folded envelope and handed it over.

On it, in pencil, was written: *Please give this to Mr. Roger Maitland.* There was no doubt in Roger's mind that it was Jennifer's writing.

With quick, nervous fingers he tore open the envelope and took out a half sheet of paper. The message was a brief one, and not in Jennifer's handwriting, but in block letters, written in ink.

> *The girl's all right so long as you behave*
> *First chance you get, ring Putney (London) 03124.*
> *Don't tell the police.*

After a long silence, Bryce asked in a hoarse voice:
'Is she all right?'
'I think—' began Roger, and then broke off abruptly, for from outside the window a gruff voice sounded:
'Everything okay up there?'
Don't tell the police, ended the message.

CHAPTER NINETEEN

HELP FROM FOLLY

'Are you all right up there?' called the policeman again, and Roger pushed past Bryce and looked out of the window. The policeman was cranning his neck upwards, his face making a faint blue against the darkness
'What's the trouble?' asked Roger.

'I thought I saw someone moving about, sir,' said the policeman, 'and then I saw your light go on.'

'Everything's all right here,' said Roger, 'except that I can't sleep.'

'Good night, then.'

'Good night,' echoed Roger, and closed the window before he turned to look at Bryce. But now the emergency was past Roger was concerned only with the message. He studied the envelope again. Jennifer's writing could be easily copied by a capable penman, there was no guarantee that this was hers; yet it appeared to have been written hurriedly, and he wanted to believe she had written it.

Bryce stood silent.

'This is a letter from the people who took her away,' Roger told him. 'They want me to get in touch with them. Who brought it to you?'

'A stranger to me,' Bryce told him. 'I was abed, and heard the knocking. The fellow wouldn't come in. He said Miss Jennifer had sent a message, and told me to bring it here.' Bryce's lips curved in what might have been a smile. 'He even offered me money.'

'Did you get a good look at him?'

'Not so good,' Bryce said. 'I had but a candle in my hand. He was a small man, I can say that. He went up the lane to the main road and I heard a car start up. Then I came straight here, reckoning it would be urgent.'

'Thanks,' said Roger. 'You may tell the police about this, if needs be.'

'If it will help Miss Jennifer,' Bryce said sourly.

'Well, now, we've got to get you out of here without the police seeing you.'

'So you're not going to tell them yet?'

'Not until I've thought about it.'

Bryce nodded.

'I'll get out wi'out any trouble,' he said, confidently, 'if you'll put out the light—'

'That window won't do,' said Roger. He gave a fleeting smile. 'I'm not trusted by the police, either.'

'If I'm caught, I'm caught,' said Bryce, flatly. 'I'll say nothing until you give the word.'

'I'll let you out by a different window,' Roger promised. 'We'd better not go downstairs. I think they've a man on duty all night in the hall.' He went to the door and looked out. The landing light was on. Roger beckoned and Bryce followed him to a bathroom, above the kitchen.

'There's a porch roof beneath you,' Roger said.

Watching Bryce climbing out of the window it occurred to Roger that the man was remarkable at getting in and out of houses. He waited until he saw the shadowy figure on the ground, then turned back to his room.

The blast of a police whistle broke the silence.

Roger swung round. There was a thud in the hall, as the policeman there jumped to his feet. A door opened and someone called out:

'What's that?'

The whistle sounded again; shrill, urgent.

Roger hurried down the stairs in time to see the night duty sergeant fling open the front door, and rush outside. He stood in the hall, looking out into the darkness, hearing the sound of moving branches and a scuffle. A man's voice called out jubilantly:

'Got him!'

Roger's heart sank.

'Who is it?' a man asked.

'It's Bryce.'

'The poacher?'

'That's him.'

'What are you doing here, my man?' asked the first speaker.

Bryce did not answer.

'It won't help you, being awkward,' said the policeman, sharply.

'It won't help me if I answer,' Bryce said. 'A man can walk about if he wants to.'

'At half-past one in the morning!'

'Well, *you* were.'

'That'll do. We won't have no witty answers,' said the policeman severely.

Bryce caught Roger's eye.

There was a slight, hardly perceptible shake of his head; and then he looked away.

'Sorry you've been disturbed, Mr. Maitland,' said the sergeant, 'but Bryce was caught loitering outside the house.'

'What's on down there?' That was Peter, from the landing.

'Bar says she heard a police whistle.' That was Paul.

'It's all right,' Roger said. He had a last glance at Bryce, and hurried up the stairs. Peter and Paul, in their dressing-gowns, were standing on the landing, while Lucille, in pyjamas, was standing in the doorway of her room; Barbara was not in sight. 'Bryce was found in the grounds,' Roger said, hurriedly. 'I don't know what he was up to.'

'The silly ass,' said Paul. 'He's asking for trouble.'

'He'll get it,' said Peter, meaningly. 'He's a fine shot – and knows the country like the back of his hand.'

'You're letting your imagination run away with you,' said Roger, sharply.

'I think there might be something in it,' said Paul, blinking. 'When you come to think of it, Bryce had a pretty good reason for hating the old man. Tippett was telling us about it.'

'But he doesn't travel about in a Chrysler,' Roger pointed out, impatiently. 'He'd no more love for the old man than we had, but he wouldn't do murder—'

'You've suddenly grown strangely fond of Bryce, haven't you?' asked Peter, with an edge to his voice.

'He's had a raw deal already,' Roger retorted.

'Was he, or was he not, caught hanging around the grounds?' demanded Peter.

Barbara appeared in the doorway of her room.

'My dear Peter, what a time for discussion. Do leave *something* for the police to do.' She stifled a yawn. 'If Bryce *is* the man—'

'He isn't,' said Roger, 'but you're quite right, we have talked enough. Two o'clock's a bad time for argument.'

They went into their rooms, but Roger did not go back to bed immediately. Several times it had been on the tip of his tongue to tell the others what had happened; and the note from Jennifer seemed to be burning a hole in his pocket; something, he hardly knew what, had made him keep back the truth. He wanted time to think about the possible consequences of the letter and the instructions to telephone the Putney number. As he sat brooding, he decided that his reticence had been wise. If he did telephone the man, it would be better that no one else should know about it.

He was uneasy in his mind because Paul and Barbara had been out when Uncle Lionel had been shot; he did not know why that thought came then, but it persisted. Would Folly be satisfied with the story that they had gone to London, spoken to no one who knew them, and returned? Or would Folly, knowing now about the white feathers and the mental anguish which the old man had tried to create in Paul, think that Paul had planned his murder?

On the face of it, that seemed absurd. If the murder had been committed in a less cold-blooded way, after a struggle, for instance, or in the heat of the moment, the motive might stand out, but—

Why was he thinking so much about Paul who, if the truth were told, had less reason to want the old man dead than anyone? But was that true? Hadn't Paul rushed back to England the moment he had heard of the threat to Jennifer? Roger remembered his own surprise at that; he had not thought that Paul had so much regard for Jenny.

He smiled wryly.

He was seizing upon anything to get his mind off the immediate problem – whether or not to telephone Putney 03124.

There were other problems, too.

He could not let Bryce remain suspect for long; the man had not only said that he was prepared to say nothing if he were caught, but, downstairs, had made it clear that he would carry out his promise. But, if Peter had been quick enough to see the possibility that he might be deeply involved, the police would hardly be likely to miss it. There was danger for Bryce. There must be no risk of tonight's escapade leading not only to his arrest, but to suspicion of murder.

Roger hurried downstairs. The policeman and the sergeant on duty were standing in the hall, near the open front door. The sergeant looked round.

'Can't you get off to sleep, sir?'

'No. What's happening to Bryce?'

'They're sending out for him, sir. You needn't worry about him any more. Ah, there's the car, I can see the headlights.'

'I'd like a word with Bryce,' Roger said.

He turned and hurried to the morning-room. Surprise made the sergeant hesitate long enough to enable Roger to open the door and enter the room alone. Bryce was sitting on an upright chair. He looked up quickly as Roger entered.

'Now, don't you—'

'I won't leave it long,' Roger said, in a whisper.

'Leave it as long as needs be.'

The sergeant was now at the door.

'I'm afraid he's determined to be obstinate, sir. I wouldn't waste any time on him, if I were you. Come on, Bryce, the car's here.'

It was nearly three o'clock before Roger got back into bed and put on the light. He had still not made up his mind what to do, but one thing was evident: there was no possibility of telephoning Putney until the morning, and if he allowed himself a few hours' sleep, his mind would be clearer. He was glad that he had not confided in the others.

He woke to find Barbara standing by his bed, with a tea tray in her hands.

'Why, hallo,' he said, struggling up. 'You on duty this morning?'

'Lucy's already getting breakfast, we let you sleep on,' said Barbara. She put the tray down, poured and handed him the tea.

'You're spoiling me,' he said.

'It's time you had some spoiling,' Barbara told him. 'Did you sleep fairly well?'

'Once I got off, yes, thanks. There's no news?'

'No, nothing at all.'

'Oh, well,' said Roger.

As he bathed and shaved, he pondered over the fresh problems created by Bryce's visit, and was surprised to find that he could do so with a fairly clear mind and a comparatively light heart. The black mood of the night had lifted, although nothing had materially changed.

'Hallo, you look cheerful enough,' said Paul, as he entered the dining-room.

'I've been thinking about Bryce . . .' Peter said.

He had thought about Bryce to such good effect that he had the poacher tried and convicted of all three crimes, with motives which were at least plausible; and Roger, anxious not to start a serious argument, did not contradict him.

Roger telephoned the police station immediately after breakfast.

It was, perhaps, unfortunate that Mrs. Harris had seen the milkman before Folly arrived. Without preamble, she called him a fool. Folly was startled. The wind, indeed, was taken completely out of his sails, and before he had time to gather more, Mrs. Harris went on from strength to strength.

'And the two policemen I work my hand to the bone in feeding are as much to blame as you yourself,' continued Mrs. Harris. 'First of all you arrested an innocent lad, and then you let him get murdered, and now – now you have to take a father away from his motherless children and leave them to starve. It's a crying shame, and I say it for all to hear.'

'Come, come, surely it would be better to restrict such an unstinted output to a few well-chosen recipients?' suggested Folly, urging her towards the dining-room as if shooing a recalcitrant hen. 'Good morning, gentlemen. Eating your heads off, as usual, I see. Is there a spare cup – ah, I see there is.'

Folly sank to a chair and put forth an eager hand.

'Ah, delicious! How few know how to make a cup of tea! Now, Mrs. Harris, I don't want you to be under any misapprehension. Bryce was foolishly venturesome last night. He was trespassing, let there be no doubt about that. He is being detained – but not for long. Take my assurance that immediately he can be released, he will be returned to the bosom of his family.' He cocked an eye at her. 'Not, however, that his reputation for looking after his family is remarkably high.'

'Do you blame him for that?' demanded Mrs. Harris, fiercely.

'I see it would be as much as my life is worth to do so,' murmured Folly.

'Give a dog a bad name, and hang him,' snapped Mrs. Harris. '*I* don't keep my eyes shut and my ears stuffed with cotton wool.'

Folly raised a hand. 'Mrs. Harris, I give you my solemn word that I will help Bryce in every way I can, and if the local police have indeed persecuted him, I will have something to say about it.' He beamed at her.

'That's something,' conceded Mrs. Harris. 'Then tell him from me not to worry about the children. I'll keep an eye on them – and it had better not be for long.' She sailed out of the room, and Folly grinned at the two sergeants.

'Well, young men, how are you feeling this morning. I need hardly ask if you have heard about Bryce.'

They nodded.

'Would it surprise you to know that, according to the statement of one of the policemen on duty at the house last night, he thought he saw a man climbing into Roger Maitland's room and, when assured by Maitland that all was well, heard voices in the room? And, further, that in his opinion – not yet accepted by anyone else – Bryce was caught after he had climbed out of a window above the kitchen?' Folly paused to allow plenty of time for exclamations of astonishment, then went on:

'*And* Roger Maitland made an excuse to exchange a few words with Bryce before he was taken away from the house. We make progress, don't we?'

The telephone bell rang in the hall.

Abbott answered it. A moment later he called out:

'It's from the office, sir. Roger Maitland's just telephoned for you, they thought you might be here. He's holding on.'

Folly called back testily: 'Tell them to tell Maitland I will be at the house in half-an-hour. And that means that we must hurry,' he added. 'Bennison, come with me. Abbott, I want you to go to London and make inquiries about the Chrysler belonging to this friend of Lionel Chard's, the man who saw him at Hilbury station. Oh, and another thing. While they were in London, the Briscoes separated for an hour, but forgot to tell us so. When they reached Hilbury, they had a furious quarrel, which was overheard by one of your men, and Mrs. Briscoe got out of the car and walked part of the way to the Lodge. He picked her up later, apparently, as they arrived together. We must find out why they quarrelled.'

'Why don't you tackle them about the London trip?' asked Abbott.

'Because,' said Folly, airily, 'I would much rather know what happened before I talk to them. So that's that. And now you'd better be on your way. Don't be too surprised if Roger Maitland is under lock and key when you get back tonight!'

CHAPTER TWENTY

FOLLY IS HELPFUL

'AND so you want to see me?' Folly asked pleasantly.

'Alone,' said Roger.

'I see no reason why not.' Folly nodded to Bennison, who rather disappointedly went out, shutting the door of the morning room behind him. 'Do sit down, my dear fellow. You had a disturbed night, I fear.'

'Yes,' said Roger. 'I didn't get much sleep early on. This is why I wanted to see you. Bryce came to see me.'

Folly's mouth dropped.

'*Did* he, then!'

Roger thought: He had guessed it, and hoped to score. In spite of the circumstances, he grinned.

'Yes. And so the sooner you release Bryce the better I shall like it; he did what he thought was the right thing.' Roger took the envelope out of his pocket. 'He brought me this. The envelope is in my cousin's handwriting, and the letter inside speaks for itself.'

Folly took the letter, and read it.

'Well, well!' he exclaimed. 'And have you telephoned these people?'

'Not yet.'

Folly looked at the telephone.

'You were wise to consult me first. How did Bryce get this note?'

Roger told him Bryce's story.

'I see. Plausible, if not wholly convincing,' commented Folly. 'This man Bryce is a shrewd fellow, I have not yet

169

entirely made up my mind about him. We shall see. Now, the obvious thing for you to do is to telephone the writer of this note, find out what he wants from you, and tell me. He must not think that you have confided in me, but of course you know that.'

Roger crossed to the telephone.

'Just a moment!' exclaimed Folly. He opened the door. 'Bennison! Oh, there you are. Use the other telephone, Bennison, call the Yard, ask them to find out the address in Putney which has the telephone number 03124 – have you got that?'

'Yes, sir.'

'They are to have the house watched.'

'Very good,' said Bennison.

Folly closed the door and went back to his chair. Sitting down he folded his hands patiently across his stomach.

'We'll give Bennison a few minutes' start,' he said. 'We want to be sure the man hasn't left, and he's sure to wait until you've telephoned.'

They waited for what seemed hours.

'Now!' said Folly.

Roger lifted the receiver.

The operator put him through, and then Roger heard the ringing sound, and his heart began to beat fast.

A man said: 'Hallo.'

'This is Roger Maitland.'

'I'd almost given you up, Maitland. I'm glad you've seen how the land lies. Are you alone?'

'Yes.'

'Have you told the police?'

'No.'

'I hope that's the truth,' said the man in London, and Roger thought there was something familiar about the voice. It was overbearing and very confident. 'Because if it isn't, I wouldn't like to say what will happen to your cousin.'

'Will you get to the point?' demanded Roger, sharply.

'I want to see you.'

'Don't be a fool. The police watch me wherever I go. I've had to sneak out to make this call.'

'I tell you I want to see you,' said the man at the other end of the wire. 'Don't argue about it. And I want you to find out the conditions of your uncle's will, whether you and the others benefit, how much Jennifer gets – everything that affects his money and especially everything that affects his business. Understand that?'

'Yes, but I can't—'

'Nonsense,' said the man, roughly. 'You find those things out, and then telephone me again.'

'At the same number?'

'No, I'll let you know what number later. Do what you're told, make sure the police don't know you're doing it because I've told you to, and be at the house tomorrow night after seven o'clock. Is that clear?'

'Yes,' said Roger.

The line went dead.

Roger replaced the receiver slowly. He was acutely disappointed because everything was so vague, but Folly did not seem particularly put out.

'We could hardly expect anything more at this state,' he said. 'I'm very glad we got so much. Someone is evidently very interested in the will. That is curious – why should it concern anyone outside the family?'

'I have no idea.'

'There again, we shall have to find out,' said Folly. 'And I think, with co-operation from the solicitor, we shall do so. Hmm – yes, Miss Jennifer's—'

Roger snapped: 'What of her?'

'Well, if she becomes a nun, her inheritance, I understand, will be negligible, whereas if she marries, her husband will become a very wealthy man indeed.'

Folly shot Roger a quick, sly look of remarkable cunning.

He was hinting again at Roger's regard for Jennifer, and he wanted to make Roger angry. He showed no particular resentment at his failure, indeed, his manner became almost dove-like.

He leaned forward.

'Do you know of any reason, apart from the obvious one, why your cousin Paul and his wife went to London yesterday?'

Roger was taken off his guard.

'No. No, I don't,' he said.

'Ah. It occurred to me as a little odd that they should go out this morning, when there was so much to be discussed, so much on their minds,' said Folly. 'Mr. Maitland, I ask you again to be frank with me. Do you suspect that they are in any way concerned?'

'I do not,' said Roger, stiffly.

'I am going to take your word for that,' said Folly. 'And indeed I hope that I am wrong in thinking there might be something strange about their visit to London. Now, about Bryce. He has been in touch with you quite a lot lately, hasn't he?'

Roger frowned. 'I suppose he has.'

'How well do you know him?'

'As a boy, I used to know him very well indeed,' said Roger, 'but I hadn't seen him for years until I came here the other day. He's—' He broke off.

'Go on,' urged Folly.

'He is sour and bitter, but he has been very badly treated.'

'Due to your uncle?'

'And to the police.'

Folly shrugged. 'Could well be. Did he appear to be sincere when he came here last night with that message?'

'He *was* sincere.'

'Dear me, we can't be so certain as that,' piped Folly.

'But I think we can,' said Roger obstinately. 'He's done you a good turn – the second one, by the way. If it hadn't been for him we wouldn't have had that Putney telephone number.'

'I think perhaps they would have got in touch with you by

some other means,' said Folly, gently. 'Bryce's behaviour has been suspicious in many ways.'

'Are you telling me that you're going to hold him?'

'For the time being, yes,' said Folly. 'And you need waste no tears on his children. The excellent Mrs. Harris has gone to the cottage to see that they are well-fed, and I do not doubt that she will make a better job of it than Bryce. Mr. Maitland, be sensible. I am not at all happy about the part which Bryce has played in this business, don't sentimentalize over him.' He paused, but Roger made no comment. 'As soon as I have had a call from London, I think I will go and visit that cottage,' he added, 'there might be something of interest there. Mrs. Harris won't approve, but I shall take my courage in both hands.'

Folly received his telephone call from London half-an-hour later. Putney 03124 was the number of a small private hotel, near the Common. Twenty minutes after the telephone call between Roger and the stranger had been made, a man had left the hotel and gone to a nearby garage, from where he had taken a Chrysler car. He was being watched on the road by police patrols, and he was heading south. The hotel proprietress said that he had been staying there for the last three days. He had registered under the name of Browning, and as far as she knew, he was coming back.

All this, Folly told Roger, as they drove to Bryce's cottage. It was at the detective's suggestion that Roger went too. Bennison sat in the back seat of the car, looking a little rueful.

He was wondering what Marlin would have made of this move; and also why Folly had taken Roger with them.

They pulled up outside the cottage.

A girl in her early teens opened the door.

'Who is it?' called Mrs. Harris, from inside.

'It's three gentlemen,' said the girl, in a startled voice, as she watched Folly's exquisitely-shod feet picking their way up the narrow path.

'You see, I cannot leave you for long, Mrs. Harris,'

carolled Folly, 'I had to come and see you. My word, you *are* putting the place to rights!' He drew nearer. 'My word!' he exclaimed again, his eyes flitting over a scrubbing brush, a pail of soapy water and a pile of upended furniture. 'And what do you think of this?' he asked Bryce's daughter.

She stood mutely in front of him.

'What do you *want*?' demanded Mrs. Harris heatedly, 'Haven't you made enough trouble for the man, without—'

'Supposing we leave you to your arduous task, and go round the back,' said Folly hastily. 'You'll show us the way, little girl, won't you? What is your name?'

The child stared.

'Hilda,' said Mrs. Harris, 'and—'

'Come along with me, Hilda,' said Folly, and, dipping into his pocket, he drew out a slab of chocolate. He broke it in two. 'There you are,' he said, giving half to the girl. 'Share and share alike, that's fair, isn't it? Do your father's friends ever give you any chocolate?'

Hilda shook her head.

'How often do they come to see him?'

She considered the point, then shook her head again.

'No one comes here.'

'Oh,' said Folly. 'No one, ever?'

'There was a man last night.'

'And he didn't give you any chocolate?'

'Silly,' she said, 'he didn't see me. I was asleep, only Belle was sick and I was awake, and I hear him talking to Dad.'

'Oh. So it was late last night.'

'It musta' been. Dad went out soon after.'

'And what time did he get back?' asked Folly.

'He ain't been back,' she declared, blending a look of mingled scorn and impatience on him. 'They've took him to prison again.'

'Oh, well,' said Folly, comfortingly, 'perhaps he won't have to stay there very long this time, Hilda. Now, do you seriously mean to tell me that none of your father's friends—'

174

'He ain't got no friends,' said Hilda flatly. 'He's got me, and that's enough.'

'I'm sure it is,' said Folly. 'And he hasn't had any other visitors lately?'

She shook her head. 'Why are you asking me all these questions?'

She was shrewd, thought Roger; and she had the same native wit as her father.

'I want to help your father,' said Folly. 'Does he ever write any letters?'

'Sometimes. He used to write to the pools every week, but he never had any luck. That's the trouble with my Dad,' she went on, 'he never has any luck.'

'We'll have to put that right,' said Folly. 'Where does he write these letters?'

'Indoors,' said Hilda, 'where else can he write them?'

'In which room?'

'We've only got *two*,' said Hilda, and pointed to the window of the room which Mrs. Harris was cleaning. 'In there – and I ought to go and help the lady,' she added.

'That's right. You run along,' said Folly.

His glance ran over the garden without much hope of finding anything.

A few scraggy hens were scratching about outside a fowl house. Near it was an old pig-sty. Roger looked at it, thinking of the well-kept piggery at Home Farm.

Suddenly Bennison clutched Folly's arm.

'That pig-sty,' he said, in a hoarse voice. 'There's something in it!'

'Well, what—'

'A shoe,' said Bennison, and moved forward. Roger turned towards the sty, and saw the shoe, dirty on one side, bright on the other; the type of shoe that Jennifer would wear.

Bennison got in front of him, and peered into the sty; and then he cried out in a strangled voice:

'There's a body in here!'

POOR JENNIFER

At Bennison's words Roger went cold from head to foot. He stared with horror at the shoe, unable to move. Bennison had gone down on his hands and knees, inside the sty. His voice came thick and muffled.

'We'll have to take the place to pieces.'

'Come along, Maitland,' said Folly. 'It will be easy, the building is rotting. Come along.'

Still Roger did not move.

'Who is it?' He could hardly hear his own voice, and was surprised when Bennison answered:

'It's a woman.'

'Come along, Maitland!' insisted Folly.

Tight-lipped, Roger joined him. It was easy to wrench off pieces of the rotting wood from the roof. Soon Roger was able to look down, into the sty; the girl was lying full length, and although he could not see her face, he saw her corn-coloured hair.

The last of the wood was off, and Jennifer lay in front of him. He bent down, and lifted her, carrying her to a patch of grass. Bennison took off his coat and rolled it into a pillow.

There was no colour in her cheeks, no hint of movement. He could see a bruise on her forehead and another on her neck, dark and ugly; he thought that she had been strangled. Folly said in a reasonable, matter-of-fact voice:

'She's alive, Maitland.'

Roger turned, furiously. 'Don't—'

'Of course she is,' Folly said, quietly, 'or you couldn't have

176

moved her like that, she'd be stiff.' He bent down and felt her pulse. 'It's weak,' he said. 'Take her to the car.'

'Can't we—'

'We can't do anything here,' Folly said, 'we'll have her home in five minutes. Bennison, go to the telephone in the village, and call Coppinger to the Lodge at once – if he can't come without delay, get another doctor. Then telephone the Lodge and tell them to get her bed ready. Shall I take her, Maitland?'

Roger shook his head and lifted Jennifer again, passing Mrs. Harris and Hilda, their mouths agape. Folly glanced over his shoulder.

'I think she's all right,' he told them. 'I'll see you soon, Mrs. Harris.' He hurried after Roger, who was near the car, and pulled open the rear door. Roger lifted Jennifer in; she had not stirred in his arms.

Arriving at the Lodge, two policemen hurried forward, but Roger would allow no one else to touch Jennifer. Tippett was in the hall, looking shocked. Lucy was half-way down the stairs.

Roger carried Jennifer up to his room, and left her in charge of Lucy.

He turned away abruptly.

Folly met him on the landing, with a glass in his hand.

'You need this,' he said. 'Now don't worry, I tell you she is alive, and Coppinger will be out in a very few minutes. I'm used to death in all its guises, and your cousin isn't dead.'

Roger took the glass in an unsteady hand.

'Thank you,' he said. 'I hope—'

'You might go downstaris and telephone the station for me,' said Folly. 'I want to know whether there is any further news of the man Browning. Be a good chap, and find out for me, will you?'

Roger looked at him vaguely.

So Folly thought that he needed something to take his mind off what had happened. Folly had made it clear that he did not think he could stand up to this shock without help. And Folly was right.

The morning room was empty, and the door open. Roger carried out his errand punctiliously, but there was no further news about Browning. Replacing the receiver, Roger's thoughts turned to Bryce; and he knew that this discovery would probably make things worse for the poacher. He felt concern for the man, believing strongly if without reason that Bryce was not personally involved.

He put in a call to Tubby Edwards, and had to hold on for several minutes. Idly, he played with some papers on the table. He was thinking of Jennifer, and of the shoe lying so pathetically in front of the sty.

He saw the words 'Paul Briscoe and wife' on a manilla folder, as Tubby came on the line.

'Hallo, old chap. How are things with you this morning?'

'They're not too good,' said Roger. 'Jenny's been found – unconscious but alive,' he added hurriedly. 'The thing is that Bryce has been taken into custody for being at this house last night. I want you to see him for me, tell him that I'm looking after everything I can but he's not to be surprised if the police spring something on him. Is that clear?'

'Yes,' said Tubby. 'Why the brief for Bryce?'

'He's been very helpful. Don't make difficulties.'

'All right, Roger. I'll give you a ring and tell you how I get on.' He rang off, while Roger stared at the Paul Briscoe and wife' and then, on impulse, opened the folder.

In the front was a typewritten note:

Briscoe known to have left his wife for nearly an hour while in London. Neither has volunteered this. Interview earliest opportunity and make sure where Briscoe went

Roger's heart missed a beat.

He closed the folder quickly as Folly came into the room. There was a certain satisfaction in his expression as his eye took in the scene.

'I thought I heard the doctor's car,' he said, his voice carefully casual. 'Yes, here it is. I've had another look at your cousin, Mr. Maitland, and I really don't think you've much to worry about.'

'What happened, do you know?'

'I can't be sure, but it looks as if there was an attempt to strangle her. Not a very powerful attempt, I should say. Now I'd better lock this door,' he added, with a playful smile, 'I can't let you loose among all our secrets, can I?'

Roger smiled dutifully in turn.

Jennifer – Paul – Barbara – Bryce – all seemed to be struggling for supremacy in his mind. He was surprised how worried he was about Paul; and, for that matter, Bryce; he could not get it out of his head that Bryce was being deliberately implicated. Thoughts of Paul predominated, and he wished he and Barbara had not gone out. Now he came to think of it, Folly had passed a pretty broad hint about Paul earlier that morning.

Coppinger and Folly went upstairs.

They were still there when Paul's car turned into the drive. Both he and Barbara were smiling until Roger went to meet them and they saw his expression.

'Now what?' asked Paul, roughly.

'We've found Jenny,' said Roger. 'She's been hurt. Coppinger's with her.' He was conscious of Barbara looking at him steadily, as he added: 'I think she'll be all right. I must have a word with you two before Folly comes down again.'

'But Jennifer—' Paul began.

'I must see you two,' Roger insisted.

He led them into the drawing-room, and did not notice that Bennison was standing outside the open window. Bennison's expression was tense, because he was remembering what Folly had said to him immediately he had returned.

'I've set a bait for Maitland and Briscoe, they'll probably go into a huddle. Don't miss a word.'

Roger thought that Barbara was looking unnaturally pale.

Paul was undoubtedly annoyed; angry, even. Roger wondered whether his own manner had been too abrupt. He could not get over the shock of seeing that brief note, and the realization that Paul had not only kept something back from the police, but had lied to him and the family.

'Now what is this all about?' Paul demanded, with an edge to his voice. 'You say Jenny—'

'Let's forget Jenny for a moment,' said Roger. 'Where did you two go yesterday?'

Paul's head jerked up.

'What the devil do you mean? You know where we went yesterday.'

'You went somewhere else,' Roger said.

Paul clenched his hands. 'If you've been prying—'

'Don't be an ass,' said Roger, impatiently. 'After we'd agreed last night that the police should know everything, you lied to them about what you did in London. It was crazy.'

'You seem easily convinced that we lied,' said Paul.

'Didn't you?'

'Paul—' began Barbara.

'I'll handle this,' said Paul, abruptly. 'What makes you think we lied?' he demanded.

'I know you did, and so do the police,' Roger told him. 'They know that you left Bar on her own for an hour while you were in London yesterday.'

Paul exclaimed: 'They *can't* know. They—' He swung round on Barbara. 'You fool,' he said, bitterly, 'you've told Roger, and he's—'

'No one told me. The police found out, made a note of it and I saw the note,' Roger said. 'It's sitting on the table in the morning-room.' He was shocked at the way Paul had rounded on Barbara. But why was he so furious? Why were his nerves so on edge?

'I see,' said Paul, acidly. 'It hasn't occurred to you that the police might have made a mistake, I suppose?'

'No, it hasn't. They don't make that kind of mistake.'

'Your trouble is that you trust them too much.'

'Yours seems to be that you don't trust them enough.'

Barbara stood up restlessly.

'What *is* the point of going on like this?' she demanded. 'If you two start quarrelling—'

'I don't want to quarrel,' said Roger. 'God knows, there's trouble enough without wrangling, but where are we going to end if we can't trust each other?'

'There's a lesson in that for you,' Paul said. 'Judging from your manner, you certainly don't trust me.'

'Paul—' began Barbara.

'Will you keep out of this!'

Roger said firmly: 'Paul, listen to me. Folly first made a dig or two about the fact that you were the only male member of the family who can't be accounted for during the time of the old man's murder. That *is* a fact. No, don't snap!' he exclaimed, when Paul began to speak. 'Hear me out. Whatever the truth, wherever you were, if you can't give a convincing account of whatever you did at the time, you're in some danger of being suspected, if nothing else.'

'Well?'

'What you didn't know is that I had a message about Jenny during the night,' went on Roger. He explained briefly what had happened. 'After I'd weighed that up, I told Folly about it. I deliberately kept it away from all of you because I didn't want the police thinking there was a conspiracy of any kind. I may have been wrong,' he admitted, slowly, 'but I thought that the best thing to do. Folly suggested that I should go to Bryce's cottage, to see whether there was any evidence there to support his suspicions of Bryce. We found Jenny in a hut at the back of the cottage. I thought she was dead. Folly assures me that she isn't, and will recover, but – well, imagine my frame of mind when I saw this police note about you two.'

Paul, moving towards him, held out his hands.

'My dear chap! Of course. It was absolutely under-

181

standable! The marvel is that you've kept your wits about you at all. And Jenny—'

'Folly's pretty knowledgeable, and he says she'll pull through.'

'Well, that's something,' conceded Paul. He smiled wryly. 'The trouble is, all of us do what we think's for the best. I'm prepared to agree that I shouldn't have tried to put you and the police off the scent about what I did yesterday, but I didn't want to add to the confusion. Besides, it seemed such a trivial thing. I still don't know how they found out that Barbara and I parted for an hour!'

Roger said: 'It wouldn't surprise me if Folly wasn't watching Peter's flat.'

Paul whistled. 'That might be it!'

'There was a man sauntering along outside,' Barbara said. 'I remember him because he was the only person we saw near the flat.'

'And I arranged to meet you at Hyde Park Corner an hour later,' Paul said, throwing up his hands. 'The fellow must have heard it, and seen me drive off and you walk away.' He drew a deep breath. 'You're right about one thing, Roger, it isn't safe to keep anything from the police.' He looked ruefully at his wife. 'As a matter of fact Barbara wanted me to tell them, and I refused. We had a flaming row when we reached Hilbury, and she walked out on me!'

'I suppose what you did in that hour doesn't greatly matter,' Roger said.

'It concerns Peter and Lucille.'

'*What?*'

'You see, I didn't want to add to the troubles,' Paul said, 'and I knew I was likely to if I talked. I went to see that man Kennard, you know the fellow – the man who bought the picture at the farm.'

Roger stared.

'Peter had told me he had an office near Bond Street,' Paul went on. 'I wanted to find out the real value of these daubs of Peter's; whether he was really considered to be a coming

182

man, and whether I could help him surreptitiously. I couldn't tell Peter that, could I?'

'No,' admitted Roger. How Peter would rage! But, in the forefront of his mind were the questions: how could this small thing affect the chief issues? Why had Paul thought it wise to withhold it from the police?

'And I got a shock,' Paul went on. 'According to Kennard, that picture he bought is—'

'The value of a picture is what's paid for it,' said Roger. 'Peter's might not be worth a great deal, but if Kennard allowed himself to be bluffed into paying heavily, that's his own fault.'

'It isn't the price,' Paul said, and there was a strained look on his face. 'Kennard says that Peter didn't paint it.'

'What!'

'The original, I mean. He says it's a copy of a well-known modern French picture. And he also said that he'd bought it in order to find out what Peter was offering for sale, and maintain the good name of the trade. He also said that he had suspected that Peter wasn't offering originals, but was imitating other artists, and he wanted this particular picture to prove it. He went to the flat to get it, but Lucille wouldn't part without Peter knowing. What's more, he says that Peter was drummed out of Paris for this kind of cheapjack work, and that there was a prosecution in the offing about selling his own work in another man's name. And it seemed to me,' added Paul, 'that if there were, it would explain Lucille's fear of the police. Don't you agree?'

CHAPTER TWENTY-TWO

PETER

ROGER felt the shock so much that he could not speak. He watched Paul as he went on talking. Surely Roger would see why he had kept this from the family as well as from the police, Paul said. It would do no good, it had no bearing on the crimes except, of course, that if Peter knew that there was no future in his paintings, he would be more than ever eager to get his hands on the old man's money.

'I still think mine was the right decision,' he finished abruptly. 'If it hadn't been for that beggar lounging about outside the flat, no one would have known anything about it.'

Roger said: 'Kennard will make trouble—'

'He won't,' said Paul, emphatically.

'What do you mean?'

'The good name of the trade, to Mr. Kennard, means only one thing,' said Paul. 'Lining his own pocket. I squared him. I bought the picture back for five hundred pounds, and gave him a cheque he was able to cash yesterday afternoon. We won't have any trouble from Kennard.' He looked quickly at Barbara, then went on: 'I was going to get this business over first, and then take it up with Peter. I'm not worried about what he may have done in the past, but it isn't a thing only that can go on, you know.'

'Of course it isn't. I always knew that he was a young fool, but—' Roger broke off. 'We're rather taking Kennard's word for all this, aren't we?'

Paul laughed. 'I saw the original.'

'Oh,' said Roger, slowly. 'Well, there it is. I wish we hadn't to tell the police about it, but I don't see that we can keep anything like this back from them. We might gloss over the details, but I'm afraid Kennard's name will have to be divulged. The police will ferret it out somehow, and if they find out from someone else, we're only going to brand ourselves as hopeless liars and be discredited in whatever else we say. That seems inevitable, doesn't it?'

'Does it?' said Paul, doubtfully.

'Well, I'm sure of this: if we tell Folly, he'll take a sensible view of it and won't make trouble for the sake of it. Folly is interested only in finding out who killed the old man and Corcoran – and, to a lesser degree, who took Jennifer away. He won't be malicious for the sake of it. But we must definitely tackle Peter right away.'

'Need we?' asked Paul. 'Haven't we enough on our plate? He'll go right up in the air.'

'He's in the air already, and it's time he got his feet on solid earth,' Roger said, grimly.

Folly was coming down the stairs followed by Dr. Coppinger.

'Ah! Mr. Maitland. We've some news for you. You'd better hear it from the doctor's own lips, you're more likely to believe him than me!'

Dr. Coppinger smiled.

'There's no need to worry, Maitland. She was brutally attacked, but the injury is comparatively slight. It wasn't any bodily injury which caused her to be unconscious for so long. She was given an injection of morphia. She'll be stiff for a few days when she comes round, but in a week she'll be none the worse. I expect her to wake up sometime during the afternoon or evening,' he added, 'and I've given instructions that she's to be kept warm and not harassed with questions until I've seen her again. Telephone me the moment she comes round.'

Folly patted Roger's arm.

'Now you'll want to go and carry the good tidings to your cousins,' he said. 'I, too, am glad about it, although I felt sure that you had nothing to worry about.' He looked over Roger's shoulder and saw Bennison in the front doorway. He gave Roger a friendly push towards the drawing-room door, and then nodded to Bennison.

Roger went back into the drawing-room.

'Well, what is it?'

'Quite a story,' said Bennison. 'There's been some trouble with Peter Maitland, he's up to funny business with his paintings. It wouldn't be a bad idea if you tackled him before his brother gets to him.'

'Possibly.' Folly considered. 'Yes, we can ask him to come to the morning-room for questioning, and you can tell me the story while he is kicking his heels in there. What of Paul's London trip?'

'It ties up.'

'Well done, Bennison, my boy,' approved Folly. 'I thought we'd get something if we let Roger see that note! Was a man named Kennard mentioned?'

'Yes,' said Bennison, slightly deflated. 'How did you know?'

'One puts two and two together and sometimes they make four,' Folly said smugly. 'Well, gather up Peter Maitland and his wife and ring them in the back way. I'll stay here and make sure that Roger doesn't go to the studio. Hurry!'

Roger entered the drawing-room, the good news of Jenny ousting every other thought.

'Apparently she was drugged, and that was the chief cause of the trouble, and Coppinger is quite sure she'll be all right in a few days. It doesn't seem to matter so much now whether we ever find out who took her away or not.'

'*I* intend to find out,' growled Paul.

Roger smiled. 'Yes, of course. I wasn't speaking literally.' He sank into a chair. 'I'm too stodgy to take kindly to so much emotion,' he said, laughing.

'Then I'll fetch Peter,' offered Paul.

Looking strangely alone, Barbara sat on the window seat.

'Roger, may I suggest something?'

Roger smiled. 'Of course. What is it?'

Barbara hesitated. 'I think it would be wiser if you saw Peter on your own. I'm afraid that Paul might say something silly and upset him.'

'That's a point, certainly,' agreed Roger judicially. 'I'd better go and see Peter, in the studio.'

But when he reached the studio, Peter was not there. Tippett was washing the car near the old barn, and put down the hose as Roger approached him.

'If you're wanting Mr. Peter, he went off with that sergeant,' he volunteered.

On impulse Roger glanced in the barn. He could see a picture on the easel. It was a full length portrait of Lucille. There was a savage realism about the work; it was Lucille and yet it was not her. An unflattering picture, yet powerful and fascinating. Roger could not take his eyes off it.

'If he can do that, he really has something,' he mused, as he went back to the house.

Peter and Lucille were taken into the morning-room, and the door was closed on them.

A constable called out in a loud whisper: 'He's coming, sir.'

'That's all for now, then,' Folly said. 'We'll leave the door open an inch, so that Roger can hear what we're saying.' He grinned. 'The man wouldn't be human if he didn't stop to listen!'

He pushed open the morning-room door, as Roger entered the hall.

Roger was thinking of that portrait as he entered the house. The effect was still strong on him.

He saw Bennison disappearing into the morning-room, and his thoughts changed. Why had Folly sent for Peter?

'*Well*, sir,' Folly was saying in a booming voice which no one could have failed to hear, 'now perhaps we shall have the truth from you.'

There was a short pause; and then Peter demanded in a sharp voice: 'What the devil do you mean?'

'What do *you* mean is the question,' boomed Folly.

Roger stood near the foot of the stairs, determined not to miss a word of what was said. If Peter handled this on his own, there was no telling what might happen.

'So you are a poseur, Mr. Maitland, a cheap trickster who lives on the art of other, greater men.'

Into Roger's mind there flashed two words: '*He knows!*'

Folly boomed on: 'Of all baseness, the baseness of a man who pretends to be what he is not is the lowest, and I intend to let the world know what you have attempted to do.'

Roger thought: Peter, be careful. He moved quickly towards the door, sick at the realization that Folly had discovered the truth, but too worried to wonder then how he had managed to learn it. He expected a fierce outburst from Peter. He reached the door and his hand was actually thrust out to push it wide open, when Peter spoke; and they were the last words Roger expected to hear.

'Are you sure you're all right, Superintendent?'

The voice was calm, the tone slightly derisive; they startled Folly as well as Roger.

'I will have you know, sir,' said Folly, 'that I have now received a report of the interview which your cousin Paul had with the man Kennard yesterday afternoon, and I know *everything* about the picture that you sold to him, the fact that it was copied, and—'

'Oh, don't be an ass!'

Folly paused.

'Mr. Maitland, this is not a matter which can be dismissed lightly or facetiously.'

'I don't know what Paul's been up to,' said Peter, and there was now an annoyed note in his voice, 'but if he or anyone else believes that the picture I sold to Kennard is a copy, he's crazy. Why, Lucille saw me paint it.'

'*Copy* it!' snapped Folly.

Peter laughed. '*Copy* it?'

'I am assured, sir, that your copy and the original were together in Kennard's office yesterday,' Folly declared.

Peter said: 'Oh, were you.' His voice grew sharper. 'In that case, I'll break Kennard's neck.'

Folly gasped: 'You'll *what?*'

'Because if there was a copy in that office, it certainly wasn't my work,' continued Peter. 'So that's why the beggar wanted to get hold of it! Kennard's a nasty piece of work, I've always known that.' He was making a praiseworthy attempt to maintain his self-control but there was a new edge to his voice. 'If he's going to flood the market with copies of my stuff, I'll—'

'Break his neck,' Folly said, and the words seemed like an echo.

'I'll drum him out of the trade,' snapped Peter. 'Which will amount to the same thing.'

'Well, well,' said Folly. 'You almost convince me.'

'*Almost!*' snapped Peter. 'I'll have you know—'

'All right, all right!' exclaimed Folly. 'You *have* convinced me, and don't blame me for this accusation, I am only passing on what I have heard. What I can't understand is why such an accusation should be made if it is not true. It defeats me – and it is seldom that I acknowledge defeat. Bennison, you're quite sure that you heard aright?'

'Heard what?' asked Peter, suspiciously.

Roger thought: So that's it. He thrust the door open. Folly showed no surprise, while Peter grinned at Roger – the grin of a man who was quite confident of himself.

'Have you heard this latest nonsense?'

'Yes.' Roger shot a quick look at Folly. 'You've misfired this time,' he said. 'You've planned this from the beginning, haven't you?'

Folly looked a little uncomfortable.

'You sent me in here so that I should see the note about Paul, and so started the whole thing off,' Roger said. 'I can see it now.' He laughed. 'Peter, the truth is that Paul went to see Kennard yesterday, he wanted to find out more about the market value of your stuff, and Kennard pitched this story about the copy. Presumably Bennison overheard Paul telling me about it just now, and Folly thought he'd got you nicely.'

'What was Paul doing with Kennard?' Peter demanded.

'I've told you – and don't start going off the deep-end,' said Roger. 'Paul only wanted to help. It's a good thing for you that he did, or you wouldn't have realized what was happening so quickly. Don't you agree, Folly?'

Folly began to smile; he actually chuckled.

'Yes, I do, I do indeed,' he said. 'And I must admit that I *was* completely deceived – as, I have no doubt, you were. I shall have to have a word with Kennard.'

'You're right about me,' Peter admitted.

'I'll send word to London immediately to have Kennard apprehended,' Folly promised, 'the matter must be thrashed out. The chief problem, as you have pointed out, Mr. Maitland' – he looked at Roger – 'is to relate this remarkable affair to the other mysteries. I will admit that I was chiefly concerned because I could not understand Mr. Briscoe's reticence about his sortie while in London. I think I can understand it now.'

'That's something,' Roger said.

Peter brushed his hand across his hair.

'Now that's over, I'm going back to do some work,' he said. He was in a surprisingly good mood. 'I'm working on the best thing I've ever put on canvas,' he said expansively, 'and when it's finished you can all have a private view.'

For fully five minutes Folly had not uttered a word. He looked at Bennison, who maintained a discreet silence. Then he shook his head, slowly at first but with increasing momentum, until his three chins began to quiver.

Bennison still stood silent.

'Well,' said Folly, 'haven't you *anything* to say?'

'Nothing useful,' admitted Bennison.

'Then I suppose you had best remain silent,' said Folly. 'Young Bennison, I feel deflated. Never have I been so completely bewildered as I am now. Do you know the solemn truth?'

'That we don't know much,' said Bennison.

'Oh, do be more careful in your choice of phrase,' said Folly testily. 'We now a great deal – a very great deal. But nothing which points to the murderer, nothing which really helps us.'

'That's what I meant,' said Bennison, defensively.

'The you should learn to say what you mean.' Folly glowered. 'For we have here a most curious effort to draw a red-herring across the path.'

'Red-herring? Path?' repeated a bemused Bennison.

'My dear fellow, *think!*' cried Folly, surveying him coldly. 'Have you lost the power to recognize a red-herring when you see one? Haven't we now to find out why Kennard has endeavoured to blacken the name of Peter Maitland? Haven't we to dispose of the mystery of the fake which was not a fake, before we can go ahead with the rest of the affair?' He stood up, and began to pace the floor. 'I have never believed in a series of disconnected events. The affair of the picture can only have a bearing on the rest as a red-herring, a second deliberate attempt to make us look foolish.'

Bennison asked: 'What was the first?'

'Haven't I told you about Roger Maitland's telephone call to Putney, and the fact that a man named Browning pretended to want to know the contents of Lionel Chard's will before he would release Jennifer?'

'If I knew exactly what had happened, I could form an opinion,' said Bennison, dryly.

Folly stopped in his pacing and glowered at him.

'That remark is quite unnecessary,' he snapped. 'I am

about to tell you.' He did so, adding with withering scorn:
'Well, does that enable you to form an opinion?'

Bennison said evasively: 'It doesn't seem to make sense on
the *surface*. Of course, the man who kidnapped Jennifer
might now have realized that she'd been taken from where
he had put her and been put in Bryce's pig-sty—'

'Heaven save me from fools!' exclaimed Folly, piously.
'Bennison, don't be absurd. Until the discovery of the girl, I
was prepared to believe that Bryce, perhaps in conjunction
with Roger Maitland, was behind all this. We may have
liked Roger Maitland, but it could have been argued that he
had a motive for wanting both the old man and young Corcoran dead; that he considered that the girl was being
influenced by the old man, and he desperately wanted her to
stay out of the convent, presumably so that he could marry
her. Jealousy could have been the cause of his killing Corcoran. I once thought that was possible – what are you looking like a stuffed owl for?'

Bennison gulped. 'That – that's almost word for word
what I said to Abbott only yesterday morning!'

'Why keep these priceless jewels of thought from me?'
asked Folly. 'However we must now dimiss the possibility I
have outlined and you have so generously agreed with.
Perhaps we should never have given it serious consideration,
for we have now to face a bewildering array of facts. Just
where and how does this man Kennard come into the mystery?'

Bennison thought it discreet to make no comment.

'And if Browning thought that he could hold Jennifer until
he had learned the terms of the will, why was she eventually
left in a place where she might be found at any time? The
difficulty,' went on Folly, 'is that we cannot relate one fact to
another, and yet they must be related. Supposing Roger
Maitland is concerned – or, perhaps more probably that
someone *wants* us to believe that he is concerned. Again, can
we find an answer to the question: why was Jennifer Briscoe
left in Bryce's back garden? To get the answer, we should

have to follow the sequence of events, something like this:
Bryce had been moved, or persuaded, to keep a fairly regular
touch with Roger Maitland; suspicion, therefore, has
cleverly been pointed towards them both. Bryce was sent
here with a message for Roger, and caught near the premises
– which eventuality, with so many police about, was obvious
from the beginning – and, presumably while he was away,
the girl was put in his garden. Therefore, whoever put her
there, wanted Bryce to be blamed for her disappearance. We,
the police, might be expected to think that the story of the
letter, in fact the letter itself, was a fake, to distract our
attention from the fact that Maitland and Bryce were working together. We have no proof, except the word of the child
Hilda, that Bryce received a visitor last night, and it is possible that the child was instructed what to say about that. So,
we can build up a pretty picture. It is even possible for us to
theorize about Roger Maitland wishing to confuse the
issue, and arranging the conversation with the man Browning – it was, as it has proved, a pointless one. As a red-
herring, it would confuse us, but I can see no other point in
it. Thus, we could answer all three problems: we could say
that Maitland is the guilty one and that Bryce had been
working for him and actually shot Chard. Bryce, when as-
saulting Jennifer, might have been rough because she
struggled, and Maitland himself might have given her the injection. That *is* possible, isn't it?'

'I thought you said that Roger Maitland—'

'I did, I did!' I am now *trying* to work the situation out in
my mind,' cried Folly. 'What I am about to say is this: we can
build up a circumstantial case against Roger and Bryce, but
it does *not* square with the picture red-herring. And the
motives are somewhat tenuous, to say the least. I wouldn't
like to take it to court, would you?'

'No,' said Bennison, emphatically.

'And although the prima facie case against Roger Maitland and Bryce might, if supported by fresh evidence, be a
telling one,' went on Folly, 'it does not fit in with the other

red-herring, Uncle Lionel's encounter with a stranger at Hilbury Station and its effect on him. Also, it leaves unanswered this matter of Chard's financial acrobatics, the fact that, in my opinion, there is reason to believe that in his financial juggling, he had made enemies of whom it could be said he was desperately afraid. It *is* teasing,' he added, irritably. 'There must be thread connecting them all.'

Bennison said in a sharp voice: 'There's one I think we've forgotten.'

'Indeed? What is that?'

'The Chrysler,' said Bennison. 'I – look here, give me a moment, will you?' He did not wait for approval, but turned and hurried out of the room.

Folly sat looking at the open door, a monument of patience. He heard Bennison open another door, and then heard him ask abruptly:

'Mr. Maitland, when Kennard came to Home Farm for that picture, what car was he driving?'

After a pause, Roger answered: 'A Chrysler.'

'God bless my soul!' exclaimed Folly.

CHAPTER TWENTY-THREE

THE TRAIL OF A CAR

'ALL right, all right, I heard,' said Folly, waving a hand, 'be quiet a moment, Bennison – you've done well, sit down and pat yourself on the back. Now, the Chrysler. The first apearance of the car was at Home Farm, that seems to be established. The second appearance of a large car was, according to Bryce, on the morning of the first attack on Lionel Chard. And we discovered that a Chrysler had been seen in the district at an early hour. Let us assume that is the Chrysler's appearance Number Two, so to speak. The third—' He paused.

Bennison said quickly: 'At Hilbury Station.'

'When Chard was accosted by a man who said "How are you, Lionel?" and gave the old man a heart attack,' said Folly, dreamily. 'Yes, that is right. The fourth appearance of a Chrysler, and surely it must be *the* Chrysler, was – presumably – after Frank Corcoran's death. A powerful motor car was waiting at the roadside for the men who ran away and avoided Paul Briscoe and the policeman who chased after them. Right. And the fifth appearance was at Putney, when a man called himself Browning, and drove off after the telephone conversation with Roger Maitland. Well, well! Bennison, be honest with me.' Folly finished making notes, and looked up. 'What made you think of the Chrysler?'

'You,' said Bennison. 'You've always insisted that these things are connected, and the only connection seemed to be the big car. Call it a brainwave.'

'My dear fellow, don't under-rate yourself,' said Folly. 'That wasn't a brainwave, that was the subconscious co-ordination of known facts, or, as I should say, the use of *memory* in investigation and deduction. So Kennard has a Chrysler. Well, well! Push that telephone a little nearer, will you?'

As Bennison touched the instrument, the telephone bell rang.

'What a nuisance!' said Folly, whipping off the receiver. 'Hallo, Folly speaking, who – oh, Abbott.' He broke off.

Bennison could just hear Abbot's voice coming from the instrument, but could not catch a word of what he said. Folly seemed impressed. He began to smile.

'Yes ... Yes ... Yes ...' he said. 'That's all right, Abbott, that's very good. Where are you now? ... I hope they are looking after you at the Yard, but never mind that just now, I've another little job for you. You remember the picture dealer, Kennard, who was mentioned early in this affair?' He waited impatiently. 'Good, good. He has an office, under-

195

stand, in the neighbourhood of Bond Street. And he has a Chrysler. I want you to tell Inspector Anderson that I am very anxious indeed about him, and he must work quickly. I want a detailed description of him, a photograph if possible, and I want to find out whether he could have been at Hilbury Station last Monday evening, when Chard returned from his trip to town. Find out, too, if Chard and Kennard were previously acquainted, whether Kennard was at Hilbury on that day or not – have you got that? – there's a good fellow. Oh, has Anderson got the description of the man Browning ready for me? Yes, read it out—'

Folly began to make notes.

'Excellent, excellent,' he said, when Abbott had finished. 'You're doing well, my boy, and Bennison hasn't done so badly here. I'll make policemen out of you both yet!' He replaced the receiver, and beamed at Bennison. 'Ask Roger Maitland if he will be good enough to step in here for a moment, and – no, I'll go and see him myself. Come along.'

Roger and the rest of the family were still in the drawing-room; none of them looked pleased when Folly burst in.

'I'm sorry to worry you, Mr. Maitland, but I wonder if you will listen to this description of a man, and tell me whether you have ever seen him. Ready?'

Roger nodded.

'About five feet ten, corpulent, dressed in dark clothes and yet somehow appearing flashy, a florid face, very blue eyes, small and wide-set, pendulous under-lip, a sharp ridge at the bridge of the nose, and straight hair, growing rather low on his forehead.' Folly paused. 'Well?'

Roger frowned.

'It's rather like—'

'Kennard!' exclaimed Peter.

'Yes,' Roger said.

Neither of them noticed Lucille, who had turned abruptly at the name. Now, white-faced and trembling, she looked out of the window. Folly did not appear to glance at her, but he saw what the others missed.

'Are you sure?' he asked, mildly.

'Yes,' said Roger, 'I am sure. It's Kennard to a T.'

'It certainly is,' said Peter.

'Ah,' said Folly. 'Most gratifying. Then I think that the law will look after Mr. Kennard for you, Mr. Maitland, you will have no need to break his neck! For Kennard is none other than your Mr. Browning.' He beamed at Roger.

'*What?*'

'I thought that would startle you.' Folly waved the slip of paper. 'Now, I do want all of you to give your fullest attention to this request: try to remember whether, at any time, Kennard was acquainted with your uncle or with your uncle's friends. This may be of the greatest importance. And you might ask the staff,' he added, 'they are a little suspicious of me, you know.' He beamed. 'Thank you very much indeed. Come along, sergeant.'

He went out.

Peter said in a strained voice: 'This doesn't make sense.'

Paul laughed.

'Folly thinks he's got something, but it wouldn't surprise me if this wasn't another of his hair-brained ideas. I wouldn't trust Folly far, if I were you.'

'Oh, I don't know,' said Peter. 'I'm coming to like the fellow.'

Paul shrugged. 'Please yourself, but don't forget that Kennard is tied up with you, Peter.'

'What do you mean?'

Paul said slowly: 'I mean that in my opinion, the police think that one of us is responsible for these crimes, and that they will twist anything they can in order to prove it. What connection would the old man have had with a picture dealer?'

No one spoke immediately. Paul had taken the latest development more to heart than Roger had expected, and succeeded in throwing cold water on the hopes that had suddenly arisen. He had shown distrust of Folly, but Roger could not rid himself of the feeling that Folly knew a great deal more than he yet admitted.

Peter stirred restlessly in his chair.

'I ought to go and do some work,' he said, 'I can't get that portrait out of my mind. There's one thing, though, "Dealer" is too loose a word to use for Kennard. He doesn't trade in the usual way. He introduces business to a lot of dealers, I believe, and he's been known to buy up a young artist. I mean, advance him a few hundred and pay him a low price for each picture, which eventually sells for a good sum. Most dealers are pretty honest types, but Kennard's just a shark. He's interested in the cash side of the business only.'

Paul had not mentioned to Peter the price he had paid to "buy back" the picture; he scowled, but made no comment.

Barbara said quietly: 'Whatever we think of Folly, we've got to leave it to him, and I'd rather have him to deal with than Marlin.'

'Well, well,' said Peter, 'let's wish success to both of them. I'm going to do some work. Give me a shout if Jenny comes round, won't you?' He linked his arm in Lucille's and made for the door.

'He's a self-centred beggar, isn't he?' asked Paul plaintively. 'Give him a tube of paint, a brush and a bit of canvas, and he's as happy as a sandboy.'

'We're getting away from the subject,' Roger said thoughtfully. 'I wish I knew what connection there was between Kennard and the old man. Who's the most likely one to help us? Tippett?'

'Ask him what the man at Hilbury Station on Monday was like,' suggested Paul.

Tippett, being approached, agreed that the man who had said 'How are you, Lionel?' at the station was very much like the description of Kennard, but there was nothing Roger could do beyond that.

For the first time, he saw a disadvantage in having divorced himself from the old man's business. He was not even known at the office. Folly would surely be in a better position than he to make what inquiries he wanted. He remembered how cleverly Folly had induced the admission from Paul; *was* this yet another trick?

Whether or no, it explained why Paul felt sour about the Scotland Yard man.

Paul said: 'I've one or two letters to write, I may as well do them now.' As he went upstairs, the postman arrived. There were only two letters, one for the old man and one for Paul.

'They do follow Paul about,' said Roger. 'I suppose the fans in Hilbury know all about him being here by now. It's a wonder the newspapers haven't played his part up pretty heavily. We've that to be thankful for.'

Barbara did not answer.

'What's the matter?' asked Roger.

Barbara said: 'I don't like the feel of this letter.'

'What—' began Roger.

Suddenly, Barbara tore it open, and turned it upside down.

Several white feathers fluttered on to the floor.

Barbara tightened her lips, and, after a pause, Roger said in a bewildered voice:

'So the old man *didn't* send them?' There was little point in speculating. They told Folly, and then went upstairs to see Paul. He was coming out of Peter's room, and raised his eyebrows when he saw them.

'What's worrying you now?' demanded Paul, and his face darkened as Roger told him.

Folly was unusually discursive on the way back to Hilbury. In his pocket were the feathers and the envelope, although so far he had said nothing to Bennison about them. He talked a great deal about the Chrysler, and more about what he hoped to learn from London.

Bennison said little in reply, and presently Folly shot him a sideways glance.

'No doubt you think I'm keeping some things back from you, Bennison. Up to a point you're right, but I shall place all the information at your disposal before the day is out, and you'll have a chance, just as I shall, of making the right deductions.'

Bennison gave a slightly aggrieved sniff.

'As a matter of fact, Bennison, as I told you before, *all* I know about Lionel Chard in London is that he was suspected of being one of a number of people who have been sending money out of the country illegally. And if a man will do that, he might send other things.'

'Such as?'

Folly shrugged his shoulders—

'Precious stones, pictures. Stolen goods, in both instances.' He concealed a smile, as Bennison started.

'*Stolen?* You didn't tell me—'

'My dear Bennison, use the brain the good God gave you! I told you of illegal transactions. I told you that Lionel Chard was a surprisingly wealthy man!'

Bennison sniffed again.

Folly swept on: 'At the moment I am most interested in that man Kennard. I wonder why he *did* make that detour to see the picture, and why he made up that fantastic story about Peter Maitland. There's something odd about it. It's one which can so easily be checked and disproved if it's untrue. No sensible man would have cast such an aspersion – except, of course, that he might have thought that the Maitlands would not inquire too deeply, things being as they are, and that Briscoe was prepared to pay him well to hush the thing up. But that would make it an isolated matter, and I'm sure that it ties up with the rest somewhere – even his journey to Home Farm with the picture. That was the first appearance of this Chrysler, and I'm pinning a lot of hope on that car. We'll see.' He concentrated on his driving for a few minutes, and then said abruptly: 'There is the other annoying development – the white feathers. I had concluded like everyone else that Chard had sent them. Now they have popped up again. The intention appears to be be to get Briscoe on edge, like the others. Then, when Kennard's name was mentioned, Lucille changed colour. She fears him, I think. And she could undoubtedly have fired that shot. Moreover, Chard barred her from the Lodge. And – she is French. There is a French angle on this business. Finally, she first brought Kennard and the Chrysler on the scene.'

He turned into the station parking place, alighting, not without difficulty.

'I'll see you later,' he said to Bennison, and went along to the Superintendent's office. Marlin was sitting with a thick pile of reports in front of him, and as Folly dropped into a chair, he said:

'I've been trying to get something from these reports, Folly, but so far—'

'A difficult and highly skilled job,' said Folly. 'That's why I'm so grateful to you. Nothing else of importance, I suppose?'

'Edwards came into see Bryce, and said he would look after his interests. I imagine that Roger Maitland arranged that.'

'Probably. What has Bryce to say?'

'Nothing at all.'

'Does he know where Miss Briscoe was found?'

'*I* haven't told him,' said Marlin. 'Oh, there is a message from Scotland Yard, it came a few minutes before you arrived. Will you telephone Anderson?'

'I most certainly will.' Folly stretched out for the telephone, and was soon connected with Inspector Anderson.

'Well, my dear fellow, what have you got ready for me now?'

'Plenty,' said Anderson.

'Ah!'

'About Kennard.'

'Oh!' said Folly. 'And what's that?'

'He's flown.'

'Flown? Literally?'

'Figuratively,' said Anderson, drily. 'He's left his office and his flat and it's obvious that he doesn't intend to come back. What's more, he's sold his car.'

'The Chrysler!'

'Yes – he sold it to a nearby garage this morning,' said Anderson. 'I've arranged for a watch at all sea and airports and stations.'

Folly breathed heavily.

'And now suppose you tell me what you really have in your mind,' he said.

Anderson chuckled.

'All right, sir. We've enough on Kennard to put him inside for seven years. He's a fence in a big way – yes, I can give you chapter and verse about that. He was in the French jewel business, too. What is more,' went on Anderson, 'we've picked up a couple of men who have admitted kidnapping Jennifer Briscoe for him, and putting her in Bryce's back garden. You can't complain about lack of results this time.'

'Good gracious me,' said Folly, in a startled voice. 'So Kennard – well, well! Have you had Abbott's message? Has he asked you to find out whether Kennard and Lionel Chard were associated in any way?'

'He has, and I have, and they were,' said Anderson. 'Kennard was a partner in Chard's broking business until two years ago, when they had a quarrel and Kennard went out – on his neck, I gather.'

'What a wonderful afternoon's work,' breathed Folly. 'And I have been down here doing – well, never mind. I—'

'I've got something else for you,' said Anderson.

'My cup's running over,' said Folly. 'Go on.'

'Kennard's had a number of telephone calls from Hilbury in the last few days,' Anderson said. 'The girl in his office took them. One of those people down there is undoubtedly mixed up in this.'

CHAPTER TWENTY-FOUR

FOLLY'S TACTICS

'Undoubtedly someone in the family is deeply involved,' Folly said to Bennison and Abbott, all three of them sitting over the remains of an excellent supper provided by Mrs. Harris. 'It is equally certain that Kennard is involved, that Lionel Chard was afraid of him, and that a member of the family – or at least someone at the Lodge – knew of the association between Kennard and Chard. Do we all agree?' The other two men nodded. 'So far, then, all is well,' went on Folly. 'The question is – which of the people at the house is concerned? Oh, Abbott, let us hear the results of your interview with Mrs. Rampling, the housekeeper whom Chard so summarily dismissed.'

Abbott grinned. 'She certainly had it in for Uncle Lionel! Apparently she was looking for whisky in his bedroom, and she found a small box of white feathers. He caught her, and went off the deep-end.'

'But Briscoe's had feathers by post since Chard's death,' Bennison objected.

'True,' said Folly. 'A puzzling fact which will no doubt be sorted out in time. Meanwhile there is little doubt that Kennard has taken fright because something serious has gone wrong since Chard's death. I think it likely that whoever has worked with him at the Lodge will also get in touch with him again – or, perhaps, Kennard will try to get in touch with his friend at the Lodge. Do you agree?'

'It's no more than a hope,' said Abbott. 'You've got something, though.'

'Thank you,' said Folly, humbly. 'Most gratifying that you should think so.'

'I mean, something *new*. What put Kennard into a panic?'

'Unfortunately that is not known.'

Bennison leaned forward, his elbows on the table.

'It's probably something that happened *here*,' he insisted. 'Could it be the arrest of Joe Bryce? If Bryce were working with Kennard, who was seeking revenge on the old man, that would explain a lot, wouldn't it?'

'I must admit that I had not thought of that,' said Folly. 'Hmm, yes. However, there is another possible reason for Kennard's panic.' He paused. 'Jennifer Briscoe is not dead, though someone undoubtedly tried to murder her and thought they had succeeded. That is one of the reasons why there are so many policemen at the Lodge tonight, I do not want Jennifer Briscoe to be attacked again, and if an associate of Kennard's is at the Lodge there may well be an attempt. That is why I arranged for the police nurse to stay with Jennifer.'

'But I thought you thought she was mixed up in it!' Abbott declared.

'My dear Abbott! That was before she was found. When she was found, badly hurt, it was immediately apparent that she was a victim. Moreover Marlin saw something which you two appear to have missed!' He beamed at their obvious discomfiture. 'He pointed out to me the name of Jennifer's closest friend.'

'Corcoran!' exclaimed Abbott.

'Precisely,' agreed Folly. 'Frank Corcoran, who was murdered, and Jennifer, who was nearly murdered. Two people who saw a great deal of each other may well have been in each other's confidence, and shared a secret which was – and is – of vital importance to the assailant. Corcoran was blinded through love of the girl, but might have come to his senses and talked. The girl is a different proposition. She is unworldly, and thus her loyalties will not be conventional ones. She might never disclose the truth, but you can take it from me that she has the key to this problem. That is why she is being so closely watched.'

Bennison ran a hand over his head.

'Do you really think she's still in danger?'

'*Grave* danger,' Folly assured him, 'and that from someone who professes to have a deep regard and concern for her. Well, I must go. Early bed is indicated, because it is at least possible that we shall have a call during the night. We shall, metaphorically speaking, have to sleep with our boots on.'

Roger did not feel like sleeping at all. He had no doubt that Folly suspected one of the family; he could not rid himself of doubts of Peter and Lucille. He felt disloyal and unhappy. He felt disloyal, too, for other reasons. He tried not to think about them but they persisted. Now that he knew Jennifer was not badly hurt, his thoughts had flown to Barbara. From the first time he had met her, he had been drawn to her. He wished it were not so, wished that there was not a suspicion of disloyalty, even in thought, to Paul. But there it was: disloyalty, a trait he hated; to Paul, to Jennifer, to Peter, all in different ways.

A man could not help his thoughts; could not easily turn from sudden, unpredictable and uninvited thoughts; yet he must.

Had he never loved Jenny?

Oh, this was nonsense! In a few weeks, at most, Barbara would be back in Hollywood, with Paul; he must give his whole attention to trying to change Jennifer's mind about the convent.

He tossed and turned, until at last he decided that he would go downstairs and make a cup of tea.

He saw no one on the landing, which surprised him; he had expected to find a policeman there. There was no policeman to be seen in the hall, either; perhaps they were deliberately hiding. He went to the kitchen, made the tea and carried a small tray upstairs.

Reaching the top steps, he saw somebody in white flitting across the landing.

Peter's door was ajar.

He looked inside. Peter was sleeping on his back, just visible in the light from the hall. Lucille was not there. Well, Lucille might be restless, as he was. She had not been happy earlier in the evening. Peter, he thought, was exhausted after the events of the day and after the tremendous burst of energy he had put into painting the picture of Lucille. He heard whispered voices.

He stood quite still, listening intently.

One voice was Paul's. It was raised for a moment.

Paul – and Lucille. This was fantastic!

Paul and Barbara had the room almost opposite Roger's That door was ajar too. He went into his own room, put the tea down, and went back to the landing. Lucille was whispering now, but he could not catch a word. He peered round the door of the room opposite. Barbara was lying in her bed; she seemed to be sleeping. Paul's bed was empty.

Where were the police?

Roger backed into his own room, and, a moment later, saw Lucille flit across the landing; there was a faint click as her door closed. The Paul went to his room and closed the door.

Roger poured himself a cup of tea, and tried to adjust his thoughts. Paul and Lucille – why had they talked together, why had they met so furtively? He must see Paul, who surely knew that, although the police were not in sight, they could be watching.

There was a faint tap at his door. It opened and Paul appeared.

'Hallo, Roger. I thought I saw a light. Good heavens, tea!'

Roger forced himself to speak calmly.

'Like a cup?'

'No thanks!' Paul closed the door carefully. 'Roger, I'm worried.'

'Aren't we all?'

'There's something else.'

Paul walked restlessly about the room, and stood for a moment looking out of the window. Then he turned abruptly.

'It's about Lucille. She came into my room twenty minutes ago, and said she must speak to me. I told her to keep it until the morning. She insisted. Bar didn't wake up, thank goodness. Lucille's as jittery as a bean in a fire. She said she couldn't tell you, you are so stern, and she daren't tell Peter.'

'Tell us what?'

'What she told me. Roger, she was mixed up in a big jewel robbery in Paris a few months ago, that's why she's scared of the police. And this man Kennard also came into it somewhere. I didn't get the rights of it, she's off her head with anxiety.'

Roger said: 'You mean to say that she and Kennard knew each other before the trip to Home Farm?'

Paul nodded.

'She says he made her take him to Home Farm. She doesn't know why. But there's something else that's obvious enough.'

'What do you mean?' asked Roger.

'My dear chap! If Kennard and Uncle Lionel did business together, we now know why Uncle Lionel wouldn't have Lucille in the house.'

'Yes,' said Roger, slowly. 'I was thinking of that. What a situation! Why on earth did she pick on Peter!'

Paul lit a cigarette.

'Apparently she was ordered by these thieves to ask Peter for work as a model. She got as far as telling me that, and then flew off into wild protestations that she was in love with him, she won't do anything to hurt him, and she's afraid of him finding out the truth. It looks to me—'

Roger said savagely: 'It looks to me as if someone wanted to get at the old man through Peter – and succeeded.'

'Yes,' said Paul, 'and if Folly once gets onto this, there'll be the devil to pay.' He paused, and then added with a harder note in his voice: 'I suppose you're going to say that we ought to tell Folly.'

'I don't know,' said Roger. 'It's something more than I'd bargained for. One of us, Barbara I think, will have to get the whole story from Lucille first thing in the morning when she's not so worked up. When we know everything we'll be able to decide what to do. But we'll have to be quick about it, for the police undoubtedly saw you and Lucille talking to-night.'

'I didn't see anyone.'

'They're keeping out of sight, but they're watching,' said Roger.

He broke off as a door opened and a woman's voice, low-pitched but carrying called out:

'Sergeant, are you there?'

Another voice came: 'Yes.'

Roger and Paul went nearer the door, as the first speaker said quietly:

'I don't like the look of the Briscoe girl. I'm going to telephone Dr. Coppinger.'

Paul gripped Roger's arm.

'What's the matter with her?' demanded the sergeant.

'I don't know. Her pulse is weak. She was sleeping, now she's unconscious. I thought I'd let you know. Watch her room, won't you?'

'I'm watching all right,' said the sergeant.

The night nurse went downstairs, while Roger and Paul looked at each other with growing tension. Suddenly Roger pulled open the door and hurried in the wake of the nurse. He waited until she had put through her call.

'I want to see Dr. Coppinger immediately he's seen my cousin,' Roger told her, abruptly.

'Very good, sir.'

It seemed an age before the doctor's car sounded on the drive. Roger and Paul were sitting in Roger's room. The nurse had returned to Jennifer, but had refused to allow either of them to see her.

They heard Dr. Coppinger go into the room; and then, from downstairs, an all too familiar voice.

'I was afraid we would be disturbed, Abbott. Never mind, we've had a little sleep.'

Paul started. 'Folly's here!'

'Yes,' said Roger, slowly. 'I wonder—' He broke off, help-lessly.

They heard Folly walk up the stairs and go into Jennifer's room. The door closed, and silence followed; a nagging, mis-erable silence. And then the door opened again. Heavy foot-steps walked across the landing and Roger's door was thrown open. Folly stood on the threshold.

'Someone in this house has poisoned Miss Briscoe,' he de-clared. 'She is gravely ill, and is to be moved at once to hospital. I want to know who poisoned her.'

CHAPTER TWENTY-FIVE

KENNARD

ROGER's head was aching unbearably, his eyes were heavy from lack of sleep. Even now that Folly had gone, he could not rest. Invariably he came back to the same question: who had poisoned Jennifer? There was no doubt about the poisoning; she was now at Hilbury Hospital, and doctors were fighting for her life; the drug, it appeared, was morphia – the same drug as she had been given before. Folly had seen every one of the family, and gradually one thing had become evident; for half-an-hour Jenny had been in her room alone. During that half-hour one of the household had given her a drink of milk. No one admitted having done this, but all of them could have done so.

Folly had put question after question, now blustering and threatening, now wooing and cozening; but he had got no further.

He had torn asunder any hope of keeping Lucille's talk with Paul quiet. A policeman had seen them, but although Roger did not think the man had heard what was said, Folly had worked first on Paul and then on Lucille until he had the whole story.

Roger went over it again and again, trying to understand it, trying to understand Folly's tactics.

Once they had reached the Lodge, neither Abbott nor Bennison had grumbled about being called out at half-past two in the morning. They were in the morning-room with Folly, two hours later; and they saw a new and terrible Folly, for he blamed himself for this second attempt to murder Jennifer Briscoe. Folly remorseful was a revelation to them; and they listened to him in awed silence.

'Well, that is the truth. If that child dies it will be my fault. There is no doubt about it. Finding the poisoner will not console me.' He paused. 'Now we have the final proof that the poisoner is one of this household, and we can rule out the maid. That leaves us with the family.'

Bennison ventured a suggestion. 'Lucille.'

Folly waved a hand.

'You are not at your best, Bennison. Let us piece her story together. At the order of Kennard she made the acquaintance of Peter Maitland. He wished to have a strong hold over Chard. That is clear, and sent this woman to Chard's nephew. Then Kennard's plans were awry, if we are to believe the chit, and I think we must. She fell in love with Maitland, and he with her. They got married and came to England. Kennard told Chard who the girl was. Therefore, Chard refused her admittance to his house.'

Abbott murmured: 'What about the trip to Home Farm?'

'Yes, yes, I know. Kennard called on her, and insisted on being taken to the farm, insisted on buying this one picture. I do not yet know why. He insisted, moreover, on seeing the family, for, as she was frightened out of her life by Kennard, had he not wanted to visit the family he could surely have taken the picture from her in London. I think we can assume that Kennard wanted to talk to, or assess, one of the people whom he met at Home Farm. Don't you agree?'

'Yes,' said Abbott.

'It might have been any one of the three men,' went on Folly. 'We can rule none of them out, and one of them, working through Kennard, has plotted and planned this thing from beginning to end. It is now clear that Bryce was made to appear as the collaborator, to save the guilty nephew. That failed, since Jennifer did not die from the first attack. The child knows much; she can name the villain; and the second daring attempt was made and I failed to prevent it.'

'You're a bit hard on yourself,' Bennison said.

'Hard! I cannot be hard enough. After this, I shall retire. My brain is slowing down.' He waggled a finger at them. 'Let me tell you, young men, that if ever you make such a serious error, retirement is the only honourable course. Never again shall I—'

A shot cut across his words.

It startled all of them, and they sat still, looking at one another. A second shot broke across the silence in the room, and Folly leapt to his feet.

'That's outside! Come along!'

He rushed to the door and flung it open, reaching the front door yards ahead of the others. Policemen appeared on the stairs and from the kitchen. Folly plunged into the garden.

A third shot sounded; they saw the flash. It was near the field where Corcoran had been killed. Folly ran towards it,

Bennison turned the car and switched on the headlights. Abbott, following Folly, glanced over his shoulder and saw Paul, and Peter and Roger on the porch. Next moment, the men had disappeared.

Folly tore on.

Bennison had a little trouble with the headlights, and by the time he had them shining towards the meadow, all three of the nephews had passed him. Everyone was looking towards the scene of the shooting, and but for a chance glance towards the house, Bennison would have seen nothing else.

As it was he saw a woman move in the opposite direction.

He started, watched, and then followed. She had slipped from the porch, and quickly disappeared into the bloom.

Bennison thought he heard footsteps behind him.

'Who's that?' he whispered.

No one answered him. Bennison looked round. No policemen were in sight, everyone had gone in the direction of the shooting. He went on, walking across the rough grass at the side of the drive. The lights from the house shone on the vague figure of a woman ahead of him.

Then he heard a man's voice.

It was unfamiliar to Bennison, and held a coarse, frightened note.

A woman gasped.

A torch shone out, and fell upon a man who was standing under the shelter of a tree. Bennison had no difficulty in recognizing Kennard. It seemed clear to Bennison that the shooting had been a deliberate distraction. Kennard had been waiting here, to meet the woman, to make the contact which Folly had expected.

Bennison felt a surge of elation, he would get Kennard, he—

Out of the darkness someone struck him on the back of the head. One blow was enough to make him pitch forward;

another, and he lost consciousness. The last thing he heard was a loud report; and he thought that he had been shot.

On the other side of the grounds, Folly and Abbott heard the shot.

Roger, too, heard it.

The blast of a police whistle cut across the garden. Roger turned towards the fresh outbreak of trouble. Peter joined him, and together they reached the drive, and crossed it. They could hear voices, a man's and a woman's. Peter stiffened. Roger put a hand on his arm quickly, but Peter pulled himself free.

'That's Lucille! What the devil—'

He rushed forward, as Lucille's voice rose in protest; she was speaking in French, and Roger could pick out only a word here and there. Soon, he was near enough to see Lucille struggling in the grip of a uniformed policeman. At their feet was the body of a man.

Folly's voice could be heard above all others.

'So we have Kennard. A dead Kennard.' He straightened up and looked at Lucille. A policeman held one of her arms, Peter the other. 'And you shot him.'

The evidence seemed clear. Bennison, who had quickly recovered, reported having seen the woman leave the house and hurry towards Kennard. No one needed telling that the shooting on the other side of the grounds had been a distraction to cover Lucille's visit to Kennard. Lucille herself broke down; yes, she had received a note early in the evening, and been told there would be a disturbance, during which she was to slip away and meet Kennard. She was so frightened of the man, she admitted, that she had not hesitated to obey. No, she had not told Paul. No one knew how frightened she was of Kennard, frightened that he would tell Peter, and her hopes of happiness would be over.

With almost every word, Lucille strengthened the case against herself.

The gun was hers. Inside the handle several morphia

tablets had been found. She said she had left the gun in her suitcase, and not brought it out that night. Knowing her fear of Kennard, that was hard to believe.

Peter, dull-voiced and dull-eyed, agreed the gun was hers. She had always carried one in France. It was the gun which had so worried her when the police had called to see her about her passport. It carried a few smeared fingerprints, all Lucille's. Only one shot had been fired.

Lucille had been sent into Hilbury. Peter seemed overcome by the shock.

It seemed clear enough that, in her fear of Kennard, Lucille had killed him. It seemed equally clear that Chard had known of her true identity, and had told Jennifer; and Lucille, that night, had poisoned Jennifer. The earlier crimes had been Kennard's – helped by the 'mobmen' now under arrest in London. Folly confirmed that view to Roger, Paul and Barbara, together and separately.

With Peter, Folly was more gentle, but Peter seemed to have accepted the inevitable.

For the first time, Roger and the family heard the whole story. Of Jewels first looted, then stolen from the Germans, and stolen again from the Maquis by French thieves working with an English contact – Kennard. For a long time valuable *objets d'art* and jewels had been smuggled from France to England and then to America, and Chard had been the chief English agent, with Kennard his chief aide, until he and Kennard had fallen out. Thereafter, there had been a struggle between the two men, Kennard gradually gaining the ascendancy. Folly said that it seemed clear, now, that Kennard had boasted to Chard of his influence over Peter, through Lucille, that Chard had struggled to the last in a vain attempt to regain his influence. Folly drew a vivid picture of that losing battle, of Chard soured, and vengeful, blaming his nephews for his plight because they had never helped him, nursing that grievance, venting his spite, striking out at those he could most easily wound. And the connecting thread through all the crimes, said Folly, had been

Kennard, who had used Lucille at every opportunity until she had turned upon him.

There was the effort to implicate Bryce, the red-herring of the telephone call to Putney, which was to make the police think that the men who had taken Jennifer away were interested in Chard's will and nothing else.

'A clever move,' Folly said. 'And yet, in the long run, a foolish one. I have no doubt that if Miss Jennifer can be prevailed upon to talk, she will implicate Lionel Chard, she will also show us that she knew something of what he was doing, something of Kennard; and there is little doubt, I think, that Corcoran was killed not because of anything he knew but because Kennard, who first attacked Lionel Chard, saw him and thought that he in turn had been seen. A strange and tragic business, and I am sorry – for you all.'

'Sorry,' said Peter, in a dull voice. 'Sorry.' He stopped, then threw out his hands. 'But Lucille—'

Roger and Paul shepherded him out of the room; and Barbara followed.

Folly sat looking at his fingernails when the door had closed. Marlin had arrived, his expression prim and expectant. Folly turned towards him.

'Are you satisfied, Superintendent?'

'Quite satisfied,' said Marlin. 'And I shall have to make an early report to the Chief Constable. Is there anything I can usefully do here now?'

'I don't think so,' said Folly. 'No. There are a few odds and ends to clear up, that is all. Just a few odds and ends. These two young men can stay and help me. I do not think we need the uniformed men at the house, there will be no further trouble. We must hope that Jennifer Briscoe will come round, and confirm all that we suspect.'

'I will call at the hospital on my way to the office,' said Marlin.

'Good fellow! Abbott! See the Superintendent to his car.' Folly waited until the sound of Marlin's car engine faded, then turned to the window.

'We must have some daylight on the subject,' he said, testily, and pulled the curtains. The clear light of dawn spread over the eastern sky. He swung round. 'Are you two as easily satisfied as Marlin?'

Abbott gasped.

'But – you've worked it all out!' gasped Bennison.

'I don't think I can recommend your transfer to Scotland Yard after all,' said Folly testily. 'Of course I haven't worked it all out. This case is not settled yet, though I have tried to make the family think it is. Oh, Bennison, Bennison! You, of all people, should know that there is something here we do not understand, that someone else was near Kennard and Lucille, the man who attacked you – and who, in my opinion, shot Kennard after sending Lucille the note to meet Kennard in order to frame her. The man whom Kennard really came to see. The man who poisoned Jennifer the second time. The man who has been in this business from the beginning, who worked for a while with Chard and, then, I have no doubt, did what Kennard did and deserted him. Few people could remain loyal to Lionel Chard. Oh, it is so clear, yet proof is difficult to obtain. But we must get it. We must not let Lucille Maitland pay. The child was forced to do whatever she has done. You know everything that I know, now. Everything. Think if you can.'

There was a long, heavy silence.

'Let me help you,' said Folly, wearily. 'There is one member of this family whose actions have, to say the least, been puzzling. Who – good gracious me!' cried Folly. 'Must I give you his name? A successful man, a wealthy man, whom Chard hated, whom Chard cut out of his will, the only one, except Peter Maitland, who has seen Kennard secretly, who actually paid Kennard good money, on a footling excuse – I've never believed the story of the copied picture, the story of—'

'Paul Briscoe!' gasped Bennison.

'Of course,' said Folly, 'of course. Listen to me—'

CHAPTER TWENTY-SIX

JENNIFER WAKES

'LISTEN to me,' breathed Folly, spreading his hands out on the desk. 'Paul Briscoe flew to England ostensibly to help his sister; actually, I have no doubt, because there was trouble in England, the trouble being the quarrel between Kennard and Chard. He reached England, he made generous gestures, he "forgave" his cousin Peter for gibing at him about cowardice, but have no doubt, he knew who was sending the white feathers. Have no doubt, either, that at first Paul was the receiver in America, the man who sold the jewels. Look at the evidence of enmity between Paul and Chard. The feathers – the will – the quarrels. Then look at the clever way he worked to throw suspicion on Peter and Roger – Roger first, through Bryce, Peter as a second line of defence, through Lucille. It is fiendishly clever and I do not use the word lightly.'

Neither of the others spoke in the pause which followed.

Folly went on: 'Look how he worked, I say. He fetched Kennard down here through Lucille, so that if Kennard were ever discovered, Lucille and Peter would be the contact, not Paul – oh, never Paul. He prompted hot-headed Peter to talk of murder – do you remember what the maid at Home Farm told Marlin, about that talk? And how she had listened and heard practically all that was said? Paul brought his wife with him, a good woman, and persuaded her to keep silent about his second visit to Kennard, and when he found out, he thought she had given

217

him away – he quarrelled with her again. Remember that, Bennison?'

'Yes,' said Bennison.

'These little things are so important,' Folly said, impatiently, 'you forget so easily. Now. Paul went to Kennard to perfect their plans, to see that Jennifer was kidnapped and killed. Kennard did the dirty work, but Kennard was getting alarmed and wanted money, so Paul gave him a cheque which could be cashed at once, and then told us a cock-and-bull story about it. True, Kennard could have denied that story, would probably have done so had we caught him alive, but by then Paul had decided to kill him and put the blame on Lucille. As for the picture – I have no doubt he told Kennard to buy it. I think it possible we shall find jewels hidden in the frame, which will appear to incriminate Lucille and Peter; if Paul has made a mistake, it is that he has been too careful, he has tried too many different ways.'

Abbott said slowly: 'You may be right, but it's Paul, he's been clever enough to prevent us from getting proof.'

'No, no! We must get the proof. But clever – yes. He doubtless taunted Lucille or somehow made her see him furtively tonight and then got her to confide in him and immediately told Roger, knowing that Roger would, in due course, tell us. Doubtless Paul hoped that no one would notice that Jennifer was dying. With her dead, I do not think there would be a chance of proving this case against him. With her dead—'

Folly paused.

He stared at each of them in turn, and then stood up abruptly.

'I see how it can be done,' he said, slowly. 'It is not orthodox. You must not be a party to it. I will demonstrate in front of you, that is all. Abbott, telephone the police station and ask the operator to call me back. Tell him not to be surprised what I say into the telephone, and to hold on until I ring off. Is that clear?'

Abbott went to the telephone.

Folly turned to Bennison and spoke in a low voice.

'When the telephone bell begins to ring, open the door. You and Abbott must go out. Go to the drawing-room, where, I think you will find, the three men are waiting. Open that door too and keep it open. Say I am coming to see them. Is that clear?'

'Yes,' said Bennison.

Abbott replaced the receiver. 'He's going to ring through in a moment,' he said.

'Good! Off with you,' said Folly, and he strode to the door and opened it.

Roger, and Paul and Peter were in the drawing-room. Barbara had gone up to her room. The three men had little to say.

As the door opened, Paul muttered:

'I can't bear the sight of any more policemen!'

'I'm sorry to worry you again, gentlemen,' said Bennison, 'but Superintendent Folly is coming to have a word with you.'

Roger nodded.

The telephone-bell in the morning-room was ringing loudly. Peter snapped: 'Can't someone answer it? At the same moment Folly's voice rang out, clear as a crystal.

'Yes . . . Yes . . . Yes . . . She is? Wonderful!'

Roger sat up. Paul turned and looked towards the door. Peter sat with his eyes closed.

'I really do congratulate Dr. Coppinger,' went on Folly. 'If he had not acted so quickly, she would not have recovered. Yes, yes, it is good news indeed for the family, I will tell them . . . when will she be able to talk?'

Paul put his hand to his waistcoat pocket.

'What?' cried Folly. 'She *has* made a statement? . . . Good gracious me, already? . . . You mustn't try her too much, we know the truth . . . Lucille Maitland—'

Peter got up, and stood with clenched hands.

Folly's voice fell to a hiss, conspiratorial in sound, but of great carrying power.

'What's that? ... Her *brother*? ... Yes, yes, go on. But naturally I will see to it that he doesn't get away, I—'

In the drawing-room nobody spoke. And then Peter's voice came, harsh and unnatural.

'So it was *you* who poisoned Jennifer!'

Paul snapped: 'Don't be a fool, Jenny's not sane! She never has been. Who's going to believe—'

'You – swine,' said Peter.

He leapt at Paul.

Abbott and Bennison rushed forward and dragged him away.

Paul leaned against the window, gasping for breath. He put a hand to his mouth, and swallowed convulsively.

Roger started to speak, but broke off as Barbara came into the room. She looked straight at Paul, her face white and set. Peter stopped struggling in the grip of the two sergeants, and Folly came walking across the hall.

He said simply: 'Paul Briscoe, it is my duty to arrest you in connection with the murders of Lionel Chard, Frank Corcoran and Kennard, and I have to warn you that anything you say may be used in evidence. Take him away, sergeants.'

Abbott and Bennison went forward and took Paul's arms and led him out. Folly waited until they had gone, and then turned to Barbara.

'I am sorry, Mrs. Briscoe. Truly sorry. And I wish I had better news in other respects. Miss Briscoe's exertions have caused a relapse. There is good hope, however.' He looked at Peter. 'Mr. Maitland, I do not think that there will be any charge preferred against your wife in this country, and I have little doubt that she was forced to do what she did in France. I should not worry.'

Peter's eyes were glistening.

Folly turned to Roger.

'Mr. Maitland, I want to say how warmly the police appreciate your frankness. It is a rare attribute. I am going to say this: I believe your uncle seized upon Miss Jennifer's desire to take her vows as an opportunity to ensure her silence. These crimes were widespread, but the greatest crime was your uncle's malice towards his family. But I am becoming prosy. I wish you every good fortune, sir.'

Barbara was standing very still.

Then suddenly she turned to Roger and his arm went round her.

Paul Briscoe was dead, killed by his own hand, but the case against him continued to be built-up carefully and with damning effect; although it was not until a cable from Hollywood, confirming that he had got rid of a great many jewels there, nor until a man was arrested in London and was identified by Joe Bryce as the caller at the cottage, that the case was sound. It was proved, too, that Paul had sent the final lot of feathers to himself, so anxious was he to appear a victim.

In the frame of Peter's picture, jewels were found. And it was proved that Kennard had visited Home Farm, to see Paul and to get the jewels without stealing the picture. Lucille, knowing him, had passionately refused to let him have it without Peter's consent, hence his pretended reluctance. Peter had told the police that he had lied about Lucille being at home Farm when in fact she had been in London only because he knew – without knowing the reason– that she was nervous of the police.

Jennifer had made no statement. She was unconscious for three days, and on the fourth regained consciousness only for a few minutes. It was a month before she was out of hospital and, still wrapped in her uncanny serenity, visited Roger at Home Farm.

He led her indoors and told her about Paul.

She said quietly: 'I am glad you know, Roger. It was a great anixety.'

'So – you knew.'

'Yes,' said Jennifer. 'I knew that Uncle Lionel was not –

honest. I knew that he was friendly with Paul until four years ago, when they quarrelled. I knew he sent the feathers. I knew that he believed that Paul and this man, Kennard, were working together. I knew he hated them both. Frank Corcoran knew, also, but I persuaded him to say nothing. I did not think it was for us to speak.'

Roger said nothing.

Jennifer said: 'I loved Uncle Lionel, Roger. He was always good to me. I pleaded with him not to be malicious towards you and Peter, but he would not listen. I was afraid that there would be such an ending as this, a tragedy that I was powerless to stop—'

'But Jenny!'

'I was afraid, when the man Kennard came and attacked Uncle Lionel and Frank was accused, of what would come. Until then, I did not think of violence, Roger. Uncle – begged me not to say who it was. I obeyed him, as I have always obeyed him.' She paused. 'Roger.'

Roger said: 'Yes, Jenny?'

'The world will blame me, I know, for what will be called my misplaced loyalty. But you and the others left me to Uncle Lionel, and he has never said an angry word to me, and always done for me what he thought best. I promised him I would say nothing, and I kept my promise. I did not like the things he did, I did not like the world he lived in. I do not like it now. I shall never raise my voice against Uncle Lionel or against Paul. Do you understand?'

'Yes, Jenny.'

'Roger, I am going to take my vows as soon as I can. I cannot – cope – on my own. I knew that when Uncle Lionel died. I would not be happy anywhere but – in a different world. I can do much good. I will do all the good I can. Don't fight against me, Roger.'

After a long pause, Roger said: 'It's your decision, Jenny.'

'I'm glad you understand,' she said. 'I do so want you to.' She stood up. 'I am to enter the convent this evening. Now I must go. I don't want you to come with me, Roger. I know that I am right, and I want to say goodbye to you in the home which you love – to remember you always, here. Goodbye, Roger.'

She kissed him lightly and was gone.

After she had left, Roger went out to the gate. A car was drawn up on the far side of the road, and, as he looked at it, Barbara opened the door and got out. Roger, watching her, felt something of the serenity which she had always brought to him, serenity which he was beginning to think was but another name for love.

They were having tea, when Peter and Lucille arrived.

Roger laughed a little self-consciously.

'This is almost the first time I haven't wanted to see Peter,' he said.

Lucille flung herself at him.

'Roger, isn't it wonderful! So wonderful!'

Peter was grinning.

'Ze pictures,' cried Lucille, 'zey sell an' sell, Peter cannot paint enough of zem, ever since ze newspapers tell of ze story – wow! All ze world wants zem!'

'One of the funniest things is that Folly's bought one,' said Peter. 'He looked in this morning, that's why we came today. There's one thing he told us that you'll never believe. Bryce is going to get married. To a Mrs. Harris, who—'

Roger chuckled. 'Who is coming to live in a cottage on the farm and look after Bryce's brood and me until I make a more permanent arrangement,' he said.

W24
Add 2000
LC 2016
#C 7

DISCARD

F
C8604   4-14-76

Creasey
  Let's kill Uncle Lionel